THE SECRET of VILLA FAVONI

LEPORELLO
books

Published in the UK in 2022 by Leporello Books

Paperback ISBN 978-1-7399995-0-6
eBook ISBN 978-1-7399995-1-3

Cover design and typeset by SpiffingCovers

THE SECRET *of*

VILLA FAVONI

MAGGIE MORRIS WYLLIE

To Royo

'It's not a good idea, sire.'
I feigned puzzlement.
'What you're about to do.'
I held up my hand to stop him before he went any further.

Simone da Benno, Florence September 1488.

PROLOGUE

They arrived in a snowstorm; tiny black dots against the quickly whitening valley. The moment that would change my life, though of course I didn't know it.

Winter had come early that year; November having brought with it a kind of cold that could not be remembered, which only added to my torments.

Clad in my thickest cloaks, I had spent a long and frozen week upon my painting tower, amidst bowls of pigment and brushes, pondering upon my Virgin. I had no idea what I'd manage to tease from my brain, but tease I'd have to; time was passing. I was still thinking when Tomma came running to tell me that travellers had been seen on the road. Nothing so very strange about that, but for the fact that they carried a pilgrim's banner.

Such interruptions being blessed indeed, I followed him out onto the campo. A crowd had gathered at the gate. Horses struggled up the hill path; I counted seven, with behind them a string of laden pack mules.

We stood back as they rode through the watchtower below us – four women, hoods hiding their faces, two older

1

men. Having proclaimed themselves to the guards, word spread like wildfire.

'English,' I heard murmured. 'English. English,' as they appeared on the campo.

I followed them to offer my services, for though they had a guide with them he looked a simple sort.

The stable boys came forward to help them dismount. One of the older men, mistaking me for a member of the Duke's household, gave me a little salute.

'I'm at your command, sir,' I said. 'How may I help you?'

'I am Mortimer... of York,' he replied, and though he looked frozen to the very marrow of his bones he managed a smile. 'I value your counsel, sir. I haven't heard my language spoken so well since we left Dover.' A claim I found dubious as I had received but four months of instruction. This had come by way of Richard Lesley, a mercenary in the pay of the Scalieri, with whom I had once shared a dungeon. But that is a tale that will wait until I have need to tell it.

'We are pilgrims.' His face remained straight though what he said next was lunacy. 'On our way to Assisi, in the company of the Abbess of the Convent of...'

My skills in Sir Richard's language being too poor to understand the rest of its name, it seemed to my unpractised ears something close to a gate with no bishop.

'...and come to seek safe passage from the Duke Umberto.'

CHAPTER ONE

All men have enemies, but I had more than most. It is not that I am an unpleasant fellow or possessed of looks that foster envy. My hair is not black, nor does it fall in curls upon my shoulders but is of tallow hue and sticks up at odds from my head as often I forget to comb it.

The Florentine accent escapes me, mine is of Bergamo far to the north. The one feature, or should I make that plural, there being two of them, which enhance my appearance are my eyes; somewhere between green and blue, akin to the colour of Aaron's cloak in my fresco in Santa Maria dei Poveri.

Being from those northern parts, I stand a good half head above others who call themselves tall, but I am not beautiful in any sense of the word, though happily for me my rough looks are different and that difference is but a key that opened the hearts of both maids and their mistresses.

When first I came south, I found the gentlemen of Florence more gorgeous than even the women, though soon I was to discover that banded hose and silken doublets, velvet caps set upon seraphim locks, are but a disguise for they can hold sway with their blades like the very Lucifer himself.

'Mistake not those prancing popinjays for anything other than killing machines' would be my advice to any young lad intent on making his way through the maze of intrigue and double-dealing for which that city is known.

And so it was too in our own painters' world: workshops vied for patrons and patrons were but mortals to be cajoled, tricked, won over, swindled and duped. As far as our rivalries were concerned, ideas were ripe for pilfering, spies would be sent into each other's camps. We artists may not be skilled with swords but we have a deadlier weapon which goes by the name of imagination.

No, I knew my enemies, or the most treacherous of them should I say, for in the world of painted walls and portrait panels we were all foes.

I don't set myself above the others; I was in the game too. In fact, I claim to have been champion amongst them. But, as with all champions, complacency sets in, you let your guard down and in the end it was my own deceits and trickery that forced me to escape the city.

It was a boy who broke me. Or a boy's father, should I say.

For all the reasons I've covered already, our workshops were closed to each other, but Ghirlandaio and I were still friends. I had gone to talk to him for I'd received word, as he must have too, that we were to vie for the commission to paint a new altarpiece for the church of Santa Maria Novella. In my heart I knew that my Lord de'Medici would choose me for the task... and why would he not, for in my painting of Aaron he had glimpsed genius. But I didn't want this competition to cause enmity between us. No, I'd present a generous and noble demeanour and tell him that no matter the outcome, we'd still be friends.

It was the end of August. The sky was blue, birds were singing. I'd been busy working on the last section of my fresco. Why, then, did I bend to temptation?

I blamed him for a while, for is it not always convenient that it be someone else's fault. His door should have been locked, his boys instructed to let no one in. But it wasn't and they did.

'Your master's not here?'

'No signore.'

And this is where I should have left. But my devil jabbed me with his trident, as often he was wont to do. I could take a moment, could I not, to see how my competitor's new work progressed?

I turned and almost fell over the boy. Where the others were at work mixing pigments, he was crouched on the floor. A new face, but why was he not with the others? 'Porco miserie,' but then I saw what he was up to. A scrap of paper in one hand, chalk in the other, the little sod was drawing.

Paper being a costly commodity is not for an apprentice's hands. I prised it gently from his fingers. He got to his feet and gaped at me anxiously.

I had forgotten too quickly; had I not been the same myself as a lad lost in dreams? And so I smiled and told him, in jocular voice, that he should get back to his work and stop idling.

And often I ask myself, what if I had thrown that heaven-sent scrap away? How would my life have unfolded? I'd have stayed there in Florence and my altarpiece would have been proclaimed the finest ever painted. But when I got back to the workshop I had it still, in my hand.

'What's that, sire?' asked Tomma.

Tomma Trovatello, who as a newborn had been found on the steps of a church in Naples, was a boy of strange character whom I'd taken on as an apprentice the year before. I had painted a small crucifix for the brothers of Certosa di San Martino and they sent him to me by way of payment. At the time I thought it an ingenious way to rid themselves of both settling a bill and ridding themselves of an unwanted juvenile. But it hadn't taken long to discover that they had rewarded me as if I had painted all the walls of all the churches in that city, and in Florence too. Where my other lads were nervous youths, eager to please, tripping over their feet to bring a rule or stick of charcoal, he wasn't afraid to say what he thought. 'It's too intense, sire,' being the first words he uttered upon coming into my service.

I had found him staring at the deep shade of blue shimmering down from the wall, in front of which he was standing.

'Oh, you think so, my lord?'

'Yes,' he continued, unruffled. It was clear, even at this early stage in our relationship, that he and irony were at odds. 'Added to which is the fact that if you were to dilute it, you would save yourself cost.'

He was wrong about the blue, but right about the cost, lapis being a pigment more precious than gold.

So, when Tomma asked what I had in my hand I should have known better than to say 'Nothing' and drop it on the floor to be brushed up with the rest of the flotsam at the end of the day.

I was halfway across to the table when I heard him

whistle through his teeth. I turned and saw he had picked it up and stood staring at it as if frozen.

'We'd be grateful if you'd kindly join us here at the mixing table, dear Tomma.'

Still he stood.

'In other words, get your arse over here.'

No sign of movement.

I strode towards him. '*Dio conservami*', but when I saw what held him, fixated, I too was caught motionless, staring.

It was done in red chalk, an arm curving round, a shoulder, a face turned towards me. A flash of movement caught in time. Exquisite. Perfect. As if its creator had managed to sneak inside my head and stolen my vision.

Until that moment I had thought myself the finest artist in all Florence... or all Italy for that matter.

The lads were beside us now, staring too, and where normally there would have been a babble of comment, even they were struck mute.

I walked to the river to think. And though the sun beat down upon me, my soul was grasped by an icy hand. With no more than ten strokes, an unprepossessing, pimple-faced boy had caught that elusive concept of movement, of motion, which in its full-blown state had eluded me thus far. I, a man of twenty-eight years, who had been painting for longer than he'd been alive.

The altarpiece was lost to me, did I not know that the balance had shifted, Ghirlandaio had a new and deadly weapon in his arsenal... and I had wanted to keep him my friend.

If I had been a braver soul, I'd have thrown myself into

the torrent. Wild thoughts of murder came into my mind. I closed my eyes and saw again the lad crouched on the floor, head bent over his drawing, oblivious to the world around him.

The sun sank in the sky, darkness fell, and still I stood staring into the water when Tomma appeared by my side. Of all my boys, only he would be brave enough to come searching for me.

He stood in silence for a while then he said, 'His name is Michelangelo Buonarroti.'

He let me absorb this information before continuing. 'He started a while back with Master Ghirlandaio. His father lives here in the city.'

Facts that made me feel no better. I turned to Tomma, and as I put my hand on his shoulder, a fantastical thought burst into my mind... could I not steal him?

He gave me one of his warning looks. 'It's not a good idea, sire.'

I took no notice of this advice.

Steal him... and lock him away. And I could lock myself up beside him and watch as he put his heaven-made marks onto paper. And perhaps a tiny spark of his genius would rub off on me.

At least the idea made me smile.

Consumed by the concept of that *cazzo* drawing, I became a man obsessed. For two days I thought of naught else, taking it out from the lining of my jerkin to examine the turn of the shoulder, the arm moving forward. The arm moving... until the chalk was so smudged I could barely make out its lines.

On the morning of the third, I woke with a brainwave.

So excited was I, I could neither eat nor drink but paced the floor until time came for action.

I would not recommend that any man set on a mission should do as I did then. By which I mean drinking not one drop of water on a sweltering morning like that. By the time I reached Santa Croce I was struck with a thirst of raging proportions and found myself in the Gatto d'Oro where I downed a jug of new wine, and half of another whilst I was at it. Never would this have been sufficient to addle my mind in the slightest, but perhaps it somewhat blunted my judgement.

I found this Michelangelo's father, this Signor Buonarroti; his house was not far away. He was of modest appearance, but had my mind been in better order I'd have known he was an intelligent man. Or to put it another way, I'd have grasped the fact that he was an even more devious schemer than I. I put a proposal to him; let his son leave Ghirlandaio's workshop and come to mine. If he agreed, not only would I forgo the cost of his apprenticeship, I'd pay him a wage. I wouldn't fix on a sum at that moment, but we would talk about it later.

Why yes, he would think on it.

I left, elated.

Only a few hours after this conversation, Tomma appeared by my side.

'Sire,' he said, 'something's happened... I have to tell you.'

His voice had and urgency to it which I had not heard before. He had left for the church with the brushes and pigment we'd need for that morning, and half a day's measure of plaster, there being but a small portion at the edge of the wall to be finished, as, perhaps, I have said. I saw the bucket was still in his hand.

'It's important,' he added.

Hearing this, Guido and Celestino rushed forward, not wishing to miss a word.

'When I got there,' he began, 'some of the masters were gathered together. They seemed angered by something. Master Pecci was shouting. I knew you'd want to know what had upset them, so I moved close enough to find out.'

'And?'

'They're after your blood, sire.'

What was he talking about?

'It seems that when he heard your proposal, Signor Buonarroti went straight to Ghirlandaio to demand a wage for his son.'

'*Figlio di puttana.*' I knew what was bound to come next.

'And now all the masters are up in arms; they think that their own pupils' fathers will act in a likewise fashion. They're so enraged, they'll kill you this time, sire. I swear it.'

'Or have you killed,' whispered Celestino.

And he was right, for who amongst those spineless shitheads would dare to do the deed himself when there are as many murderous hands for hire in the city as fleas on the arse of a rat.

I stood, head in hands. 'My fucking luck.' But luck had nothing to do with it; I should have been blaming my fucking stupidity.

Tomma pressed his hand upon my chest, an action which had a somewhat calming effect, and said, 'Just think, sire, men like Lampeduso Pecci won't have troubles like this. Would you prefer to be like them?'

I must say here that Pecci was a plodding painter of unremarkable talent.

'You have to get away, that's all.'

His words hit me hard; to leave the city now, when that prize beyond dreams was within my grasp, to say nothing of the bounty attached to it, namely fortune, fame... adulation. There might be something else I should add, but I can't think of it at the moment.

'I know,' he said, 'but there's time.'

And at my lack of response, he sought to prompt my memory.

'Till the first of January.'

What had the first of January to do with anything?

He looked at me with gentle compassion; his poor master was losing his mind.

'Remember, sire... The Lord de'Medici's birthday.'

The date crept, slowly, into my brain, for then it was that Ghirlandaio and I would, in happier times, have presented our finished designs to our gracious prince and the good friars of Santa Maria Novella.

'You can work on them anywhere,' he continued. 'It doesn't have to be here.'

Gesu, he was right.

'Three months, sire. You have three months.'

I would have kissed him had he not been too sober a boy for unrestrained shows of affection.

Hope returned, a new strength filled me; those arseholes weren't rid of me yet, for then it was I resolved to create a design of such wonder as to shake the very ether in which their spheres orbited... that would be acclaimed the most wondrous yet seen... that would set measure of the insurmountable heights of excellence required of those other poor bastards.

And would not my lord command that I came back to his city? And when he did, no man would dare oppose me.

A vision rose up in my mind. There was I, as startling as Signor Polo returned from the lands of the Orient, striding through the doors of the Novella, Tomma at my heels. Boys looking up from their grinding bowls, a murmuring engulfing the space. 'Who's that?' I could almost hear them whisper.

'Simone da Benno,' would come the reply. 'It's that son of a bitch... Simone da Benno.'

Their masters' shocked faces peering down from the heights of their painting towers, with looks of puzzlement then disbelief. Is not Vengeance the sweetest of words?

There was, however, one detail dear Tomma seemed to have missed. 'And what of the Buonarroti boy?'

'Oh he will be long forgotten by then.'

And now you know the whole balls-aching story of why I had to flee Florence.

CHAPTER TWO

I arrived in Montevecchio on the third day of October, in the Year of Our Lord Fourteen Hundred and Eighty-Eight with a folder of drawings and Tomma, for though he was small and misshapen, by now you will know that his mind was sharp as a tack, and minds being of far more importance than bodies, who else should I chose to take with me on the road that, pray *Deo*, led to my salvation?

It being common knowledge that the Lord Umberto of that city set in the mountains a good day's ride north sought a master to paint a great work in his church. It was of consolation to me that Umberto was known as a thorn in Florence's side and though his fiefdom was too small to be more than an irritant to the great city, the thought of it gave me at least some little satisfaction. And so it followed that's where we headed. Had I left Florence in happier circumstances I'd have carried with me a commendation from my patron telling of all the sensations created by me, describing, especially, Aaron's cloak, of that deep and glistering blue never before seen on a wall, be it in Christendom or beyond.

'If things turn out well, I'll send for you,' I had told Guido and Celestino. I felt a great pull at my heart for there was no choice but to leave them behind.

Guido put on a brave face. Celestino only scuffed his toe along the dusting of chalk on the floor.

'Go to Master Sandro.' That possessor of genius, who went by the name Botticelli, had stood by me through far worse than this. He would take care of them. 'He'll be most happy to have you…'

I emptied the jug of its stash of coins and gave them both a handful, the rest I stuffed into the lining of my jerkin.

Apart from those few coins, most of which turned out to be soldi, we left with only the clothes we stood up in, along with some of my drawings. Tomma, with usual presence of mind, had scuttled around collecting the best of them, squeezing them into the first folder he could lay his hands on. Guido ran out to hire us horses and strapped it onto the larger one's flanks. Moments later we were through the city gates, galloping north.

The road from Florence is not easy even in daylight; the river crashes and thunders beside it, its gullies and rocky outcrops being hazardous in the extreme, to say nothing of having to pass by way of Pistoia, where robbers and cut-throats lie in wait for passing trade.

With a change of horse you can make the journey in a day, as I have said, but we had left late and there was no choice but to break our journey. And so it was that, far enough beyond that place where dwell those enemies of Heaven, and still in possession of our lives, we reined our horses in a field and, uncaring what might befall us in the fast-creeping darkness, threw ourselves upon the ground and fell into a sleep of the dead.

Unlucky for Tomma, he passed his sixteenth birthday

the following day, and even though little by way of intoxicating liquor had ever passed his lips, we should have spent it at the Gatto d'Oro. Instead, stiff and miserable, we rose with the dawn and set off again, reaching the foot of what I can but describe as a gigantic rock, with clinging to its peak the citadel of Montevecchio, the planes and facets of its buildings shining like mirrors where the sun struck upon them.

Our ascent up its treacherous path is etched in my memory still. We led our horses, their hooves sparking and skidding on the stony path with no idea of how far we had yet to climb, for the wooded way above us shielded sight of our destination.

A fierce heat beat down upon us, but mountains being familiar to me I knew that winter would bring with it even deeper snow than in Florence, and fires would be kept stoked well into April. Hard to imagine with the sun glaring down on us now. It sat at midpoint in the heavens when, above a row of pine trees, a massive rampart came into view. We entered through it by way of a well-guarded gate tower, and the fortress opened out before us, or should I say 'up'. I could see that the place earned its reputation, being as true a stronghold as ever I had encountered with its maze of alleyways soaring skywards. What ill-led army would risk attacking? The sole method of wresting surrender from its good inhabitants would be by starving them out.

The sergeant on duty asked our business. Perhaps it should have been a warning that he and his detachment of men seemed somewhat bemused when I gave my reply. Up through a warren of alleys we reached the summit and my jaw dropped. No doubt so did Tomma's, though I was too busy gaping at the scene set out before us to affirm that indeed it was true: for there at the summit stretched a great campo. On one side stood Umberto's palace, on the other, a bell tower beside a church of ancient design, where no doubt the fresco was to be painted. And in between the space was filled to overflowing with what I could but assume was any man who cared to attach the appellation 'artist' to his name. And all, it would seem, with the same aim in mind: to win the commission for the job. This was a problem neither of us had contemplated. And what about lodgings? Every room, be it in a hostelry or shopkeeper's home, or good wife's little cottage, was taken by vast entourages. *Sangue di Dio*, why did they need such hordes of attendants?

And so it was back down through the alleyways, past the guards at the gate tower where, as in a winter evening's play, we settled in a stable in the company of our horses, the farmer taking as much from us, excluding our livery charges, as had we been bedded in the Prior's own cell in the monastery of Sant Severino.

The second morning of our venture saw us picking our way along a dusty track and onto the perilous road, with strapped once more on my horse's flank my folder of drawings. Through the gate tower and up the alleyways to the campo we joined the throng, and here I took stock of what I would once have regarded as no more than deluded losers, but by the number of the motherfuckers, now seemed more like flies in the proverbial ointment, their retinues crowded around them, turned out in all their glorious best; brocades, pleated tunics, hats with feathers jutting up on their crests. And they having set out long before us, we found ourselves at the edge of the crowd, all eyes fixed upon the palace gate in front of which stood sentries taller than I.

'*Santa Madonna,* let's find us another wall that needs painting, even if we have to ride all the way to Siena.'

'No sire,' Tomma peered up at me. I perceived a look in his eyes. 'You don't want word to reach Florence that someone else has won the commission. They'll know you're here. And you have no way of explaining the fact that you left of your own choice.' Luck might have abandoned me, but not him. 'It's simply a case of waiting; none of these men is competition.'

His statement, which was certainly valid, was marked by the fact that in all the months he had been with me, never had I heard him utter words of flattery... or false encouragement if it came to that.

'But perhaps it's better to go back down the mountain,' he continued, 'find a place to eat... make a plan.'

We tethered our horses at a tavern, but I was too dejected to think about eating.

'Those men in the campo,' Tomma asked when we found a space at a crowded table, 'what do you notice about them?'

To save me the effort of finding my voice, he answered the question himself. 'Rich clothes, washed faces.'

Rising above my instinct to throttle him, I held my tongue.

'The painters among them are twenty at most; their servants make up the numbers. You stand out, sire. You're not like them. If all were put together, alongside yourself, who would you notice?'

His question, being of a rhetorical nature, did not need a reply. I waited to hear what next he would say.

'Don't comb your hair, sire, or dust down your clothes. Stay as you are. Sooner or later you'll catch their attention. Oh, and don't ride. We should walk the road. Someone will be bound to say, "Who is that madman, struggling on foot?"'

'And pray what to do with my drawings?'

'Strap them to your back, which will only make sure you stand out even more.'

It was then I knew that in Tomma I had treasure greater than all the gold in the newfound lands of the Spanish.

On the third morning we joined the crowd and pushed ourselves into its centre, and just as we did, the gate opened. A guard appeared through it and called out a name. Only then did it strike me that all those clustered around us must surely have submitted petitions. How else would they know which one amongst them to summon?

His servants thrusting and jostling their master's way to the palace gate, he entered through it.

This continued for two more days. 'Don't give up hope, sire.'

Hope? What about the will to live? 'No, Tomma, this is a balls-aching waste of our time.'

'What else are you doing?'

Grazie a Dio, I was too tired to argue, for at the next morning's circus when the gate opened the guard pointed at me. 'That man,' he shouted. 'There, with the bundle strapped to his back.'

My heart lifted and would have flown from my body had it been a bird.

With all the cocksuckers gaping upon us, we were led through the sentry-guarded gates, and found ourselves in a courtyard, at the end of which loomed Umberto's palace.

I sweltered under my jerkin, helped not by the weight on my back. Up massive steps, and through a carved, iron studded door. Along a columned walkway and I saw I'd been right about winters in these parts; heavy hangings, drawn back to let air through the open windows, would in times of frigid weather be closed fast. I found myself greatly surprised at the opulence surrounding us, which equalled any in Florence.

Into a sumptuous chamber. A man stood beside an open window. My knowledge of such places and their inhabitants told me he was but some bumptious factotum. An elaborate silk cap was folded in pleats about his forehead, more ornate than any sported by my so-called rivals waiting outside on the campo. In the barely abated heat, it seemed to me like an instrument designed for torture.

'What is your business, signore?' he demanded in a languorous, apathetic tone as if eager to display his boredom.

I cared not for his manner, surely my business required no explaining.

'I come to make submission to paint the fresco for the Lord Umberto... signore.'

'Ah, a man from the mountains.' This he said in a mocking, and should I add exceedingly poor rendition of my accent.

I didn't reply.

'You have not done so before now?' next he enquired; a detail I happened to know already.

'You're right. I haven't.'

He looked me over as a judge would a thief dragged

before him, making great play of the fact that my appearance offended his eyes every bit as much as my diction.

'And your name is?'

I wouldn't be slighted by a one such as he. 'Simone da Benno... And yours?'

Startled at being addressed in this manner, a moment passed before he answered. 'It is of no importance to you.'

'Aye, signore, but it is.'

His lips tightened. 'You are exhausting my patience, Signor... da Benno.' Clearly my name meant nothing to him.

And now it was that I felt that old and time-honoured fury seethe up inside me and would have turned back along the way we had come, across the courtyard and down the mountain, had not Tomma started scrabbling behind me, wrenching the folder from my shoulders. He had it off now, and kneeling on the floor proceeded to open it, unrolling the first of my drawings with its sweeping patches of colour.

As if he were a connoisseur of all things to do with a painter's craft, the dickhead put his hand to his chin.

A moment passed before he proclaimed, 'We have seen enough... You may go.'

He was a dullard who had seen nothing. Knew nothing. This fact was clear.

But Tomma wasn't about to give up. 'Please, signore. My master has worked in the court of the Scalieri and that of the Medici. Look again, and you'll see...'

The arsehole turned away.

'Come Tomma.' I pointed at the drawings, indicating that he should gather them up. 'No point in casting pearls before swine.'

'You call me a swine?' The ludicrous hat took a step

towards me.

'You may not be one,' I retorted, 'but your knowledge is of porcine capacity.'

'You offend me, signore.'

'Impossible... signore... you have nothing worth offending. I simply state what I see.'

'And I see a lout standing before me. You waste my time with such... monstrosities. I consider them the jokes that they are, and would laugh if I had the energy.'

Tomma, aware of what was bound to come next, grabbed hold of my jerkin in a brave attempt at holding me back. His efforts were in vain, however. Forward I lunged and seized my tormentor by his throat, closing my fingers about it. His face turned the same shade of puce as his cap. A guard ran towards us, others appeared. And though my little apprentice knew nothing yet regarding penalties linked to such actions – I refer to dungeons stinking of piss or bodies hanging from gibbets – his mind was working like mine. By now he had given up on my jerkin; we glanced at each other and ran. Up we leapt, in unison, and out through the open window.

I can't say how many of my nine lives I had squandered thus far. If this were the tenth then pray the Dear Lord would help us. Our legs made running motions. We stretched out our arms as if we were flying, the fast-approaching tree tops our only salvation.

I made impact first. Tomma came toppling behind me. The branches gave way, one after the other but, thank *Gesu*, with each agonising bump our velocity diminished and, the last one above us now, we crashed to the ground with a little less force than would have been required to kill us.

I heard a loud crack; it seemed to come from somewhere in the general vicinity of my shoulder. A pain of the searing variety ripped through it. The world went blank. Who knows how long I lay there. In due course I heard a small voice saying, 'Sire.'

'Sire,' it repeated.

Fighting the agony, which all but overwhelmed me, I summoned strength enough to turn my head towards it.

'Open your eyes.'

I would have surrendered myself to oblivion, but for its insistence. I forced them apart.

Adjusting my vision, I could see Tomma stretched out beside me and watched as, akin to an upended insect that once I'd observed under a glass bell in my Lord Leonardo's cabinet of experiments, he moved first his arms then his legs.

I endeavoured to follow suit but my limbs would not respond. I strove to force the word 'Tomma' from my mouth. 'Aa... Aa', being all I could manage.

He crawled towards me and looked down at my face.

'Sire.'

'Aa.'

He took my arm and raised it upwards.

'Aa... Ma...' Now I could form the sound 'M.'

'Ta... Ma...'

Agonising pain hacked deeper into my shoulder.

Slowly, gently, he pulled me up, though I would have preferred to be left on the ground. And there we vomited, together.

As we were thus engaged, a very great screaming started somewhere below us.

'They're coming!' There was a deal of terror in Tomma's voice. But we had a far greater problem than the guards he imagined, for I knew that sound as I knew no other.

'Run!' And though my words were indecipherable, he got the gist of them. Fright caused our legs to function enough to get us up the slope, just as a boar, the size of a small pony – had my words about swine summoned the monster up from some hell? – came charging towards us. Our only refuge being the treetops, we clambered, Tomma up one, I up another, struggling to find footholds, white hot daggers stabbing through me.

We smelt it even above our vomit, so much like rancid pork was its odour. Tomma's tree was but a slender sapling compared to mine. For some unfortunate reason the boar decided to charge and hit poor Tomma's a thundering whack, a step or two back and, now having measure of his target, hurtled forward again, battering his massive head against it.

'Hold on!' I yelled, language miraculously recovered.

I was thinking fast now; how to deflect the monster. I snapped off a branchling and threw it down upon its great back.

The colossus withdrew, but as he lowered his head to launch himself at Tomma again, my selfless act having been in vain, a new sound arose – a scuffling from the forest below.

Distracted, the boar held his ground as a group of peasants appeared through the trees, long staves balanced upon their shoulders. At the sight of them, our foe grunted, and shot off like an arrow, pursued by a pack of silent, slathering dogs. The peasants would have followed were it not for the sight that beheld them. They stopped in their tracks and looked up at us, flummoxed.

Now a young man emerged from the undergrowth, his clothes in perfect contrast to his companions, though his stave was of similar design. He followed the gaze of the gawking assembly.

'Well, I'll be damned.'

He started to laugh. As if now having permission, the peasants laughed too.

'Don't stand there you worthless bumpkins, help these good gentlemen down.'

The words 'good' and 'gentlemen' did much to restore my spirit, there seeming little that could mend my body. Tomma went first, hands reaching up to help him as he slid down.

My turn now. Like a man encased in iron armour, and weighing thereof, I managed an inelegant descent, and despite the proffered hands, walloped onto the ground.

'You look in pain, signore?' As well I might, having leapt from a window a great way above.

But I could say nothing of that. 'Getting into the tree…'

'Thank goodness you did… those are brutes when their blood's up.'

Try to make conversation, Benno. 'You were after it?'

'No, clearing nets with my dogs. They got the scent and there was no stopping them. They're trained not to bark, which is why you didn't hear them approach.'

'I thank your dogs, signore, but for them we would have been stuck up there for *Dio* only knows how long.'

'I am Donato Favoni.' He held out his hand.

'And I Simone da Benno.' I managed to grasp it. 'And

this is Tomma.'

'Ah.' He looked at me doubtfully. A grown man and young boy, out here in the forest.

I cared not what he might think, but nonetheless felt it a duty to put him straight.

'Tomma is my apprentice, signore. I am a painter...' Well-practised in the art, how quickly lies flew into my brain. '...commissioned to create a scene of antiquity, set within woodland. We came here with our slates and chalk.'

'Collect them up then, Signor Simone, and come with me. My house is not far away. We'll take a look at your injuries. My assistant has a good knowledge of medicine. And my cook makes a very good table.'

'It's too much to ask of you, signore.' I would have protested with greater conviction but even above the pain in my shoulder my stomach was growling, and I knew that Tomma's was too.

'Come,' he replied, 'gather your things, you can regale us with painters' tales.'

But we couldn't gather them; there being none to gather.

'We ran a good way.' I would have continued calling him simply 'signore' had he not addressed me by my own Christian name. 'Signor Donato. Our stuff is down there in the thicket. I can't think we will find it.'

'Oh come, let us try.'

'Please, it's of no value. Only a couple of lines had been drawn. And slate and chalk are easily replaced.'

'In that case, let us go. I'm afraid we must get ourselves down to the foot of the hill, join the road and go up it again.' And, by way of illustrating this statement, he pointed skywards.

Even in my agony I could see what he meant, for above us towered a flat plane of rock, over which we had just tumbled, the palace and its open window somewhere above it.

I tried to look grateful; the thought of that journey.

'Fortunato is waiting with my horse. You shall have it. The going won't be so hard.'

We went slowly, Tomma and I, helped along by the peasants, the pain in my shoulder increasing with every step down the buggering slope, at the foot of which, as promised, the aforementioned horse was tethered to a tree. A chubby servant boy, lounging on the grass beside it, jumped to his feet when he saw us. The peasants helped me mount, Tomma balanced behind me and off we set, the servant boy leading the horse by its rein. But, as it clip-clopped along its thudding jolts tortured me to such an extreme that, leaving the saddle to Tomma, I dismounted, better to walk.

CHAPTER THREE

I was digging a grave with Francesca when I first saw Simone da Benno. But that is not exactly right, I was doing the digging, she being encumbered with a vast belly could not so much as attempt to bend over. Instead she was giving instructions; 'Faster Sofia', for that is my real name, Maria Assunta being the one given to me when first I joined holy orders. 'Can't you go any faster?'

'No.'

I managed to stop myself adding that if she thought she could do any better, she could give it a try.

Next came a small wail of impatience.

They do say that women who are almost come to full term behave with heightened emotions. But even taking this into consideration, though it might seem a strange thing to say, as I looked up at her sorrowful face I did think that I, a poor novice, trapped in holy orders until the day that I too would be buried here in the graveyard, was the fortunate one.

Just as I set to digging again, we heard her husband's voice. It came from the road which, belonging as it did to the outside world, was on the other side of the wall. Her face changed from agitation to fury, 'In the name of all that is sacred,' she shouted, 'can't I get away from him for even a moment?'

The wall being too high to look over, I ran to fetch Corvo's box, opened its lid and tipped him onto the grass. His feathers were no longer blue-black and glossy but shrivelled and grey. I didn't have time then to think it strange that, rather than stinking as all dead things do when left to fester, he smelt of something... much like vinegar.

It needed some effort to carry it; not because it was larger than Corvo, but as it was circular in shape and therefore had no corners to grip to, it slipped from my grasp a few times and took precious moments to get to the wall. I set it down. We stepped upon it, and now could see a band of men approaching; the owner of the voice to the fore.

The box wobbled as Francesca's fury rose. 'What is he doing?' Her voice had the tone of a wife of twenty years practice, rather than barely one.

As they came closer, a tableau emerged, somewhere between a nativity and 'Christ being led to his crucifixion', Christ being a rough-looking fellow, battered and bloodied, his raiments in tatters, supported by two of a group of good shepherds, their pitiful clothes in very great contrast to those of her husband. And there at the end of the procession, Fortunato leading his master's horse, upon which a small bent figure was perched.

Clop-clop of hooves striking the cobbles. Shuffle-shuffle of the good shepherds' feet. Clomp-clomp of Christ's sturdy boots. They passed by the wall and disappeared round the curve of the road.

CHAPTER FOUR

Soon we were making the familiar ascent back up to the top of the hill. Passing through the gate tower. Other men would have baulked at the prospect of entering, once again, into the lion's den, but I had experience enough of such things to know the safest place to hide is under your enemy's nose. And I was proven right for, though we surely looked as if we had been in a battle, the guards gave us not a second glance. And why should they, being as we were in the company of a nobleman.

Up we went, through the maze of winding alleyways. Above us loomed the campo with, set somewhere upon it, the church whose wall, had things turned out differently, I would have become acquainted. But cursing my fate would not help me now.

We did not carry on to the summit, *Madonna Grazie*. Instead we turned along a narrow lane and stopped at a merchant's house of great splendour. The peasants took their leave, bowing and pulling their caps as they went. I could but surmise they had been well rewarded for their morning's work. Under a portal, carved into its stone, were the words 'Villa Favoni'. The house was handsome indeed, standing in proportional perfection at the end of a garden planted with trees. The boy Fortunato helped Tomma down. Along the path between the trees and through an arched portico, we entered a hall inlaid with carved wooden panels. I knew wealth when I saw it; the place was sumptuous.

In Florence I had cut a plain figure amidst the peacocks of the court, but cared not a jot about it. Here, however, in my tattered jerkin, exchanged in Bologna eight years before for a sketch quickly done in a whorehouse, I felt more bedraggled than the peasants who had only just taken their leave. In the midst of such opulence, in our torn and dirt-stained clothes, Tomma and I could have been *buffone*, hired to perform on the stage of the Palazzo Ducale.

'Come gentlemen.' That word again. He led us into a small, book-lined room and bade us sit. We were most happy to do so. The lad called Fortunato was given instructions. 'Go and find Signor Baldassare. Tell him to come as fast as he can... and bring his instruments. I have a patient for him.'

By now, my shoulder pained me so greatly I could no longer make effort to speak. Thanks then for Tomma.

'You have a splendid library, signore.'

Our host, much gratified by this compliment, embarked upon what might have developed into a discourse, starting with the purchase of his first manuscript, had a figure not appeared at the door, Fortunato in tow.

'Ah Giacomo, we need your help. My guests are wounded. They fell from a tree...' If our new companion wished to ask what we had been doing in one in the first place, he was polite enough not to.

'Signor Baldassare studied medicine at Padua.' This our saviour said with such pride that, though they were of equal ages, he might have been speaking about a son. Tall and black haired with eyes even darker than Tomma's and, like all the scholars I had come across up until now, an air of dour and aloof self-assurance. I can't say I immediately liked him.

'We should attend to Signor Simone. He seems in great pain.'

Baldassare leaned over me and before I had time to inform him of the fact, said, 'It's your shoulder signore.'

I confirmed that it was.

'I'll have to cut through your jerkin.'

By now I couldn't have cared had he cut through my arm along with it. He opened his bag, from which he produced a small knife, and went to work.

Fortunato was sent for water. He reappeared some moments later with a sloshing bowl. When my shoulder was bathed, my physician pressed his finger upon it, an action that produced such agony as to make me yell like a two-year-old child.

'It's broken,' he proclaimed, in his flat, indifferent, tone. I was not surprised by his diagnosis. 'We'll bind it and strap it to your chest; it's important to keep it immobile.'

'For how long?' enquired Tomma, ever the practical.

'Six weeks... maybe eight.'

Donato looked at me with sympathy. 'Oh I'm sorry,' he said.

But I was far less sorry than he for, *Gesu grazie*, my good arm was not the one put out of action for, 'like most painters,' I reassured him, 'I am left-handed.'

The binding took place, with soft linen bandages. My arm was then strapped to my chest, elbow downwards, hand close to my neck... and a miracle took place – the pain left me.

'You must stay here, Signor Simone, until you recover,' our Good Samaritan smiled down upon me. 'I'll send word to anyone you wish, explaining what's happened.'

'I thank you, but please, you must not be concerned. There is no one.'

I saw his expression and remembered my concocted tale about commissions to paint woodland scenes.

'Oh, my patron is in... Lucca... I can send him a letter.'

'But what's his name?'

'Signor Zaccari Trissino,' I said, coming up with Guido and Celestino's surnames combined.

At this he looked puzzled. 'I'm on familiar terms with the merchants of that city... I can't say I know him.'

Think fast, Benno. 'I see I have confused you. His house is there, but he's often away.'

Which was as bad, for now he proclaimed, 'Well that is lucky, I go there next week. Tell me where it is, and I shall deliver it. If he is not at home, it will be waiting for him on his return.'

It occurred to me then, my luck would run out when he went on his *cazzo* expedition.

Tomma stepped in. 'But remember, sire, he sold his house.'

'Ah yes, Tomma is right... you're right Tomma. It must be the blow to my head. How could I have forgotten? His house has been sold. He has gone to...'

'Rome, sire.'

'Rome... yes, Rome.'

Our good host had lost us by now. 'Ah well, no matter.'

He smiled. 'No, you must stay with us Signor Simone.'

'Please call me Benno.'

'And you must call me Donato. It will be a pleasure to have two new faces amongst us.'

I thanked him from the depths of my heart.

'I'm afraid I can offer only a room at the top the house. I'm a silk merchant, you see. I'm using all the others for storage just at the moment.'

It was an attic to be precise, at the top of a steep wooden staircase.

Happily, he knew nothing about the world from which we had come, or of the role of commissioned painters who, by our very employment, reflect power and prestige: we are costly, so much so, that we have been known to bankrupt a family.

The space, however, turned out to be far better than any of the fine apartments allocated to me in times before, for those I had been required to share with my competitors, and competitors being an abhorrence to me, I often chose to sleep in my workshop, as I may have told you – forcing my boys to stuff their ears with wax in order to block out my snoring.

As habit had taught me, I took my dagger from the band of my breeches and pushed it under the larger of the two mattresses set on the floor. I could but rejoice that the smaller would be more than sufficient for Tomma. I then lay upon it, '*Sangue di Dio...*'

'You must look on it another way, sire... if it hadn't been for the trees... if the signore had not been passing.'

'Pull off my boots, there's a good lad.'

He pulled.

'And undo my jerkin.' Or what remained of it, I meant. He undid it.

'What next for us now, my little friend?'

'Don't worry, sire, we'll think of a plan.'

'Sleeping is all I have plans for at present.'

But I was in for a great disappointment, for now came a knock at the door. Fortunato's cheery face appeared round it. Next came his body. Under his arm was a bundle.

'My master would like you to join him for dinner. He sends you these and hopes they will fit.' He held out the bundle, Tomma took it, and Fortunato placed on the floor beside him what, from the distance of the mattress, looked like a fine pair of boots.

CHAPTER FIVE

Would we even know who the Christ figure was? What he'd been doing on the road with Donato, where they were going? You might wonder why Francesca could not simply ask him, the answer being that she hadn't spoken to her husband for more than a month, and she wasn't about to start now.

I would have marched up the hill path and asked him myself, for never had I seen such a being. Which was but fantasy of course for, as you will know, we unfortunates shut away behind convent walls must shun life outside them, except when performing the work of Our Lord. When we do venture out into the world, it is to poor places; to tend the sick or take food to the hungry. It thus followed that on my short travels I had come across many a type, but none even vaguely like him, so wild, so fascinating, had he been. Perhaps I should have prayed forgiveness for permitting such thoughts to enter my head. But that would have meant renouncing my sin, and I didn't want to.

I closed my eyes and pictured, again, the strange procession: Donato, the Christ figure towering above him, the peasants, the horse clop-clopping along, and that's when I remembered Fortunato, leading it by its bridle. I

35

could hardly contain my excitement for then it struck me; Francesca would not ask her husband, but she could ask him.

CHAPTER SIX

'...*Dio conservami.*' This I said after Fortunato left us, along with other choice phrases. I longed only to stay there, flat on the mattress, shut my eyes and sleep forever.

'Tomma.' I pointed at the boots.

He brought them over, and with a great tugging at my legs, managed to pull them on.

By now trickles of sweat were making their way across my forehead, it being true that hot air travels upwards as had been demonstrated by Signor da Vinci or was it some Greek in the time of Archimedes.

He looked up, suddenly struck by a thought as far away from boots as could be. 'What if the Duke's men are searching for us? What if they track us down and find us here in the signore's house?'

I couldn't give him an answer, except to say, 'I don't know Tomma, you tell me, you're the clever one.'

And so it was, by courtesy of our gentle host, having acquired a somewhat sophisticated appearance at odds with my usual shambolic one, in clothes of a type never before had I occasion to wear, or even had I money enough would choose to afford, my feet clad in the boots of Morocco leather, one arm in a new silken doublet, the right side of it draped round my bandage, we made our way back down the stairway. I may add here that Tomma was swathed in a tunic and breeches which once had belonged to a person of far greater bulk. Woven from fine marbled wool, he had knotted them at his waist to prevent them falling down to his ankles.

Fortunato stood waiting. He managed to keep his face straight when he saw us, or, in this case, should I say Tomma. We followed him along passageways as intricately carved as the hall. Halberds and flags hung upon it. There was no doubt that our Signor Donato was even more prosperous than I had supposed; one thing I'd discovered in my travels being the level of ostentation placed upon households by those in command.

At the very top rung are the noble families, and so it follows, in possession of fabulous wealth. Their palaces are hung with tapestries, covered with graffito decoration, filled with carved and inlaid furniture. Mosaic pavements are under their feet. They are born in beauty and die in it.

A rung down are the old patricians, no longer rich. They have money on which to live comfortably, but their rooms remain furnished in times of the past. Were this order to swell in number, my livelihood would be at stake.

The profit of painters comes from the first lot, or the third who, like my gentle host, have wealth but recently made. All in their houses is new and expensive; a sideboard is chosen not for its beauty or delicate lines but for cost. Lavish spending does not result in tasteful surroundings, however, this being the finest example of what I am talking about.

The dining room into which we were led was as opulent

as any in Florence owned by a man of new money. A beaten silver table stretched its length, at the far end of which sat an elderly gentleman, with, beside him, Donato.

'Ah Benno!' He jumped to his feet. 'Come and join us. But first let me present my father.'

Signor Donato's father had the look of a man who had worked, rather than fought, his way into fortune, with none of the corpulence that afflicts those who sit back to enjoy the fruits of their plunder. His largish head sat upon a thin frame.

'Do you remember I told you that I have invited Signor da Benno to stay here with us for a while? He is a painter.'

Paper, quill and ink sat beside Donato's hand. 'A painter,' he repeated, and wrote the word down. His father's bleary eyes followed the quill as words took shape on the paper. He then studied my arm in its bindings.

'Don't concern yourself father. You are left-handed, are you not Benno, by the grace of God?'

'Oh yes. The old man held my gaze. 'A painter. I have often heard of them, but I have never met one.' He spoke with an accent akin to my own, belonging as it did to a lower order. A self-made man. A type I admired.

'My father is deaf,' continued Donato, before I had time to reply. 'He became thus afflicted in later years, but if you speak slowly, by watching your lips, he can follow something of what you are saying.'

In the midst of eating, Donato would put down his fork – aye they had forks, with ivory handles – and jot down a sentence or two for the old man, who would add a few words to the conversation.

'For whom do you work, signore?'

I paused too long as never I should when a lie is to be told. 'Oh I take my trade where I can find it.' I pronounced my words with deliberation. Had I been less preoccupied with my answer, I might have noticed his wary expression.

As if to absolve me from answering further, a sound came from the passage beyond and the physician entered the chamber. I could not but observe that he looked somewhat agitated.

Donato waved him forward. He approached apprehensively; it was clear he preferred not to speak in front of strangers, by which I mean Tomma and me. He whispered into his master's ear.

'I beg you to excuse me.' Donato was on his feet in a flash. 'I'm afraid I must attend to something.' And with that he left us alone with his father. I could think of nothing to say to the old man. Tomma tried. 'You have a most beautiful house, signore.' But there was no answer. An uncomfortable silence settled upon us but the feast that followed went a long way to help us ignore it.

I summon from somewhere in the depths of my memory roast goose and a sauce made of cherries. This we attacked with a fair deal of relish, for over the preceding month of relentless work in order to finish my fresco we had eaten simply to keep us alive. In the midst of our feast, the old man broke the silence. Putting down his fork, he started upon a long list of questions; where did we come from? How long had I been engaged in the painters' craft? Did I belong to a guild? I shouted my answers but it was plain it made no difference.

The third course had only just been cleared when there came a sound from the corridor. The old gentleman called,

'Francesca. Francesca.'

I might have dwelt upon Tomma's puzzled look but there was no time, for a young woman stepped through the door. I say woman but she would be better compared to an immortal concocted by Sandro. We artists spend lifetimes in search of perfection. We paint portraits and it's our job to change plain features to fair. But extreme beauty is not simply prettiness intensified; it must beguile, enchant, it must captivate utterly. Nor is it immediate; you can't simply hold it in your mind's eye, sum it up in a moment. You know you must look at it again, and again, until you get its measure.

My silence wasn't lost on Tomma. Perhaps I should mention the other detail assailing my eyes, this being that she was most enormously pregnant. He nudged me. I got to my feet a man bewitched. She gave a startled look when she saw me, and had I not known it to be impossible, I might have thought she knew who I was.

'Come and meet our new friend,' said the old man. 'Signor Simone da Benno.'

Still I stood.

Tomma prodded me violently enough to rouse a response. 'My lady.' I bent my head. 'I am honoured.'

If she was pleased to see me, she made a good job of hiding it. Nor did she seem curious about the fact that my doublet was open, my bandages only partially hidden beneath it. Close to her now, I studied her face, as artists are wont to; wide forehead, made wider by eyebrows shaved in the fashion of the day, small chin and a thick glob of what looked like dried mud on her cheek.

She stood by the table's edge saying nothing, her expression not greatly unlike Baldassare's. The old man clenched his jaw as if to stop himself uttering words he would later regret.

'Signor da Benno is an artist,' he made great effort to explain. She did not seem interested to hear it.

'But,' the old man managed to ignore her, turning to me; it was clear he'd been struck with a sudden idea, 'you must let us sample your work.' He pushed the paper and quill towards me.

'My daughter-in-law is a worthy subject, are you not... my dear?'

I leaned across the table, turned the paper to its clean side, and picked up the pen. A moment later I pushed it back to him, foretelling his reaction, for Sandro aside and, perchance, Mantegna, I was the finest in all the land. I do not include da Vinci, of course, but he is more magus than mortal.

He looked at it long without speaking, then he proclaimed, 'Ye gods, but you're good.'

'Good' being a word that never before had been attached to my work, I postulated in my mind that he was impoverished of language.

'I wonder,' he said now, his eyes still transfixed to the paper, 'if you are not in employ at the moment might I offer myself as your patron?'

My mind worked like a fury to find a response. We couldn't stay here; Tomma was right, for all we knew the Duke's men were searching for us at that very moment.

'Oh,' I hesitated.

'I'd pay you well.' As if the deal had been struck, he handed the page to his daughter-in-law. She glanced at it briefly then pushed it away.

'Will you do it, signore?' he asked. 'Will you paint

Francesca?'

I heard the word 'Yes' escape from my lips before I had time to stop it.

*

'Has the Devil taken charge of my mind? What possessed me to say I would do it?' We were back in the refuge of our attic. To be stuck in a merchant's house, painting his loathsome wife; even though I knew how to treat all manner of rich and spoilt women, there was not a project less likely to tempt me. 'No Tomma, I'm made for better things.'

But he wasn't listening. 'There's something I don't understand, sire. If Signor Donato's father is deaf, how did he hear her out there in the passage?'

What was he talking about?

'He must have. How else would he know she was there?'

This was one of Tomma's unanswerable conundrums; was there not more to be thinking about?

He ceded politely, but now came one more of his observations. 'She doesn't seem keen on the thought of a portrait.'

If I hadn't known him by now, I might have thought he was trying to be funny.

'Then we shall ease her of her concerns. We're not hanging around here. We're going. Tomorrow. We'll rent us a workshop. Anywhere, Tomma, I do not care... didn't we think of Siena?'

'I'm sorry about the fresco.' Until now it hadn't been mentioned.

'Oh, I'm not. I'm glad. In fact, I'm ecstatic. No balls-aching deadlines. No orders to move the scene a little to the left... a little to the right. Change the shade of the background. Joy, my little friend, we are free.'

'But what about your shoulder, sire?'

'Oh, I'll manage.'

'Well, if you're sure, we should head for the coast.'

He had reason for saying this?

'There are ships in Livorno.'

'You propose that we sign ourselves up as deckhands?'

He answered, in earnest, that no he did not, that he had other ideas. 'Forget Siena, sire, it's too close to Florence. We should take passage to Naples.' This wasn't such a preposterous idea for, as I might have told you, it was his city and he knew it well.

I remained silent for a while, conserving my strength, better to consider his proposal, Naples being a place to which, filled as it was with immensely more passionate scoundrels than I, I had sworn I would never return... the presence there of the Marchesa Rizziola being the single attraction with power enough to tempt me.

Though not a regular occurrence, I did sometimes suffer a prick of conscience. 'And what do we tell Donato?'

'Explain, sire. Say you were carried away by the prospect of the portrait... you can't start upon it now, but you will return. And when you do, he can be sure it will be the finest ever painted.'

How did a boy of such genius come to be in employ as a lowly painter's apprentice? Yes I would tell him... we'd go tomorrow.

But plans are made to be dashed, are they not?

44

CHAPTER SEVEN

I am sure you are wondering why Francesca was part of my life. And why I was part of hers?

Let me explain this peculiar reality: my father had managed her father's vineyards and so we had grown up with each other. I look back at that time with great happiness; his house was a merry place; life had been good. But when her mother died of the swelling fever... and her father shortly after, it and its grounds and vineyards were passed to her uncle, a selfish avaricious man who wished to rid himself of her as soon as he found a way to do it, just as he planned to get rid of my father, both of which he succeeded in doing within a very short while. He betrothed Francesca to Donato Favoni and cast my father out.

I don't blame my poor father for giving me up to the convent; he was penniless by then and sick with worry as to what might befall us. And so I entered holy orders... and the vicious world that lurks behind nunnery walls.

And why, you may ask, were we able to meet, as we had the day before, when she came to bury poor Corvo? The answer is simple. Before he died, Francesca's father had given vast sums to our order, and happy to follow in his footsteps, Donato continued to do the same. So it was for this sake, and this sake alone, that our Reverend Mother turned a blind eye to the rules and allowed us to meet one day every month... though, when she had something important to tell me, we met in secret too. I don't need to add that I never had anything of even the slightest importance to tell her in exchange.

But all that had changed when Signor Baldassare came into her life, casting his spells upon her husband, for now there was too much to tell me in those brief granted, or stolen, moments. And so we had thought of a way she could do it; when the next peculiar thing took place, she would write it down in a letter – well, not a real letter which would be too large but rather a small scrap of paper – and give it to Dosolina. I should explain here that she was Francesca's old and long-suffering servant who would come to our chapel in the pretence of attending morning mass and, a little way inside the gate, would hide it under a cobblestone. And after the final blessing was given, I'd hurry out and make great show of sweeping the path, and if I was sure that the coast was clear I'd pull it out from its hiding place.

And so, the next morning I hid behind the yew tree, waiting, and just as I felt I might burst with impatience there came the rumble of carriage wheels on the hill path. It pulled up at the gate and there she was, scuttling through it, crouching down over the cobblestones as if to tie her shoelace.

I couldn't so much as think about God whilst we were at prayer, and after the Ave Maria, when Dosolina had clambered back into the carriage, I took my broom and, hardly able to stop myself running (such unseemly conduct being forbidden) hurried down to the gate as fast as I was allowed. And making certain that no one was watching pulled the square of paper from its hiding place.

As it turned out, there had been no need for Fortunato to tell Francesca about the Christ figure.

'Oh Sofia, you never will guess what has happened, when I got back to the house he was there.'

My breath stopped in my throat, but not for the reason she might have imagined.

'They're trying to make me believe he's an artist. That they've brought him to paint my portrait. They must think me more stupid than I imagined. He doesn't even look like one.'

I knew nothing about such creatures but Francesca did, her sister having been painted by a dark and beautiful Florentine who, though he was called Domenico di Doffo Bigordi, went by the name Ghirlandaio.

'I'm to be shut away with him every morning.'

A flutter of something I now know was envy rose up in my heart.

'At last they're getting me out of their way.'

She meant so that they could get on with whatever it was they were up to. We had thought long and hard about what this might be, but only when she found the book with its strange symbols did we knew it was something most evil. Donato had made a great mistake when he locked all the rooms at the top of the house where he and Signor Baldassare worked, for it only signalled to Francesca that behind those doors were things they were hiding. The household was told they were being used for storing his silk, but she knew better. One day, by mistake, they left one unlocked, which was a chance sent by Heaven. But, surprisingly, the room was quite empty except for a table, upon which lay a book, some bottles, a quill and ink pot alongside a stack of blank sheets of paper. One of the bottles contained a shiny substance. She poured a few drops onto the table, but when she placed her finger upon it, it parted and formed into small silver balls.

At this point she might have made her escape, but this is Francesca we're talking about. She opened the book. It was filled with the symbols I have told you about. She inked the quill and, taking a sheet of the paper, copied two of them as carefully as she was able. And the next day, which by God's grace was the one marked for us to meet, she brought them to show me. I studied them closely but could make nothing of them. I can only describe them as squares filled with lines.

'Could they be a code of some kind?'

'No. They're spells,' she said. 'I know it. He and that...' she stopped here to think, '...monster Baldassare have turned to the Devil.'

I had thought this the most ridiculous thing that ever I'd heard, even though we knew they'd killed Corvo.

But now, with this new revelation, I wondered if she had been right all along. Not about Devil worship, of course, but to go to such lengths to shut her away simply to stop her snooping.

'Don't worry, Sofia, I promise you something. I'm going to get rid of him if it's the last thing I do.'

I didn't have time to work out my feelings about this last piece of news, for at that very moment there came a rustle of starched linen. I looked round and my heart sank down to my toes for who did I see but Canoness Sister Veronica, face like fury, striding down the path towards me.

CHAPTER EIGHT

That night I came down with a fever. Tomma was to tell me later that he heard a moaning so loud it seeped through the candle wax wedged in his ears. I was soaked in sweat and thrashing about on my mattress as though possessed of a devil.

'My poor Tomma.'

'And though you were burning, you seemed to be cold. A shivering had beset you, yet I could feel a great heat coming up from your body.'

It occurs to me now that, unwilling to cause fuss, good lads that they were, Guido or Celestino would have left it till morning before going to seek help. But not he. I do not like to think what would have befallen me had he not acted in a contrary manner, rushing downstairs and finding the kitchen, where someone was bound to be. And he was right, the someone turned out to be Fortunato.

'He sent for Signor Baldassare. You were cursing and swearing a very great deal.'

'*Madonna Santissima*, what was I saying?'

'I can't repeat it but I told him, "I'm greatly shocked, this isn't language commonly used by my master".'

'And he believed you?'

'I don't think so. He only told Fortunato to bring buckets of water... and rags. He soaked them and wrapped them round you. I swear, sire, I saw steam rising. He took a knife and cut into your shoulder. Puss spurted from it.' More water and my profanities ceased. 'And then you slept. It's been two days, sire.'

Though many years have passed since then, I'm still haunted by the nightmare that beleaguered me during this time: I am in a vast and mysterious space, which I know must be the Novella. As I approach the sacristy, I catch a glimpse of my altarpiece through the dim light. But there is no image painted upon it, only a ground of white gesso. My brushes and bowls are set out before it. Panic engulfs me. I know I must reach it, but I can't move. The audience waits in silence. A figure steps forward. They watch as he picks up his brush.

And when he turns, I see it is the Buonarroti boy.

Over the days that followed my waking, I couldn't have raised myself from my bed had the very house caught afire. One morning, however, I stirred from my stupor. A ruffle of air touched my face. I turned my head towards its source – a large and bright oblong which, as I focused my eyes upon it, revealed itself to be a window. Its shutters were open. A pale morning moon hung in its centre; some way below was a garden laid out with neat rows of trees. Memory shuddered back into my brain: our leap from the window, the boar, the dogs, the *cazzo* journey back up the mountain, our gentle rescuer... his smiling, gracious, wife. I tried to move, but I couldn't; something seemed to be wrong with my shoulder.

I tried to shout 'Tomma', and though the sound that

came from my mouth was no more than a whisper, he heard it. Something akin to emotion lit up his face when he looked down upon me. 'Oh sire, you look better.'

He held a bowl of water to my mouth. I gulped like a castaway mariner, marooned twenty years on an island of sand. And able, now, to tackle speech, I managed a croak, 'We must go... there's no time to lose.' And as if to underline this statement, I tried to sit up.

'No... Stop... We can't...' But noting my determination he relented, if only a little. 'Here, let me help you.'

Should you ever find yourself in such circumstances, you'll be in need of assistance. Or at least until you adapt to functioning with only one arm. After the washing and pulling on of my breeches, I said, 'Let's go then. To Siena... or was it Naples?' Memory seemed to have escaped me.

'We can't,' he repeated, but added this time, 'until you're recovered. You need to rest.'

'I've rested enough.'

'No sire, you haven't. Please listen. I've worked it out. Stay here for the moment. It's a good place. You can work on your altarpiece alongside the portrait.'

And I'd thought him the clever one. 'But if they find out we're here.' I meant the Duke's men. 'No Tomma, we're going.'

He chose to ignore me. 'You can explain. Tell the signore you haven't been entirely honest with him, that you were forced out of... think of somewhere, best not say Florence. You're in fear of your life. You have to lie low, you must remain hidden. You don't want payment for the painting; only that you may be permitted to stay here in secret until it is finished.' The concept of no payment was a new one to me. 'It will take a week at most to do it, plus some days to recover enough to get started. Use this time to plan your altarpiece. We'll go, sire, but when you've got your strength back.'

My head was swimming. 'Let me think on it my little friend. I need air.' I looked down from the window. 'Perhaps we could sit in that garden.'

He seemed doubtful about this proposition. 'Can you get down there?'

I couldn't be sure but my legs required stretching; so long on that mattress I felt as if I had just stepped from a gondola onto the Rio di Meloni.

Strangely, for once, it seemed I'd convinced him. 'Perhaps you're right. You need air. And I'll bring you some breakfast.'

But food was not topmost in my mind. 'How long is it till the Medici birthday?'

He set his mind to calculation. 'Two months, two weeks and three days, sire.'

*

And so, with Tomma taking my weight (he might have been small but he was strong) we made our way down the narrow stairway to the floor below which, if the attic were disregarded, sat at the top of the house. Into a door-lined corridor where a servant was sweeping. Two more floors descent and we stood in what logic told me was the hallway into which we had entered when first we arrived. But logic and memory differ; where then it had been a place filled with early evening shadows, now it was lit by shafts of sunlight streaming in from an open door, with beyond it the trees I had seen from my window, their branches spreading great patches of shade.

I told him I could manage from here, and though not entirely persuaded, he set off for the kitchen whilst I stepped out into a pool of green. Sun glinted down through the dappled leaves. The air was filled with smells of autumn. I sat myself upon a bench scattered with cushions. Birdsong and the murmur of insects might have persuaded me to doze a little, had he not reappeared with a tray piled high and proceeded to unload it. We dined on a repast of salt beef and bread, followed by a plate of figs. I may have imagined that I had no appetite but, ye gods, just observing the feast set out before me, hunger had struck with ravenous intensity.

I was stuffing the last fig into my mouth when we heard footsteps and there was Donato walking along the path, dressed as if for a journey. Even in my invalid state I could sense his exceeding agitation. He saw us and shook himself, forcing a smile upon his face, as if delighted to have stumbled upon us.

'Ah Benno! How are you, my friend?' he asked with concern. But there was a tension in his voice.

I made to stand.

'No. No,' said he, 'stay where you are.'

'I have lain too long. I am recovered.'

'I'm so very glad. You gave us a fright, I can tell you.'

'You must forgive me for that.' I took his outstretched hand with my free one. 'I thank you again. You have rescued me... twice now, you know.'

'The first was my pleasure. As for the second, it's Giacomo who must take the credit. It seems your wound was the cause of the fever. He says it often follows injury. It may return, you know. You must take care of yourself, my dear Benno.' He paused for a moment. 'I'm sorry to say that I have to leave you. I must go to Venice. Business calls, as ever it does.'

This was news that relieved me greatly, for now there was no need to put Tomma's plan into action and talk about other, forgotten, commissions. Instead I said, 'You seem troubled.'

'Oh, it is nothing.'

Had I been a polite fellow, I might have left it at that. But I was not polite, so I continued.

'You can tell me, you know.'

He shook his head. 'It's only business, as I have said. I have problems, but it is always thus. I often wish I were a goatherd up in the hills, free of worries.'

'But then you'd have others. Wolves to start with, and then there are snakes and bandits and goat thieves, I do not wonder.'

He smiled again, but this time with feeling. 'And you have agreed to paint Francesca's portrait, or so my father tells me. You must forgive him, he should not have asked such a favour.'

'It is my pleasure, please believe me. Especially as she will be such a beautiful subject.'

'I am most grateful, dear Benno, and greatly happy. The thought of it will speed my return. I'm afraid I'll be gone for some time. Will you manage?'

'Oh,' I said, 'don't worry about us.' As far as the portrait was concerned, all I required was a panel to paint on, pigments, brushes, and his wife, of course. Along with a bright room to work in.

He looked down at us, his agitation greatly increased. 'Of course. Of course.' He thought for a moment. 'I may have mentioned that just at the moment all our rooms are being used for storage.' He stopped again, I could see his mind working. 'But that's not a problem. Giacomo will take you to find one that pleases you to work in, and it will be cleared for the purpose. Give him a list of all you require and he will find it for you. But you mustn't start yet; you cannot paint with that arm.'

'Oh it is of no consequence, for, as I may have mentioned, I am left-handed. At least the gods have not been too cruel.'

'That may be so but you are not well enough. Rest awhile, I insist,' he continued. 'There is no rush.'

As he departed, he turned. 'Promise me, Benno, wait a few days. Lie in the garden and rest.'

But, as I'd told Tomma, I had rested enough.

And so our lives do turn. We might not meet again, and for this I was sorry. But in order to preserve our lives we'd stay here in his house, at least for a while. I'd draw up my sketches for the altarpiece and leave him a portrait of his wife fit for the noblest of nobles.

Some little time would be needed before I could start on it, however, as first came the task of collecting chalk and charcoal and paper for sketching, lime plaster, a sand clock and of course pigments which, apart from lapis, that most costly of blues, are easily found in the quantities required for small works on panel, as is paper etcetera. Brushes are different, however, being as life and death to a painter; of specific length of handle, fashioned from squirrel or bristles of hogs, cut straight or rounded, or angled to give diverse effect. In Florence, I had them made to my design by the brothers Pieri.

I may have been lax in most aspects of my life, but being the son of a baker I was acquainted with the fact that prompt payment of bills guarantees credit in desperate times. I cursed God that though such a time had now come, they being back in the city and I here, cast out in the wilderness, they could not be called upon to supply me with what was needed for the job.

This I explained to Baldassare, as Donato had instructed. He'd find what he could. I can't say he sounded enthusiastic.

Tomma helped me clamber back up to the attic where I sprawled on my mattress and soon fell asleep.

When I woke, he informed me he had made a list of what was required.

'Good lad.' I turned on my side and closed my eyes again.

During those days of respite, I spent much time upon my mattress, the rest in the garden wandering its paths. All the usual ornamentation was to be found there; stone cherubs holding garlands of fruit, a topiary maze. The one thing, however, that did take my eye being a copper sundial, green with verdigris. Not so uncommon, apart from the fact that upon its surface was carved a nymph with behind her a large-pricked satyr, ready to pounce.

CHAPTER NINE

There was no sign of Dosolina the following morning, or the next. Or the one after that. You can imagine my desperation.

More than a week passed before I heard the familiar rumble of carriage wheels out on the road. As she pushed the gate open, I whispered her name. She looked round and, thank the dear Lord, she saw me by the yew tree and took the few steps towards me. What could they say if the Lady Francesca's servant wished to speak to me for a moment? She wasn't just any old woman.

She grasped my arm as if for balance. I pretended to steady her, and now she was close enough to whisper, 'Oh Sofia, I hardly know where to begin. There is so much to tell you. The portrait hasn't been started. That man who came is in bed with the fever. My Lady hopes he will stay there. She was right to think that he's an imposter. They told her he'd come from Florence to paint her. But Fortunato said they'd only just met him on the hill after he'd fallen out of a tree.'

I stared at her, mouth open.

But she wasn't able to tell me more about this fantastical story, for just at that moment the Angelus started to toll, clanging so loudly I wouldn't have heard her even if she had shouted.

CHAPTER TEN

One late afternoon, it might have been the third of this time, returning from the garden my eyes still dazzled by the sun, I almost bumped into the old signore.

As I leaned forward to steady both him and myself, he looked upon me with confusion.

I shouted, 'It's me... Benno!'

And when still he seemed confused, I shouted more loudly, 'The painter!'

Even a fish swimming deep in the sea would have heard me. 'Ah yes indeed.'

Only now did I see Baldassare behind him.

'Giacomo tells me he is collecting the materials you require. If there's anything to be added, now is the time to tell us.'

'No signore, apart from the room to paint in.' I acted out my words whilst pointing at the sun beating in through the window beside us.

He seemed to understand, but didn't look happy. In fact he looked deeply disgruntled, which only served to give the impression that he was beginning to regret the fact he had ever thought about portraits. Turning, he whispered what seemed like an order. And then he shuffled off, leaving

Baldassare to inform me that I could make use of the dining room. 'Oh, and all must be done in the mornings.'

'Don't you think it strange, sire,' Tomma screwed up his face when I told him of my encounter, 'with all the rooms in this place, you'd think he could have a less ostentatious one cleared for the purpose.'

Strange or not I couldn't have cared; the dining room had good light and large windows.

*

It was nearing the end of October by now and wasps in a stupor buzzed in the shade. There was the occasional rustle of fruit as it dropped from a tree and thump when it landed. What better prospect for contemplation? And so, stretched out on the cushion-covered bench, a breeze whispering in the branches above me, at last I could think on my altarpiece. It occurs to me that I have not yet told you its subject, so I shall now. My Lord de'Medici, having heard of the little panel Sandro was planning for the church of San Barnaba, had settled on an Annunciation, which you will surely know is a portrayal of the moment the angel appears before the Virgin to inform her that she has conceived of a child. But it was a tired old theme – the Virgin, the angel, the lily... even the garden, which was a great pity for as far as the latter was concerned was there not here in the Villa Favoni the perfect one to use as a background?

But backgrounds weren't my problem, or not then at least. Instead was the question of how to rework that too familiar image, turn the scene from one of quiet harmony into a drama filled with wild movement, explosions of riotous, gushing energy, for I was as passionate about this as I was about colour. But how to do it, that was the question? How could I rework the time-wearied, placid, static and motionless image into a vision so shockingly new as to make those who looked upon it reel back with startled expressions?

During this calm and gentle time I tried to fix my mind on the problem, but it was as blank as the altarpiece in my bastarding nightmare.

One morning, stretched out in my accustomed manner, exhausted by the battles waged in my mind, I shut my eyes... and feel that I might have been snoring. A shuffling sound. I opened them most reluctantly and who did I see but Donato's wife peering down at me.

I smiled, which seemed to upset her. A moment collecting herself and she set her expression back to its scowl. If not for her beautiful, discontented face, I'd have found it impossible to move my gaze from the protruding globe of her belly.

'Come Benno.' I stirred myself to action, for have I not said that I knew how to deal with all manner of rich and spoilt women.

'And how are you, my lady, this glorious morning?'

But damned if my stratagem didn't work. She turned her back on me and stumbled, unsteadily, back down the path. And odd though it was, the notion occurred to me; flirting and jesting with the wives of my patrons, which I counted as a routine use of my talents, would be of no help to me now.

The inevitable came, however, as inevitables ever do. The materials gathered, Tomma said, 'Sire, we should start tomorrow,' which meant there would be no returning to the garden and my aforementioned state of blissful surrender. Instead I had to shift my mind from my altarpiece to the sodding task at hand.

And though, through lack of circumstance, we hadn't discussed the topic of poses, I knew what Donato would have chosen were he around to do so. This being the usual kind of thing, a profile as seen on a coin which, harking back to a Classical past, was all the rage back in those days. But I was as uninterested in pasts as I was in fashion, and the situation had conspired to help me; he wasn't here, which meant I could paint her any way that I wanted. And what did I want? Something astonishing, something that would amaze in its skill and its newness.

It came in a flash. The little shit Buonarroti, his figure done in red chalk, arm curving round, face turned as if to look at something.

'What?' asked Tomma.

There soon started hurtling about in my mind every species of animate object. A butterfly? Too predictable. A bat? Too much a sign of darkness. A lizard? Perhaps. What about a monkey? But where would I find such a creature? True, I had come across one before, dressed in a little striped jacket, a Saracen's hat upon his head – the Marchesa Rizziola's companion. But I had not sufficient memory of the strange little fellow to paint him well enough.

Then it struck me; whatever it was would be a mystery existing beyond the panel. And it would remain so for all time thereafter.

*

Tomorrow came too fast. Having breakfasted on sweet cakes and honey, I positioned myself at my easel. I say easel though it was but three strips of timber nailed together to form a tripod. Tomma stood by a table set out with paper, chalk, bowls of pigment. Baldassare had succeeded in finding most of the items required; amongst those he had not were the brushes laid beside them. But Tomma had come to the rescue, ingeniously fashioning them from tufts of fur and sticks and twine.

Since departing Florence, apart from the sketch made that first night for the old man, I had touched neither chalk nor pen and was impatient to move my brain in an onwards direction. Drawings would come first. In these I would catch the sweep of her forehead, cheekbones, her chin. Only when I had captured her spirit would I transfer her image to the panel.

We heard footsteps and a long moment later she came waddling through the door accompanied by an old waiting woman, the folds of her gown, green as an emerald, spread round the curve of her belly. Her expression remained unchanged from the occasion of both our last and first encounter. And as she approached, I could do little to stop my eyes being drawn to a bead of sweat trickling over her collar bone, making its way to the crease of her breasts.

'Bow,' whispered Tomma. But I was too distracted.

He had placed a bench in front of the window and set her chair at an angle upon it so that when she was seated she would take up the position required and her face would be level with mine.

The waiting woman helped her onto the chair. Tomma set the sand clock.

'I don't think we should have her sit for more than one half turn at a time,' he had cautioned. And he was right, for once I started to work, a daze would enshroud me and I would be lost. A whole day might pass standing in front of my subject, with only a ravenous growl from my belly rousing me from it. But women cannot be prevailed upon thus, especially if they are pregnant.

I lifted my chalk and asked if she would be kind enough to turn her head towards me, as if she were gazing over her shoulder.

She did not comply, but sat, instead, stiff as a statue, and even though her face was in profile, I could not miss her frown. An expression that I wasn't used to. No, let me rephrase this statement... that I wasn't used to from a woman. I tried a new tactic, complimenting her on her choice of gown.

She turned, as requested, but grudgingly, and I saw her eyes. So dilated were her pupils, blocking out all but the wafer-thin circle of blue surrounding them as to give her the appearance of an other-worldly being. Such is the effect of belladonna – or of vanity – it should be said. But it would take greater distraction than this to put me off my stride.

Tomma nudged me. I moved my gaze.

Sun flooded through the window but did nothing to warm the frigid atmosphere. Observing again the beauty of her hair, clasped back from her face, I dared to make a further request. Would she be kind enough to unclip it?

Her servant set to work pulling out clasps and pins; it fell about her shoulders and tumbled down her back. And there she sat, tight lipped and sullen, staring vacantly into the distance until the sand clock ran its course.

Being locked, still, in that faraway zone known only to painters, Tomma nudged me and I heard him say, 'Thank you, my lady. I think that is all for today.'

She deigned to let him help her down from the platform and, steady now on terra firma, set off towards the door without a backwards glance.

This was too much for me. I stopped the old waiting woman, for she had been slow to rise from her stool, 'Madama...' She cast a beady eye upon me, '...may I ask what I've done to offend your mistress?'

And what did she say but, 'She's not stupid, signore. Be sure that she knows why you're here.'

This threw me, I can tell you. I stood as if stunned as she scuttled away.

Tomma gave me one of his looks when the door slammed behind them. 'Did you not think to ask what she meant?'

No, I did not. But now I had a good idea. What if we swapped places? He could be the one in charge. But instead of offering up this somewhat truculent proposal I said, 'To show us that they are as obnoxiously insufferable as each other, or that they're both mad, lest we hadn't noticed the fact.' I had come across enough crazy people in my life, I felt I knew the symptoms.

'You should have gone along with her a little.' Ye gods, he was like a dog with a bone.

'I don't intend to go anywhere with her, verbally or otherwise.'

'But you missed the point of what she said...'

'I have no care for puzzles.'

'But doesn't it intrigue you sire?'

'No Tomma.'

'Don't you want to find out?'

'What I want, my little friend, is to finish her poxing portrait and get out of here as fast as we can.'

I could see his mind working.

'I'm serious. They are deranged.'

'I'm not so sure, sire.'

And though he was wont to scare me sometimes, what could I say but, 'Well, my dear Tomma, that is where we must differ.'

Tomma may not have had enough of the Lady Favoni, but I had. That night in the attic, as I lay listening to his soft breathing I tried to push her from my mind, with no success I may add, the truth being that I wasn't used to such treatment from women, or normal women should I say. I had put on a good face in front of him, but it caused me much torment. I tried to reason with myself. 'What do you care? You've more than mad women to think about. Two months two weeks and three days.' I fixed my mind upon the image; striding through the doors of the Novella, the fuckheads' shocked faces. But I would be striding nowhere, stuck here in an attic in some godforsaken place at the back of the sodding beyond.

And so, I resolved I would go to the garden to grapple with the lumpen forms of the actors of the Annunciation not yet set upon my stage, and beg my muse to return.

I shuffled down the staircase as silently as I was able, and had ventured but a little way along the passage when a door opened and Baldassare stepped through it, followed by Fortunato. Both carried stacks of what looked like wooden drums of about half an arm-span's diameter. Not wishing them to catch me there in the corridor at that time of night. I would have turned back, but it was too late.

They stopped when they saw me. To say Baldassare looked flustered would be an understatement of monumental proportion.

'I'm going to the garden,' I sought to explain. 'I can't sleep.'

He didn't respond.

'It's a good place to think... and I need to do much of that,' I continued, forcing a cheery tone.

Still he stood, saying nothing.

'I would help you, but...' I moved my bound arm and forced an apologetic grin.

He found his voice. 'There's no need. They're empty.'

So they weren't drums. 'Oh, they're boxes?' I had never seen such a type before.

'Yes... Yes. They are.' And with this, he and Fortunato turned on their heels and hurried back into the very same room they had just come out of.

'*Sacro Cristo.*' It put me off my stride, yet I got to the garden albeit bewildered. Once there I was hit with immediate calm; it having changed from a place of green, filled with the buzzing of wasps to one of darkness and shadows. The moon was full and seemed strangely close, as moons do in autumn.

I sat myself on the bench, still covered in its cushions, and managed with some little success to move my thoughts towards the task. But, once it was there I couldn't clear it of small, trifling details – should the Virgin be seated, should the angel be to her left or her right, should his wings be wide-spread or folded, whilst the extravagant waves of motion I sought for the spectacle flew to some remote region far away from my mind.

*

'*Porco Dio* Tomma, why did he run off like that?' It was morning, and I was telling the tale of my last night's encounter.

'I don't know sire, and I don't think we should try to find out. And next time you want to go out to the garden in the middle of the night, wake me and I'll come with you.'

CHAPTER ELEVEN

The following day was no different as far as my subject was concerned. Had I been expecting even the smallest of shifts in her demeanour I was in for a disappointment.

I was happy with the sketches set out before me, now I would start on the panel, which Tomma had prepared with gesso. As panels go it was small, being but a quarter arm-span in width and less again in height; it wouldn't take long to blank in the basic arrangement. When this was done, I would work in the details, using ochres for her hair and skin tones. Then would come the green of her gown, for which, ordinarily, I'd have used verdaccio. But this being one of the items Baldassare had been unable to lay his hands upon, Tomma had set to work with a mix of yellow oxide and scrapings of verdigris from the sundial.

We stood waiting, but she didn't appear. Still we stood; no sign of her. We had resigned ourselves. We wouldn't see her that day, and were sprawled on the floor, or should I say I was the one sprawling, Tomma was sitting, back against the wall, when she appeared. Perhaps I would have got up more quickly had my arm allowed it, but perhaps I wouldn't.

Today, as if to taunt me, she wore a gown of soft

grey. She wished me to ask if she would be kind enough to go back to her chamber and change it for the one she'd worn yesterday. But ordinary members of the public know nothing of the painters' craft; with portraits you may be granted but an hour or two with your subject, why waste it on pleats and folds, on patterns of brocade or nap of velvet? No, all this is done later, which means that colours can be altered as the fancy takes you.

It gave me great pleasure to see her confusion when all I said was, 'Shall we start then?' I did not add 'my lady'.

Tomma helped her to her place.

I turned to the waiting woman but she was as silent as her mistress, and from then on she followed my every move, hampering my concentration as much as my subject's expression.

I lifted my brush to block in her skin tones, and then it was I saw them: the faintest marks upon her face, imperceptible to other than a painter's eyes, for do we not spend our lives in close examination of what is in front of us. Fine blue threads, half a thumbnail long. They had not been there yesterday, of that I was certain.

At the first half turn of the sand clock, I thought to ask if she felt quite well. She answered with an icy stare. And though I sought to shrug it off, it upset me I can tell you. And as if to add to my discombobulation, she motioned to her waiting woman to come and help her down from the platform. Tomma stepped forward and offered his hand but she chose to take her servant's, and once her mistress was steady on her feet they turned their backs and walked out of the door, leaving us staring after them like befuddled loons.

'That's it, we're going. Sod the *cazzo* portrait.'

'No, sire,' said Tomma, 'you owe it to Signor Donato. He helped us. He's a good man. You can have it finished tomorrow, or the day after. Not as you'd like, that's true, but it will be wondrous just the same.'

'I can't bear to look at her.'

'You won't have to, she won't be back. But you don't need her anyway, you've got your sketches. You're almost there. And when it's done, we can leave with our consciences clear.'

Tomma was wont to stump me sometimes. I found myself submitting, as always. I'd finish the balls-aching job, and the moment I did we'd be off.

But this was torture indeed; to labour on a portrait I had not heart to paint, with all the while my altarpiece waiting. Two months, two weeks and a day was shrunk now to two months and twelve days. Tomorrow would be two months and eleven; each grain of the sand clock counting down my fate. Two days here, one to Livorno, one to find us a ship, two days to Naples... let us call it a week, there to ensconce me in the Palazzo Rizziola, where, replete with the pleasures awaiting, I'd work on my masterpiece during the stretch of the two months and however many days left by the time we got there.

My spirits were lifted. 'Scrub your mind clear, Benno. Start anew. You need but a little quiet contemplation.' I changed this to 'a little merriment', and then to 'a little'... no, to 'a great deal of... screwing'.

It was hot up there in the attic. My mind required airing. And so I waited till Tomma was sleeping and in the still dark hours of the morning made my silent way down the stairs, along the corridor and into the garden, there to transfer the tortures inflicted upon me that day to my Virgin and her sod of an angel. I reached the bench, stretched out on the cushions and set my mind a wandering. But though I gave it permission to roam, it stayed tightly fixed in my brain. Portraits apart, my method differed from that of my rivals. I didn't start upon compositions until I had set out the scenes in my head, dreaming up great swirls of colour and movement. Only then would I commit them to paper, working with speed whilst they were still fresh in my mind. But nothing in it was fresh. Hard though I tried, I couldn't clear it of the same pissing details; should the Virgin be seated? The angel to her left, his wings wide-spread or folded? The gods had abandoned me. Inspiration had fled. I would have to run fast to catch it again.

For the thousandth time, I cursed Ghirlandaio. Why had I gone to his sodding workshop? Why had I paid any fucking attention to the little shit, Buonarroti? I could see it all slipping out of my hands, such is the turn of a moment. Dreams of that gilded tomb with carved upon it the words SIMONE da BENNO. GREATEST PAINTER OF HIS AGE seemed dashed, now, to dust.

I could not stop myself cursing most loudly. And through the ensuing silence came a moan in reply. My skin seemed to shrink. I forced myself up from the bench. The clouds parted, and in the moonlight I saw a barefooted figure, hair dishevelled as Cassandra's, weaving her way to left and to right along the path towards me.

I reached her in time, and though it was hard, having only one arm to put into action, succeeded in catching her as she fell. I tore off my bandages and carried her to the bench, and had only just laid her upon it when I heard running footsteps. It was the old waiting woman.

'Signore, Signore,' she panted. She knelt down beside us. 'Oh, my poor lady.'

No need to ask what was wrong with her mistress. Men drink; women take the poppy. It has always been thus, and thus it will be until time ends.

I turned to the old woman. 'Get Baldassare.'

At which she leaned forward, gripping my arm. 'No. Please signore.'

'Then I'll take her to him.' I lifted her up. Despite her pregnant state she was light as thistledown, and could not but notice a strong, spicy odour about her, like vinegar, perhaps.

'No, I beg you,' she continued in a desperate tone.

I'd have ignored her, but she wouldn't give up. 'You don't understand. Nothing is what it seems.' I was right, she was as mad as her mistress. All seemed plain enough to me, but I had a problem here, do as the old woman said or ignore her?

'He is the cause of all this.'

Here was a time I needed Tomma; he would have known what to do. His instruction that I should not wander out at midnight without him hit me with a whack.

'Take her to her room, I beg you signore,' she continued, gazing up at me with a look of the most utter dread.

She was a stupid, babbling old woman, and yet...

'Is it the poppy?' I asked.

And with my question, she fixed her face as if the notion had only just hit her. 'Yes... Yes you're right... She has taken too much... I implore you, please keep it a secret.'

And so I carried the Lady Francesca back through the garden, into the house, up the stairs to her chamber. Her bed was large and canopied, much like the Marchesa's. I laid her upon it.

And then I left and made my cautious way back along the corridor, climbed the steps to our attic and woke Tomma.

'It was the poppy.'

'Are you sure, sire?'

'What else could it be? And there were those marks on her face.'

'What marks?' It occurred to me that we hadn't discussed them.

'Threadlike. Blue. They were there this morning.'

'Why didn't you take her to Baldassare?'

'The old woman said not to. That he was the cause of all this.'

I need not describe his expression.

I thought for a moment, could he be the father of her child? Donato was handsome and of good nature; Baldassare dark, sober, stiff and sedate. Nonetheless, I put this to him.

'I don't really think so.'

I was glad he had said it. 'But what was he the cause of then? How could it be his fault? What has he done?'

For once Tomma seemed as baffled as I.

'It's the final straw.' I did not need to add, 'We're leaving.'

We sat for a moment, then came the inevitable, 'Sire, perhaps we should think for a moment.'

But my shoulder pained me and I was too weary to listen. 'No, Tomma. We're getting out of here. And that's the end of it.' I held up my hand; I didn't want to hear more.

'Then we should take the pigments, and brushes and paper.'

Which was a most excellent idea, for when we reached Naples we would not be as naked as we had been when we arrived in this turd of a place.

We waited till light had come into the sky. Tomma had fashioned a sack from his bedcover, which we were busy filling with the items he mentioned when we heard footsteps. We turned together and there she was at the door, face white as a phantom's. She didn't seem to have noticed what we were doing. As we stood, frozen, I clutching the cover, Tomma holding above it a stack of good paper, she came towards us. I opened my mouth to start on some feeble explanation as to what we were about, but she beat me to it.

'Oh, signore.' So, she could speak after all.

A metamorphosis had taken place in her appearance and demeanour. I loosened my grasp on my bundle; it fell to the floor. Tomma stood holding his pile of paper.

She had reached us by now. 'Thank you for saving me.'

So shocked was I at this turn of events, I may have managed to mumble something, I cannot say it was intelligible.

'I beg you, forgive me.'

Tomma took the chair from its plinth, 'Sit, my lady,' he said, 'it is better.'

'Only if you say you'll forgive me.'

'There's nothing to forgive.' This was polite talk, but I had to say something.

It was enough. She sat and looked up at me; her face white as I have said, but blotches of red had appeared on her cheekbones. 'Oh, but there is. I have behaved most despicably. I am ashamed of myself.'

Not knowing how best to respond, I kept my mouth shut. Better not to spoil things at this most delicate point in proceedings.

'I was sure that my husband had brought you to keep me out of his way,' she continued.

I'd been right, she was mad. But even so, I didn't want to hear about husbands, especially not about hers. And so, not wishing to advance this crazed line of thought, I sought to move her on to a new subject, speed her return to the door, and out of it, and let us get back to the task at hand.

But Tomma was not so easily sidetracked; he beat me to it. 'Why would he want to, my lady?'

Merda Tomma, don't get us in deeper.

She took a moment to answer. The blotches on her cheekbones grew redder. 'I know now that I was mistaken. You can't imagine he cares about portraits, but he wants you here all the same.'

'Why?' Once he had his teeth into something...

'To stop me finding out what they're up to.'

Ye gods, Benno, change the subject. I leaned over her and spoke very softly. 'But are you well now? It's all that matters.'

It worked. Donato was safe... at least for the moment. She frowned. 'I don't know what happened last night. I was awake, but it was as if I was dreaming. And I was walking. I was in the garden, but to get there from my bed knowing nothing about it? And then I felt cold. I heard a great shout. It woke me. I felt myself topple. Then someone caught me. It was you, signore...'

Her face crumpled. If I hate anything in the world it is to see a woman cry. I found myself on my knees beside her.

77

'My name's Benno. You have to be honest, I don't suit "signore".'

She gave a little tearful smile.

'And this is Tomma.'

Where once she had seen but a small, misshapen being, now she set eyes on his beautiful face. This time she held out her hand.

He took it. 'I'm glad my master was there for you.'

'If he hadn't been, I cannot think what would have happened.'

'I asked your servant to find Signor Baldassare, tell him to come straight away. But she didn't want to.'

She started to shiver. I took off my doublet and wrapped it round her shoulders. 'Poor Dosolina. But she was right.'

Tomma gave me a look which I knew meant, 'Come on, sire, you can't just ignore her this time.'

'We're good listeners, if you'd like to tell us.'

So she did.

'We were happy until he came into our lives. He turned up one day. My husband said he had met him in Padua and asked him to come and help with his silk.' She gave a little shrug. 'I don't know what there was to help with that couldn't be done by one of his workers. All had been normal till then. But only a few days after he got here, strange things started to happen. That's when the rooms were locked. My husband said he was using them as storerooms. But I knew he was lying.'

I would have butted in with, 'Oh, I am sure you are wrong.' But Tomma's look stopped me.

'Every day after that, from morning till midday my husband and... he... would go from room to room. Nothing was taken out, or put in, so there was no reason to update his lists, which is what he said they were doing.'

'So why are they locked?' asked Tomma, and I could see that I was about to be dragged into a conversation I'd rather not have been part of.

She shook her head. 'One day they forgot, and left one open. I took a chance and sneaked in. I expected to see great bales of silk piled to the ceiling, but it was empty except for a table and some things set upon it.'

I glanced at Tomma, but he was too caught up in what she was saying to notice.

'Books and boxes and bottles. One was filled with a shiny substance. I poured some onto the table but when I placed my finger upon it, it parted and rolled across it.' She looked at us as if we might not believe her.

'Quicksilver,' said Tomma.

It was clear this meant nothing to her.

'It's a liquid metal, used mostly by alchemists.'

A fact that seemed to greatly shock her.

'You said there were books on the table.' Of course it was Tomma who asked this, not me.

'Yes, with strange markings inside them. I copied one from a page that was open.' She took a scrap of paper from the front of her gown, a finger's breadth below the patch of skin where the mouth-watering rivulet had been trickling. 'I keep it here. If my husband should find it...' I noted that she chose to hand it to Tomma.

He flattened it out and we looked upon it.

'It was difficult to copy exactly.' She glanced at him anxiously, as if he were a tutor marking her lessons.

It shames me to say that, as one who lives by my eyes, I

find it almost impossible to describe what I saw, but let me try. There were two square symbols, one above the other. The top one was somewhat like a J, though more linear, with two lines stroked through it and a short line beneath, facing left. The bottom one was vaguely reminiscent of an N, with one line scored through it and three lines beneath it, facing right.

'There was a column of them, but I only copied these... they were too complicated and I hadn't time.'

I felt I had to make some contribution to the conversation. No point in saying, 'It's not Greek,' this being an evident fact, and so I proudly offered up the fact that it wasn't English. 'I'm sure about that.'

'And it's not a Moorish script,' countered Tomma.

Ye gods, he would never cease to amaze me; what did he know of such things.

'I can't read their language but I know it when I see it. Remember, sire, I'm from Naples, Araby is not far away.' He turned his attention back to Francesca. 'Was there anything written beside the markings?'

'Yes. In Latin. There was no need to note them, they are easy to remember. Hot... Cold... Warm... Dry... Damp... Light... Dark... and Shade.'

Quick as a flash, he responded, 'And the rooms, how many are locked?'

'I cannot think.'

'Well, let us do it another way. How many rooms are there in the house?'

A moment, then, 'Seventeen.'

Still looking upon the square symbols, 'And how many in use?'

She thought for a long moment. 'Apart from the servants' downstairs by the kitchen, and the attic where you are, Dosolina and I have three, my husband one, Signor Baldassare, one, my father-in-law two, the library and the one we're in now.'

'Nine.' I was glad he had counted; I wouldn't have thought of doing such a thing. 'Which means eight are left.'

He had lost me long before now.

'Eight rooms are locked. Eight items on the list.'

'Could it not be coincidence?'

'No, sire, I don't think so.'

'What is it then?'

This had him flummoxed; I could almost see his mind working.

Francesca interrupted his flow of thought. 'I tried to get that silver stuff back into its bottle, but it was impossible. Some dripped onto the floor. It's why they knew I'd been in there, why they brought you, why they asked you to paint me. To stop me prowling about when they summoned up their spells.'

Did she really believe that's what they were doing?

But fantasy didn't interest Tomma. 'What else has happened, my lady?' he asked, as if he was sure something had.

She stared at him. 'They killed my crow.'

*

'What are they?' We were back in the attic and trying to make sense of what we'd just heard, starting with the symbols. My mind was racing. 'An alchemist's jottings?' I remembered what he'd said about quicksilver.

'No.'

How could he be sure?

'I mentioned it only for her sake, sire. To reassure her. But they're nothing to do with alchemy.'

'A code of some sort then?'

'Perhaps, or a language, taking into account the fact that there were translations in Latin.'

'You think they're translations?'

'What else could they be?'

'Of what?'

For once he was baffled. He shook his head. 'We have to get into that room, look for ourselves. We might find...'

'No Tomma. If we don't get away from here before the next *cazzo* thing happens, my life will be over. And you'll be back in Florence, working for the likes of Lampeduso Pecci. We've done what we can, we must think of ourselves now and get to Naples.' I was in control again, or at least so I thought. 'We'll tell her servant... what's her name, I've forgotten it?'

'Dosolina.'

'...to throw away her poppy.' I could be the sensible one when pushed. 'And her belladonna. They're addling her mind. Ignore the crazy goings-on. Get on with our lives.'

'We might be making a mistake, sire.' I noted that he was kind enough to say 'we' and felt a twinge of conscience, but it didn't take much to push it away.

He tried one last tactic. 'But why kill her crow?'

I attempted an answer. 'Perhaps, my dear Tomma, because babies and crows make bad companions.' I was proud of my logical reasoning and felt I had redeemed myself, at least to some little extent.

He did his best to look convinced.

I changed the subject. 'How long do we have now, until my lord's birthday?'

He calculated, 'Two months, one week and one day.'

'We'll finish it.' I meant the portrait, of course. 'But only for Donato's sake. Then we're off...'

CHAPTER TWELVE

I couldn't stop thinking about the Christ figure. About his fever. Dear Gesu please don't let him die. And what of Fortunato's preposterous story about him falling out of a tree?

As if to add to my confusion, a heavy stillness hung in the air, so stifling and humid even the wasps had stopped buzzing.

The Angelus tolled. We trundled our limp and drooping way to the chapel. Two steps inside and I stopped in my tracks for there was Francesca, kneeling by the altar. My heart stopped, what could have happened? As I made my stupefied way forward, she turned and gave me a little smile. Her cheeks were flushed, and, unbound from its usual pleated coils, her hair fell loose on her shoulders.

The Lady Favoni happy for once? The other novices seemed as startled as I.

After the Ave Maria, she rose. We stood back to give her space as, eyes down, hands clasped to her breast, she made her way along the nave. Passing me, she made the sign which meant we should meet in the orchard, this being the place to go when she had something important to tell me that couldn't be dealt with in one of her notes.

I waited a moment, then fetched my broom and set off for our meeting place. Hardly had I shut the gate when she started.

'Oh Sofia,' she ran towards me and clutched my hands. Next came a torrent of words. 'I had to come. I had to tell you. I was wrong about him... So wrong. He is an artist after all. His name is Simone da Benno...'

So she hadn't got rid of him. I could not but feel my happiness rise, and pleased for hers too, somewhat begrudgingly though it was.

'They did bring him to paint me. And now I'm with him every morning.' She gave a little laugh. 'I can only thank sweet Gesu.'

Corvo... and even her old and favourite subject, Signor Baldassare, were forgotten. In their place, now, was Benno. Benno this and Benno that.

'He's so funny. So strong, and so gentle. I fell in the garden. He helped me. I told him everything. About the book... and the markings inside it. He promised to help me.'

'Oh Francesca.' I pushed my bitterness aside; I feared for her even more now.

'And you'll never guess what else has happened... he's... gone to Venice.' I knew, by her change of tone, that 'he' meant her husband. 'We're alone, apart from that toad, Baldassare.'

Is there need to tell you how confused I was by now? But she didn't want to talk about him.

She pulled a scrap of paper from her bodice and held it up, and I saw her face drawn upon it. Of such exquisite mastery was that image I reached out to touch it.

'It's one of his drawings. I took it when he wasn't looking. It's for you, Sofia. I want you to have it.'

She had offered me many things before now, but we were permitted to own only our habits and rosaries, which even then were not ours in the true sense of the word. And so I'd been forced to refuse them. But this was different for it stirred something deep in my heart; the lines drawn upon it were not delicate or graceful as others I'd seen, but wild and powerful, and though it will seem strange to hear it, and impossible to imagine, they suggested a kind of impatient movement.

No, you would have to see it yourself to understand what I mean.

Just then the dreaded rustle of linen came from somewhere out on the path. I forced my eyes away from the drawing... it didn't bear thinking what would happen if we were caught together without permission to do so.

Francesca took charge. She ran to the gate and popped her head round it.

'Ah Canoness Sister Veronica,' she cried, in a bright tone, 'the very person I wish to speak to. My husband and I were wondering...'

I cannot tell you what came next for, pushing the drawing into the fold of my habit I rushed to the gap in the fence and was through it before I was able to hear the next part of what she was saying.

CHAPTER THIRTEEN

A stultifying heat lay heavy about us. It would thunder, no doubt about it. We dragged ourselves downstairs to wait for Francesca, and could but pray to God in Heaven that nothing out of the ordinary was going to happen today.

She was there already, and wearing her green dress, I could but note, her face even paler than before.

She jumped from her chair when she saw us. 'Oh, you've come...'

It occurred to me she had thought we might not have. But where was her servant?

'I asked her to leave us alone for a while. To come when we're finished.'

'Are you well enough, my lady?' Tomma looked doubtfully at her.

She assured him she was.

Her face might have been paler, but there was a new and wondrous aspect to it: she was smiling. And as I stepped forward to help her onto the platform, I was glad to note that the blue marks were gone.

And now, with her settled into her pose, blessedly serene and uncomplaining, Tomma set the sand clock and I lifted my brush resolving that from now on I would treat her as

I would any woman sitting before me. I joked about this and that and, to my surprise, as the sand clock was turned, once, twice, thrice, contrived to make her laugh at tales of the court back in Florence, of rich clothes and pampered women, of intrigue and cuckolded husbands, dignitaries from foreign lands and, later, when our talk became more intimate, of subjects like that of the Marchesa Rizziola who danced in the temple of Serapide until the hour before she gave birth.

And she had something to say to me... or to ask me. 'What happened to your arm?'

'I fell.'

She did not look as if she believed me. 'I thought, perhaps, you had been in a fight.'

'That would be a deal more glamorous, and perhaps I should have claimed it was so. I could have added that the other man finished worse off by far. But I am sorry to disappoint not only you, but myself.'

'And you must have hurt it again when you helped me.'

'An adventure like that was just what I needed.' I was glad to see her laugh.

As Tomma was helping her down from her perch, she asked, 'May I look?'

When subjects take to inspecting their likeness, you may be sure it will turn to disaster. 'My nose is too long', when you have shortened it out of kindness, 'My chin too short', 'Eyes too small'. Need I continue?

'It isn't finished.'

'Oh please, let me see.'

And so I led her forward, and there it was, glowing out from the panel; not for me the flat colours favoured for portraits back then, the shade of her dress ground from Tomma's verdigris, being of a hue so vibrant as to hurt the eye. And absent, too, the rigid pose beloved of painters. I'd captured not a static moment in time, but movement; the Lady Francesca, turning to gaze at some mysterious entity beyond the edge of the panel.

She gasped and took a step back, which pleased me, then a step forward.

'It's not...'

'...What you expected?'

She shook her head.

'But, do you like it?'

'It's the most beautiful thing I've ever seen.' She stepped closer to it. 'But what am I looking at?' the question I wished all who saw it would ask.

It could be anything she liked. Today a salamander. Tomorrow a parrot. The next a bumble bee.

'Or,' she said, 'Corvo.'

Perhaps it was the heady mood of the moment that caused her to stumble. Or the heat, which as I have said was muggy and oppressive. Or perhaps it was simply because she was pregnant. I steadied her and guided her back to the chair.

'I'll get Dosolina,' said Tomma, amazing me as always for he hadn't forgotten the old woman's name, and he set off through the door.

I pushed the shutters wider, but the stagnant air outside it did nothing to cool us.

We sat for a little in silence and, not being of a bashful nature, when I saw she had recovered I asked when her baby was due.

'Not for two months yet.'

'You must take care of yourself. You must rest and eat well. And you mustn't worry about trifles like locked doors. You're the most important thing. And your baby.' I lifted her chin and studied her skin. I had been right, the blue marks were gone, and now, disregarding the rules of conduct, I placed a finger upon her lips, forcing her to smile.

At that very moment Tomma appeared, Dosolina in tow. I was prepared to see his raised eyebrow and later to hear the usual declaration about it not being a good idea. But it would seem he hadn't noticed; I could not but observe a strange look on his face.

I helped her to her feet. 'Sleep,' I whispered. 'And think of good things.'

When they were gone, I turned to Tomma and started upon my explanation. 'It's not what you think. She stumbled and...'

But he was too preoccupied with what he was about to tell me, for something most strange had just happened. 'When I stepped out of the door, sire, a woman was standing behind it. She was listening to us, I'm certain.'

Just at that moment, Dosolina reappeared, as if from nowhere; she scuttled towards us wringing her hands. 'I know I can trust you, signore.' She said this so quietly I could barely hear her above the old man's thunderous voice in the corridor. Her face filled with fear, 'Come to the garden tonight,' she whispered. 'I have something to tell you.' And she hurried away before I had time to stop her.

CHAPTER FOURTEEN

We did leave the Villa Favoni, though not the way we had intended. But I race ahead of my story.

It was night and we sat in the garden, waiting to hear what ominous tale the old woman was determined to tell. The heat hung heavy about us, matching my mood.

'*Gesu Cristo*, what next?' A question of the rhetorical variety which I had voiced the moment Dosolina had scuttled back out through the door.

But Tomma had answered it just the same. 'We don't know, sire, but we have to find out.'

We were going to now, whether we wanted to or not.

I had an ominous feeling; whatever this 'something' turned out to be, it could stop us getting to Naples. And in a bid to strengthen my resolve, I started again. 'I don't care what she comes up with, we're leaving and that's the end of it.' I thought of the sand clock, dribbling out its grains; two months, one week and how many days?

'None, sire.'

Thunder rolled in the distance.

'But...' He stopped for we could hear voices down by the gate. We stood up silently. Tomma walked to the end of the path, and came back with the news, 'Men, sire, with torches.'

A lantern's light appeared at that moment, bobbing up through the garden. As it drew closer, we saw Dosolina running towards us, her cap falling off in her hurry. And just as she did, the long threatening growl of thunder rumbled in the distance and rain started battering down with such force we couldn't hear what she was shouting.

What else could it be about but Francesca. Thank God Tomma was with me this time.

I was wrong, however, for as she approached her voice became clearer. 'It's the Duke's men!' she shouted again. 'They've come to arrest you.'

The old and familiar spark of energy that ignites at times like these flared up inside me. And there was I without my dagger, it being under my mattress in our attic where I had left it.

'Quick, quick,' she shouted. 'We must hurry.'

We ran beside her through the garden and reached a door set into a wall. She thrust the lantern into my hand, pushed the door open, slamming it shut behind us.

And there, by the flare of torches, we saw her. In that moment of panic I should not have found time to take note of her beauty. But, ever the painter, I couldn't help it; her hair fell in dripping strands on her shoulders, her sleeping robe barely concealing her belly, sodden and stuck to her skin. Her face, which I had noted in all its guises, scowling, petulant, enraged and tender, was filled with panic now. As we got nearer, we saw she was trembling.

'Oh Benno, don't let them catch you.' She pushed a purse into the fold of my doublet, and leading us out across the cobblestones, said, 'Go... Now ... You must go.'

She shouted for one of the stable lads, but there was no need for he had opened the pen doors already. Horses were harnessed but there was no time for saddles. Thanks be to Francesca's venture in the garden, my arm was free of its strapping, else the act of mounting, even with help, would have been beyond me.

Out then, we clattered, into the night and down through the twisting alleys. It was not yet midnight and the last bell was still to be rung.

We made it through the gate by a whisker.

Down the bastarding hill again, keeping a fair enough pace; we could not have gone faster had we been equipped with stirrups, though only when forced to ride without those master products of invention do you appreciate their worth. At least the rain had eased somewhat, but as we neared the foot of the hill the heavens broke open again, this time with ferocious intensity. A torrent of water cascaded upon us, soaking us through to our bones. The road turned into a river. A tumultuous crack of lightning above us and my horse shied. I managed to calm him, but Tomma's took fright and, helpless as a spectator at the Palio Circo, I could but hold my breath and watch as it plunged about in the torrent. He held on for a while, good boy that he was, but lost the battle. I saw him slip down into the flood. It took a moment to rein my mount in, another to wade back up through what had once had been the road but now was a coursing waterfall, the fear of Beelzebub closing in on me.

I thank God and all his angels I reached him in time, for now from somewhere beyond the rattling downpour came the sound of splashing hooves.

Tomma's horse had disappeared. Mine stood patiently

waiting, an outcome I'd have been happy about had circumstances been altered. But a lone horse on a road gives sign to the fact that its rider is not far away. I picked a stone from the torrent and threw it at him. He bolted off into the night.

The splashing grew nearer. I hoisted Tomma up, pretty roughly I own, and hauled him into a ditch. And there we lay, I pressing my great weight upon him as they passed, pebbles and clods of mud hitting us like slingshot.

When all noise had faded, apart from the rain, his voice, beneath me, said, 'Thank you for saving me, sire.'

I couldn't find mine. A pain of the searing variety ripped through my shoulder, and it took me a while to get to my feet. The night became darker, or at least so it seemed.

To our right the field stretched out into the gloom; to our left the rocky foot of the mountain shimmered a silvery grey. From the edge of the enshrouding silence came a faint reverberation. A moment's listening established it to be the fuck of a *cazzo* splashing again, instilling within me strength enough to drag him out of the ditch while still there was time. I hauled him to his feet and, steadying ourselves, we lurched our way forward.

We found ourselves in a quagmire. It was impossible to run. Our feet sank into the swamp. I lost a boot. The splashing reached deafening pitch. We stopped and stood silent, praying to every saint whose name we could muster that it would fade away to nothing, and we would be able to breathe again as they headed back up the hill.

One of them was surely listening. We pressed ourselves against a rock. A second later they passed.

'*Merda*, Tomma, that was a close one.'

Thunder boomed in the distance. At the next flash of lightning, I caught glimpse of what looked like a gap in the rock but a few paces away. I lurched towards it, pulling Tomma behind me. Stumbling and gasping we squelched through the mud and found inside it what I can but describe a dry hollow. Consumed by exhaustion, we threw ourselves onto the ground; darkness and silence did the rest.

*

Light, which I know now to have belonged to morning, seeped through my eyelids. Reality had not yet hit me. Where was I? Stretched out the ground, head pulsating, I could but conclude that I must be lying flat out on the street by the tavern Gatto D'oro, after a night of wine and carousing. I struggled to the surface of my pain and, forcing my eyes open, turned to see Tomma beside me, which seemed to me strange as never would he have been with me in such a place.

A recollection of horses neighing and skittering into the night brought me to my senses. I looked up; the curve of a cupola hung above us. We were in a cavernous chamber, reminiscent of a catacomb or the Grotto of San Justinian; the other fact of which I was certain being that a barrel of pitch had been poured on my shoulder and some sodding bastard had set it alight.

'Tomma,' I managed to whisper.

He sat, back propped against the rock, eyes closed. They opened. He groaned. I felt we had been in a like situation sometime before, but could not persuade my mind to remember.

By now the fire in my shoulder had flared into an inferno; it called for great effort to pull myself up so that I might sit beside him. With the power of language now partially restored, I asked, 'How are you, my little friend?'

'Thank you for saving me,' he said again.

I tried to make light of our circumstances. 'You aren't dead then,' I forced a smile. 'I'm most glad to see it.'

'I lost my grip. I'm sorry.'

'No, I'm the sorry one, dragging you into all this.'

'How are you, sire?'

'Alive. Like you,' which was the main thing.

'And your shoulder?'

'Oh, it could be worse,' I answered untruthfully, and somehow I forced myself to keep talking. 'So the fuckers caught up with us then.'

'But they didn't catch us,' which was a fair point.

'True. But now we're back where we started.'

'No, sire, we're even worse off than then.'

And he was right, having, as we did, no horses and three boots between us.

'But we'll get out of here,' next said he. 'Don't worry.'

I liked to think myself an optimist, but couldn't quite share his conviction. 'Yes, my little friend.' I tried to sound confident; we'd stay here till night fell then get ourselves down the rest of the poxing mountain. It occurred to me just at that moment, 'But what to do about money?' Strange that a man aged twenty-eight should be asking this of a boy twelve years younger.

'Look in the purse.'

What did he mean?

'The one Francesca gave you.'

He leaned over and with some effort took it from my doublet. 'Don't you remember?' He then proceeded to empty its contents onto the leaf-strewn ground before us; all of three golden coins and seven of silver.

'I think she liked you.'

'Us, Tomma,' I said. 'She liked us.'

He didn't credit this with an answer.

'She's saved our lives in more ways than one.' I forced the old Benno back onto the stage. 'We'll get us to Naples, then we'll get started.'

'Sire...' he said next, in a tone which by now I knew preceded one of his declarations. I turned towards him, the action paining me greatly, reluctant to hear the rest of the sentence. 'What will they do to her, do you think?

It took a moment for his words to hit me, one more to come to my senses. I might be a braggart, conceited, immoral, but I hadn't thought myself a coward. Yet I had run off and left her to face those shitheads. For all my wrongdoings I had yet to lose my conscience.

I was going back. I had to make sure she was safe before we went any further. I resolved, then, that if she had been taken, I'd turn myself in. But I didn't mention this part of my plan.

'But sire, it will make no difference. If they've taken her, they'll take you as well. And...'

'No, Tomma, you can't persuade me. If it turns out like that, get back to Florence. Go to Sandro. At least I'll be able to live with myself.'

'You may not live, sire. Aside from your shoulder,' he pointed at my bare, mud-plastered feet, one booted, one not, 'you're not going to get far like that. I'll go. It's easy for me. I'll sneak through the watch tower, find out what's happened. Then I'll come back and bring you another pair.'

'And if they've taken her?'

'Then that's the time to think what to do.'

I sat silent, wracking what little of my brain seemed left intact: go now, take that God-given boat, leave all this behind us and let the memory of abandoning her weigh upon my soul forever. Or set Tomma out on the road, for he was right, as always he was, as to the fact that I wouldn't make it.

Seeing my anguish, he got to his feet. 'I'm going sire; there's no point trying to stop me.'

No, there was not.

'I'll wait till it's dark before I come back.'

I took one of Francesca's gold coins and put it into the lining of my doublet; the rest I handed to him.

'It's too much,' he said.

'What good are they here? Take them, they might come in useful.'

'Just one thing, sire. We didn't find out what she wanted to tell us.' And when I looked at him, uncomprehending, 'Dosolina. But I might find out now.'

As he stepped out onto the road, I made him promise to be careful, do nothing foolish, when we both were aware that he should be the one giving me that advice.

I watched him disappear up the hill path, and was filled with very great melancholy.

The sun had reached midpoint in the heavens. I tried to comfort myself with the thought that he would be back by nightfall.

CHAPTER FIFTEEN

A most violent thunderstorm struck us that night. Rain battered down so fiercely it shattered the tiles on the chapter-house roof and crashed down a great many trees in the orchard. And so you can imagine how I felt the next morning; light had barely appeared in the sky when Novice Sister Cecilia came running to say she had just seen Francesca making her way up the path.

No doubt to tell me more about Benno. I did not think I could bear it.

'She looks ill. Someone has gone to find Sister Agata.'

I turned before she could say any more and hurried as fast as I could down through the cloister. Dear God in Heaven, what could have happened? Onto the path and there she was, just as Novice Sister Cecilia had said. She stopped and swayed as if she might fall. 'He's gone,' she cried as I reached her. 'He's gone.' Her face was blotched and streaked with tears and her hair was in tangles.

'The Duke's men came for him. But he escaped and I will never see him again. Oh Sofia, I'll die.'

I struggled to collect my thoughts. Yesterday, she had been euphoric. Now she was telling me she would die.

'He'll come back. Of course he will…' I could but pray

that he would, though I did not know why; there was no chance that I would ever be in his company.

'No, No…' she wailed '…he'll be far away by now.'

Sister Agata appeared at that moment, and though she couldn't know the true cause of Francesca's distress, at least she could give her something to calm it. Together we led her back up to the cloister. There was a strange smell about her. It made me think of something, but I couldn't remember what. She flopped down on a bench. Sister Agata crouched before her and lifted her eyelids.

'Have you eaten anything unusual, my Lady?' *She pushed her hair away from her face, and it was then we saw the marks upon it – blue, and thin threads.*

Francesca shook her head and Sister Agata said, 'We'll keep you here until you are better. You can't be jolted about in that carriage all the way back up the hill.'

Which was exactly what I'd been thinking. After such storms, the road would be covered in mud and loose boulders. How her coachman had managed to get down it was a miracle indeed. I should explain here that our convent was set in the valley, the citadel hung on the summit above us.

'Let us…'

But Sister Agata didn't finish her sentence, for we heard the thud of hooves, and a few moments later who should appear but the very last person I could have imagined, namely Signor Baldassare. I can only say he looked stricken. Whatever had stirred him, it wasn't Francesca. Why would he care about her?

'Thank you, Sisters, you've been too kind already.' *He was doing his best to sound like a normal person.*

'Oh please don't worry, signore,' Sister Agata said in her calm, steady voice. 'The lady can stay here with us. We're happy to help her. She seems...'

'No. I thank you. There is no need,' he cut in. 'It's best I take her home.'

We could not protest for he was a physician, not a simple apothecary like Sister Agata.

'Then let me come with you,' said she.

He smiled, as if in gratitude for her kind offer. 'I'm sorry but there is no room.'

'But you have your horse; there will be space enough for us both in the carriage.'

Here he looked flummoxed 'He's lame,' he replied somewhat curtly. 'I have no choice but to leave him with you. I'll send someone to fetch him.'

This seemed most strange, but what could we do, we being but weak and foolish women?

Francesca clung to me, trembling. 'Help me, Sofia,' she whispered. 'I'm frightened.'

'I'll come to you as soon as I can.' I said this only to calm her, for though as I may have said we did venture out into the world, it was to poor places. Visiting friends in rich houses... well that was something else entirely.

'Tomorrow ... Promise, Sofia... Tomorrow.'

'Send for me, if you need me,' was all Sister Agata could think to say to Signor Baldassare.

'I will, you can be sure of it.' And with this he made much show of helping Francesca to the gate. But when he had got her through it, he bundled her into the carriage.

'It might be the poppy, or that she has used too much belladonna.' Sister Agata looked almost as worried as I as *we watched it slip and slide up the hill. 'But I'm not sure, my dear. Her symptoms are not what they should be for that. I must think on it a little.'*

But I didn't need to, I knew what was wrong with her. Or who was wrong with her, to be precise.

CHAPTER SIXTEEN

Had all sense left me? Why *Deo Santo* did I let him go?

I set upon trying to convince myself. 'Don't worry, Benno, he's far too clever to be caught,' tried to bring logic into the debate, 'And he was right, you'd never have made it. There was no choice. We couldn't abandon Francesca; she hadn't abandoned us.'

Until then I had used God for my own ends, had painted frescoes in his churches, fashioned altarpieces for his congregations. Now, however, I found myself praying. 'Dear Lord, let him come back safe, and I swear.' I was sitting against Tomma's patch of wall, a multitude of declarations spewing out of my mouth. I would give up carousing, live life like a monk, offer half my earnings to the church. No, all of it, when I heard shouting out on the road. I got to my feet and through the gap in the rock saw where it came from – the Duke's men on foot, heading up from the valley.

'*Merda…* Tomma.'

But he wasn't with them. My heart started beating again.

It occurred to me then, I would have to hide myself somewhere out of immediate sight. I wasn't stupid enough to imagine they wouldn't be back. I looked up to the ceiling, which I had thought a cupola but now could see was a broken crossbar of stone. It evoked in my mind ruined structures in the Forum of Nerva. The ivy and ferns clinging to its surface had all but taken it over, in many parts holding it up. I shuffled further into the cave and had travelled but a few steps when I stumbled and grasped at the ivy which hung down like a curtain from the wall of rock. It came away in my hand, revealing a space behind it, and perceiving what looked like an overgrown tunnel, I pushed my way into it. A few steps and I found myself in what can but be described as a small anteroom, if caves have such things. Here, too, the walls were covered in creepers and its roof, now nothing more than a mat of woven branches, let the morning light filter down through it. I thought I could make out vague glimpses of colour, and I was right for as I pulled the scrub of leaves aside, I saw what looked like a portion of frieze done in red ochre.

Using my good arm, I set upon the creepers, tugging and wresting them from the wall. And there it was.

I stood before it, disbelieving what was before me.

For that moment, my mind was a blank. May God forgive me, I even forgot about Tomma.

A scape of land... trees, rocks and sky. It wasn't those that stopped my breath but a figure diving downwards, feet above his head. And was it the sea or a pool of still water shining beneath him?

Emotion hit me hard then; to know that I was not alone. A long age before mine, a painter possessed the same vision as I. Not for him the static imprint of a solitary moment. Had I been a different type of man I would have fallen to my knees.

But I wasn't a different kind of man, I was me. And being me, I sat myself down to study the image.

Feet above the plunging figure, right leg pointing upwards, left bent, hips turned one way, body the other, his naked back towards me, naked buttocks, naked legs, arms sweeping outward, like wings.

Those days, and nights, in the garden failing to summon the vaguest concept from my mind... yet here he was, my angel plunging earthwards down towards his Virgin.

Time passed, I sat transfixed. Above the ceiling of branches the sun was dipping in the sky before I forced myself to my feet. Released from paradise as I was, the pain of mortals hit me anew. I managed, but only just, to make my way back through the tunnel. I found Tomma's place and, closing my eyes, hoping to blank out the torment from the inferno now reignited inside my shoulder, lay down upon it to wait for dusk to fall.

I must have slept. A sword's point woke me. The fellow prodding it into my neck may have been smaller than I, but he had advantage.

CHAPTER SEVENTEEN

I ran to the Reverend Mother, caring not if I would be punished, and told her what had just happened. And, though I knew what the answer was likely to be, I asked if she would permit me to visit Francesca.

She looked up from her writing and put down her quill. And though she spoke softly, her words were like needles jabbing my skin. 'The lady is a rich and... fortunate... woman.' She didn't say 'foolish' but that's what she meant. 'You have others to care for who are not.'

But as I bowed and turned to go, she said, 'Her husband is there for her. They do not need you.'

'But Mother, he has gone to Venice.'

I could see her weigh up this information, and perhaps I am unfair to suggest it was only thoughts of his business there, and the wealth resulting from it, that caused her change of heart. I might have told you before that he gave great sums to our Order.

'Rules must not be broken.' Was I right, did the frown relax from her forehead? 'But, Sister Maria Assunta, on this one occasion I am prepared to bend them. You will join the rest of the novices clearing the trees in the orchard. I will inform Sister Agata that when you have finished she may

accompany you to visit the lady, for though she has lived in pleasure upon the earth, she too is in need of God's love.'

I hurried back through the cloister, thanking our Lord for reminding our Reverend Mother where her loyalties lay, and had almost reached the orchard when Fortunato came into view. He was perched most awkwardly on a large horse. Signor Baldassare's to be precise. I didn't think it seemed lame as it clip-clopped out onto the hill path. But, then again, I knew little of such things. He had only just disappeared from sight when the gate opened again, and Canoness Sister Veronica stepped through it.

I blinked once and then I blinked again, for limping along the path beside her was a small, misshapen boy.

CHAPTER EIGHTEEN

I sought to assure them that I would go peacefully but they dragged me out of the cave by my feet, ripping the silver sewn fabric of my new doublet to shreds. Up the bastarding hill they hauled me, through the gate tower and up the alleyways, onto the campo.

In times before, rage would have conquered all other emotion and it would have carried me through. But now, in its place, there settled an unfamiliar sense of ambivalence as to what would become of me. I only cared about Tomma.

A crowd had gathered and a buzzing rose up as if from a wasps' nest, as I was towed past them on my back. I must have blanked out at this stage. But when I came to, it took no pondering as to what kind of place I was in. Are not all dungeons of a similar style, down to their lack of furnishings?

Life mocks us, does it not; one night asleep close to the sky, upon a mattress of feathers, the next under the dome of a Roman's house, now on the stinking floor of a cell. And there I offered up a new prayer thanking God that Tomma had set out on the road, and thus had been spared this hellhole.

A fly-speck guard, devoid of teeth, leered as he held up

his lantern and slammed the door as he left me. Then came then the familiar clunk of his key as it turned in the lock. There being no glimpse of light turning night into day, I could not judge the passing of time. There was but a piss pot and jug of water, the surface of which, experience told me, would in the shortest of times be covered in flies. If it wasn't already. Just as well, then, that I could barely see it.

I started in the secure faith that Tomma would find me. That he had made it back to the house, that the old signore would set about planning my rescue.

From this happy notion, my spirits plunged, and I was filled with despair; before they had time to save me, my limbs would be cut from my body and what was left of me hung on a gibbet.

And when word reached Florence? I could but conceive of the glee this news would spawn amongst all those turds and bastards. Only my boys and Sandro would light candles and pray for my soul.

But it wasn't long before this forlorn self-pitying state of mind subsided, for now an icy hand gripped my heart. How did they find me? Only Tomma had known where I was. Terror engulfed me. I remembered the Duke's men, heading up from the valley. '*Sacro Cristo*', they had caught him out on the road. My heart seemed to stop, how much had they hurt him? Before now I had not thought that it would break for a boy. I closed my eyes and saw him again stepping out of the cave.

A heavy black serpent coiled round my soul. I had to stay alive. I had to find him. I prayed for the second time that day. 'Take me,' I pleaded, 'not Tomma. He's a good boy. He's not like me...'

CHAPTER NINETEEN

By the time I reached the orchard, the others were gathered already; they stood in a circle all huddled together. Novice Sister Perpetua turned when she heard me squelching through the waterlogged grass. 'Who is he?' I could but assume she meant the boy. 'And what's he doing here?'

'And why has the Canoness Sister left him alone in the cloister?' added Novice Sister Cecilia. 'He's just sitting there.'

'He might be a prince, forced into hiding.' Now it was Novice Sister Catherine's turn.

'Don't be silly,' snapped Novice Sister Marta. 'Princes don't have bent bodies.'

'And they don't wear breeches tied in a knot to stop them falling down,' Novice Sister Perpetua added for good measure.

There was only one way to find out the answer. You don't get a prize for guessing the person elected to do this. I found him in the cloister, as Novice Sister Cecilia had said. And though, at that moment, I could not care about anyone except Francesca, yes, it was strange he'd been left there alone.

He stood when he saw me. He was small, as I've said,

but still taller than I. And older than I had imagined. His body was twisted, but this is not what struck me, for though it was a sin even to think it, his face was the most beautiful that ever I'd seen, his eyes so dark as to be almost black. And, under its crusting of filth and dried mud, his tangled hair fell on his shoulders.

I confess to staring at him for a long moment before I heard myself say, 'Who are you?' a little too brusquely perhaps.

He seemed unperturbed at my rudeness. 'Tomma Trovatello,' he replied. His voice was deep, his accent soft and languorous, unlike any I had heard before.

'And what are you doing here?'

'I wish I knew.'

I started, then, on another tack. Our conversation went something like this.

'Where have you come from?'

He paused, before answering, 'I'm sorry,' he said, 'I can't tell you.'

But I would not be put off my stride. 'You won't tell me, or you've lost your memory?'

He paused again and looked at me with an unbowed expression, 'I may have lost it. I can't remember.'

I'd have thought him a dullard, but as I looked at his bright, clever face, I knew that I had met my match.

Just then came the sound of feet treading on the piles of wet leaves blown in from the storm.

'Maria Assunta,' Canoness Sister Veronica bellowed. 'Get back to the orchard. This instant.'

'You're saved... for the moment,' I whispered.

CHAPTER TWENTY

I fancied that Richard Lesley was sitting on the floor beside me. I saw his thickset face again, his eyes the colour of water. But here I would not be entertained by talk of England, which did seem to me a primitive realm where winters are even colder than ours. So cold is it, he had told me, that folks are sewn into chemises of wool at the start of October, and cut out of them only when Lent is well behind them.

I knew he was but an illusion conjured up in my mind from that old gaol of nightmares. Like that one, here was dark so deep it seemed as if blindness had struck me. And it had been so with him, we had taken turn to sleep, though never were we able to fall into that luxurious state beyond dreams, whilst he whose turn it was to stay awake would watch for rats, which troubled not by our presence appeared from their holes to amble fearlessly.

Often the ravenous pangs in our bellies would tempt us to catch them to eat, and perhaps in our desperate state we would have been driven to do so had there not arrived notice for our release. Months passed, my ransom was paid by my lady Rizziola, but Sir Richard Lesley was led away and I knew I would never see him again.

Just as I'd never see Tomma.

I lay in torment. A branding iron seared into my shoulder. My arms wouldn't move; for no reason other than they were shackled. Then the rats came. They couldn't be seen in the darkness, but I felt them clambering over my legs. Pain coursed through my body with rampant abandon. It occurred to me that I was in the bleakest of hells, all hope abandoned. I cannot tell you how much time had passed when the door of my cell was thrown open. Light filtered in from the passage, two figures came towards me and hauled me to my feet. With a shift, plainly borrowed from a hermit, pulled over my head and a blindfold tied round my eyes, I was led out to face the fate that waited. All was lost now for Tomma and me.

A very great fright entered my breast and in my state of trepidation it took some moments to perceive of the fact that the guards were leading me forward gently, stopping every few moments to let me gather strength to go on.

Smells altered as we advanced... from shit to dankness, to that of beeswax. Someone played upon a recorder; its music increased as we approached it and faded behind us, leaving only the sound of my chains and the guards' boots striking the floor.

I remember nothing after that.

I woke to find myself curled up upon a sack filled with straw; its grassy smell mixed with that of sweet herbs. I had a sense that I was clean. My cell had changed. It now had a window; stars shone beyond it. I felt a presence beside me. A shape leaned over me. A phial of liquid was held to my lips; it trickled its way down my throat. And as it did a bolt of energy shot through my veins. Pain left me. I felt stronger, my mind clearer, the candle flame flickered with brighter intensity. All seemed to stop, or slow to a snail's pace, and a calmness filled me.

I next woke to the orb of the sun rising beyond the window. Water, and corn bread if I remember correctly, had been left on the floor beside me. But I couldn't eat.

A second phial was held to my lips. And, as before, all things around me came into sharp focus. The sun's rays changed into shards of gold; footsteps from somewhere below the window seemed as if from a marching army. I felt myself strong enough to beat that army. Light enough to fly. Wise enough to answer all the questions ever asked...

In that lucid state my wits returned, and with it my memory; not in segments requiring of time and patience to reassemble, but all at once, and a very great panic surged up inside me as a picture of Tomma crashed into my mind. I saw, again, his face as he left me behind in the cave. How long after that had they caught him? The black serpent slithered back into my soul.

When next my protector appeared, he carried a basin of water and told me, gently, that I must wash and dress.

He spoke in an accent foreign to my ears. It wasn't English, I knew that one well. I could see, now, hovering above me a man of middle years. And though he had the bearing of a servant, he wore a nobleman's black, this colour, if I may call it thus, being, as you will know, so costly that only the wealthiest of men have means to afford it. His beard was trimmed to a long and sharp point, a fashion I had not seen before.

'They're taking you to the lord Volsini, I am most sorry to say. I believe you were unlucky enough to come into his company some weeks ago.'

I admitted I was.

'He would prefer to have seen the last of you, but men such as he have fragile egos. You shamed him, signore. The only way of restoring his honour was to track you down and make great display of punishing you. He could not allow you to be his nemesis. But you escaped him... again. You are safe for the moment. But I bid you, tread carefully.'

Had I been able to assure him I would, but treading and carefully were mismatched words as far as I was concerned. And so I said, 'You rescued me, signore. I thank you.'

'It was not I.'

I would have asked him to explain, but something stopped me.

I readjusted my brain from pointed beards to a pile of pleated silk wound round a forehead. 'That *pezzo di merda*,' I managed, a statement requiring no answer.

Had circumstances been altered, I would have rejoiced at being in the fuckhead's company for the second time in my life, so great was my blind and terrible fury. I relished the thought of strangling him properly, feeling my hands slowly crushing his neck. 'Where's my boy?' I would loosen my grip until he answered. And if he did not, my next demand would be for a blade, and once I had it firm in my hand they would lament the day Simone da Benno had crashed into their master's life. I pictured it all in my mind; his guards unable to move as I wrenched the last breath from his body. All was but fantasy, of course, for this was the end for me...and for Tomma. Here was punishment for my sins. Would they bring him up from his cell? Would we be sliced into pieces together?

But wait. Had I forgotten the indisputable fact that that

every man has his price? As had been proven so recently by way of the little shit Buonarroti's bastard of a father.

It therefore followed that the arsehole must too. I'd barter what was left of me in exchange for Tomma. All I had was my talent and so I'd inform him that, from this day forward, I would paint only for him. I would depict him on every last one of my panels, or walls, or my ceilings. I would grant him eternal life. Would this not be worth trading for a footling boy?

My protector helped me stand. My shoulder pained me less and I took in the fact that it had been bandaged again. He left me with a bowl of water. I splashed my face and neck. And as I did, I felt something caught in my hair. My fingers were useless, and it took a good while to untangle the chain and pull it over my head. But when I succeeded, I saw it was so finely worked it might have been transparent, with a bead hanging from it. I held it up to the window's light – it was fashioned to look like an eye with, etched upon the white of its orb, the blue of an iris and a black pupil.

I would have asked what it was and who had put it there. But again something stopped me.

Thus it was that, dressed in a jerkin of soft calfskin, much dissimilar from the one Baldassare had cut me out of, a linen tunic, plain hose, which, being designed for one of normal height, stopped below my knees, I limped beside a guard who led me down the same windowed corridor along which Tomma and I had travelled in high spirits what seemed like ten lifetimes before. I might say here that after laying these items of clothes on my mattress, my gaoler had held out Francesca's gold florin and placed it on the bed beside me. How it had survived its journey up the mountain was a miracle of gargantuan proportions... and it was then I knew, if proof were needed, that I'd been delivered into honest hands, though such trifles were of little consequence just at that moment, as were altarpieces and gilded tombs. But I thanked him anyway.

'I should tell you,' he said now, 'my name's Ivan Kovac.'

'And I would tell you that mine is Benno,' I smiled, 'but I think you may know this already.'

Back along the beeswax corridor, into the same small chamber. And there, as before, stood the arsehole himself, looking much as he had on the day of our first, and last, encounter, with his same long, face and scornful expression. For some reason, peculiar I know, I couldn't but take note of his hands; smooth and white with rings upon his index fingers, a fashion I despised on a man but liked very much on a woman.

'I give you your due, da Benno,' his tone was drawling and lazy, 'it took a fair while to find you.'

Was he expecting an answer?

'But we did. In the end. As always we do.'

A wiser voice than mine echoed in my head, 'Kill him, sire, and you'll be back in that dungeon. And what good will it do you there?' There was still hope if I kept my mouth shut.

'It may interest you to know the name of the man who disclosed your presence to us. Or let me put it a better way,' he closed his eyes as if summoning effort to the endeavour. 'The one who betrayed you.'

And when still I didn't respond, he continued, 'No? Ah well, I'll tell you anyway. I believe you may know him. His name is Donato Favoni.'

Did he think I'd believe his bullshit? With this insult to my intelligence something of my old bravado returned and I would have informed him that he was a *stronzo supremo* had it not been for Tomma and staying alive.

So I said, instead, 'What do you want with me, signore?' Let him speak, then start to bargain.

'I? What do... I... want? I want to have you taken onto the campo, there to have your fingers cut from your hands. Then to deal with your eyes. Have them gouged. Fair punishment for an artist. What do you think, fingers first, eyes after?'

'Fingers first would be my preference.'

'A wise decision but I'm sorry that, just at the moment, I cannot comply. You seem astonished. And well you may be, for, in the meantime, you have been granted... let us call it a stay of execution. For though I consider your drawings hideous, not all are blessed with good judgement. Another has fixed on the notion that you be permitted to make submission to paint the fresco. You will go to the church tomorrow and consider the task set before you.'

Had recent events so addled my brain that I could no longer detach fact from fiction?

'One last thing da Benno, don't think to venture beyond the campo.'

But I knew that now I was free, if only to paint the fresco, venturing beyond it never to return, was exactly what he hoped I would do.

Back in my room, upon my grass bed, I scoured my brain for answers.

Why had I been freed from the dungeon?

In order to paint the fresco.

Why now, when it was denied me in the first place? Who was Volsini's 'someone else'? Who put the eye-bead round my neck... and what was its purpose?

My mind was as tangled as the piles of string on our workshop floor, requiring of Tomma's skill to unpick it. But he wasn't there.

There was no sense to any of it, and so I lay back and consoled myself. It all was but a fantasy, and when it was over I would open my eyes and say to the boys, 'Ye gods what a nightmare.'

I would tell of the flight from Florence, the jump from the window, the tree, the boar, the portrait... the fresco...

'It was the cheese, sire,' Celestino would say, 'or it might have been the grappa.'

And then I would swear, as always I do, to start upon a new and abstemious life, for had not the Good Lord Above let me glimpse future-wise, as warning of what was bound to become of me should I continue on this course much longer.

But, as ever, when I made such a pledge, I could bet my last soldi the boys would know it would only last till the evening when the first tavern lights had been lit.

CHAPTER TWENTY-ONE

The hazy light of morning seeped through my window; and there below me stretched the campo where, all that long time past, Tomma and I had stood waiting, my folder of drawings strapped to my back. The wankers were gone; ye gods amongst all those peacocks they hadn't found one for the job. In their place, now, were ordinary, unadorned people going about their everyday chores. On the opposite side stood the bell tower, its church beside it. I could but wonder what fate had in store for me there. Or for Tomma, wherever he was.

'Where are you, my little friend?' A shuddering sense of despair filled my soul. When darkness fell I'd start searching for him, and the first place I'd go was the dungeon. But still it was day, and the next part of my ordeal lay before me.

Ivan Kovac led me along the now familiar passage. No recorders this time, but still the beeswax smell. A vast hallway. Into the courtyard and through the palace gates with its sentries. Here he left me to continue alone. Across the campo to the church. Within its pediment was carved the words 'Santa Maria del Monte'. I pushed the door open and stepped inside. It was of a usual type, small and dim, smelling of mould mixed with incense. The reek of death, I would call it.

We all have dreams; in mine I stand in a vast space, its walls unadorned, waiting for my genius to fill them with scenes of unparalleled... I shouldn't say 'beauty', that word being affixed to the work of others. No, with power and movement and colour. But in front of the only blank portion of wall, reality revealed itself to be a space no more than three arm-spans wide, placed betwixt two works of crushing ugliness produced by different hands; one of Jerome in his cave, who the other might have been I did not know, or care. Hazarding a guess, I'd have gone for the Baptist.

I gaped at it, unbelieving.

Give me a wall of favourable dimensions and I'll paint you a fresco of such blinding wonder that its church will shine brighter than any jewel ever seen in the world. I could but ask myself what malign spirit had whispered in my ear the word, 'Montevecchio'? Montevecchio? *Monte* shitting *Cazzo* would have been more precise. In normal times, ten thousand florins could not have persuaded me to make a whore of myself here. But times were not normal. I'd have to look keen until I found Tomma, which would demand the greatest feat of play-acting that yet had been seen in these parts.

A friar, of corpulent dimension, sat dozing by his lectern. He jumped when he heard me approach him, making great show of his ire at being stirred from his sleep.

I spoke to him courteously. 'I am Simone da Benno.'

'I presume you have come to see the wall that awaits decoration?' He said this in a weary drawl, feigning absorption in the psalter lying open before him; he might have been master of the Tornabuoni Chapel for all any ignorant, uninformed idiot knew. 'It's over there,' he pointed, without looking up.

I should scrape and bow and show gratitude for that pissing piece of wall? I informed him that I had seen it.

'Then I only need tell you,' still he kept his eyes on the psalter, 'that there are two other, most excellent, candidates invited to submit their designs.'

What wonder that still they were here and had not gone running off down the hill to find another to paint. Any would do.

'Your arrival means you are three, altogether.'

I couldn't count?

'The commission will go to the best. All designs must be presented by tomorrow, at midday, when they will be given to me.'

The only thing I would give him was a whacking great boot up his arse.

I couldn't trust myself to remain in his company, and so, holding tight to my tongue, I turned and walked back to the door. And as I did, I seemed to hear a muffled rustling and scratching, and a faint tinkling, as if of a bell. I stopped and looked round, but no one was there, only the Fra settling back to his dozing.

In the open space of the campo, I tried to gather my thoughts; the first being to get to the dungeon. It took great resolve to stop myself going there right then but, nothing was more certain, I'd have to wait till nightfall. I had one chance to find Tomma, I couldn't squander it in a moment of madness.

The second related to the fact of there being two other candidates and one day, only, to conjure up my design. But there wasn't time to ponder upon this turn of events, for just at that moment I saw Ivan Kovac striding towards me. 'I'll take you to the kitchen, signore.' I was getting used to his accent.

'Remember, I'm Benno.'

He smiled, acknowledging the fact. But I knew he was too formal to make use of first names in a casual way. 'You must be hungry.'

An understatement if ever I'd heard one.

With this he led me back through the palace gate, the sentries standing ramrod straight as before, and a little way across the courtyard to steps that seemed to lead down to the very bowels of the earth.

As we descended, the smell of roasting meat wrapped itself around us. At the foot was a large, open door where he left me. Had he not taken me to that place of mouth-watering wonder, my nose would have led me there by itself, for now it struck me; I was hungry. No, not hungry, ravenous. I hadn't eaten for days, and I needed strength to find Tomma.

I peered in from the doorway and beheld, as were all kitchens I'd known before, a place of frantic action. Boys scurried about with trays, plates and spoons. Old men sat, stripped to their scrawny waists, turning spits of roasting meats. Pots boiled, lids crashed, cooks shouted above noise of indescribable volume. And all against a backdrop of fires blazing and crackling with fat in their grates.

Noise dampened to a babble, then to silence as heads turned towards me. I allow that I must have cut a strange figure: a giant with a face bruised black and purple, hair sticking up from his head, in hose that barely covered his knees. Often had I been taken for a brigand, and here was no different. A young lad, whom I took to be one of the under-cooks, lifted a cleaver. Now was the time to speak, else I might have found myself back on my grass bed, with another phial of miraculous potion being poured down my throat yet again.

I said a polite 'Good day' to the company assembled before me, all with mouths open and terrified looks on their faces.

'I'm Simone da Benno,' I forced a cheery tone. 'I've come to paint the fresco.'

Faces glanced at each other. He doesn't look like a painter. From what we saw of those who came here in September, they are persons of flamboyant appearance. Take care Beppe, don't approach him, he is a starving man come to raid us.

No, he looks more like a lunatic... it was a full moon last night.

'Let me show you.' I stepped towards them; the congregation stepped back. And as I had done so often before, I ventured to prove I was what I claimed. Rubbing my finger upon the soot-covered chimney breast, and moving along to a clean space beside it, I looked round to find the best subject. And there she was, at the edge of the assembly, a voluptuous goddess, with hair dark as blackberries. They gathered round, with ooohs and aaahs as I drew her face upon it.

Here were people of my stripe, *Deo Grazie*. Amongst them might be one who could help me find Tomma, for do not servants know more of the goings-on in their mansion or palace than the very nobles themselves?

'Signore,' an elderly gent, whom I took to be head cook, said after some time had passed. 'Never have I seen such a marvel in my life... and it has indeed been a long one.'

He led me to a bench, waved a lad over to clear it of pots and of pans, made me sit, and there I devoured three plates of a stew of bacon and beans. Even now I remember ramming its bulky sweetness into my mouth, feeling its warmth make its way down my throat to the grumbling space of my stomach.

My goddess looked at me, concerned. 'You don't need to eat so quickly,' she said, 'there's plenty more in the pot.'

*

It was with an overwhelming lack of enthusiasm I departed that haven of warmth and food, a servant having appeared with the balls-aching news that he was to take me to my rivals. But he was wrong with that description; in view of my genius with a brush they were not rivals at all.

Up the twenty or so steps we climbed, into the midday light. Reaching the end of the courtyard we approached what I can but describe as a miniature building wrapped within a circle of pillars, much like the one at the end of the Ponte Rotto. It seemed far larger inside than out, and was hot as my father's forno, which only served to intensify the smell of gum Arabic hanging in the air. But, patently, it was more than a workshop for fur-strewn pallets were set at the end of the room. A table sat in its centre, with all manner of materials arranged upon it – stencilling frames, knives, pens and inks. Bowls of pigment. Drawings were stacked on the floor with ox-hide portfolios, polished, pristinely, beside them.

Santo Cristo, they were serious.

Here dwelt my adversaries; a thickset man, who informed me his name was Antoniano Carpini. His appearance attested to the fact that he cared more for sweetmeats than he did for his craft. He had with him a thin, nervous knave with the look of a rabbit caught in the jaws of a coursing hound, who went by the name of Cesare. I could not but suppose his father possessed a hearty sense of humour.

The other claimed a nobleman's title – Matteo Guistinio Da Viggo di Fassa. I froze when I saw him, for with his oiled tresses cut short at one side to better display the pearl that dangled from his ear, I took him to be a cavaliero of the Florentine variety, the very last thing I needed. Such affectations had suited Sir Richard, being in contrast to his rough looks. But this man was too pretty for baubles; he'd have better been served by a sword scar, or something of that order.

He spoke and I thanked God that I had been wrong, on one count at least. He wasn't from Florence, for complaining to the servant that he'd been assured that he and Carpini were the sole candidates, he spoke with a Roman accent. He was without assistant, which seemed appropriate, it being apparent that he enjoyed his own company to such an extent he was loath to share it.

My appearance apart, Carpini seemed untroubled that I had materialised out of thin air. Laying his chalk down, he bade me good day.

When I informed his rival that my name was Benno and that I was included in their company, being too self-respecting to refer to it as a competition, he looked at me, puzzled.

'But signore,' he said, 'you have only what's left of today and half of tomorrow.'

I told him I knew it.

'You've submitted your drawings already?'

No, I hadn't started on them yet.

He sought to cover his consternation with a new query. 'You've seen the church?'

I told him I had.

And what was my opinion?

'Oh, it's as I expected.'

'You expected it would be so meagre?'

He thought it meagre?

Mystified by my response, he told me he did. 'And then there's the question of the frescoes on either side of the space.' He wished me to remark upon their ugliness.

'Jerome,' I said instead. 'And the other, might he be The Baptist?'

Da Viggo di Fassa looked up from his drawing. 'He jests with you, cannot you see it?'

Ah, now he understood. He returned my smile; there was humour in his eyes. I smiled back and, seeing his bundle of chalks, asked if he would be so kind as to let me have one.

'We are in competition, Carpini. You are under no obligation to furnish him with materials.'

Carpini returned my look, raising an eyebrow to show he cared nought for this piece of advice, and passed me a handful.

Di Fassa face remained expressionless. But for the fact

that I had to force myself to behave, at least for the present, I would have taken the so-called materials and thrust them down his gullet.

And the subject to be painted on that turd of a wall? The Coronation of the Virgin, Carpini informed. Rejected sheets were strewn about him, his final effort, to which he was adding finishing touches, was coloured well enough, but too tightly constructed. His Virgin's eyes rolled back in her head; but where he had hoped to portray a state of ecstasy, she looked as if she'd been struck by a fit. Had circumstances been different I would have been happy to help him. But they weren't, and so I resolved to repay his kindness in some other way.

I thanked him and took a chalk from the handful.

The Coronation of the Virgin? There being no time for creative endeavour, I trawled old images from my mind, Lippi... Angelico? Grave and serious depictions but I'd have to start somewhere, and having no paper proceeded to draw on the table, doing away with the clouds, the host of worshippers, the throne.

Carpini watched in fascination. 'It's most ...' at last coming up with '...unusual.' The word pleased me greatly for, as I may not have mentioned, 'unusual' is good, 'usual' is the thing that sinks us.

Aware of Da Viggo's hostile gaze, I rubbed my arms across the chalk and with the image firm in my mind, stood up and walked out into the courtyard. I had set myself thinking how to get back into the buggering dungeon when I heard footsteps. I turned to see the boy Cesare behind me. 'Signore,' he whispered and took from his shirt several small sheets of paper. 'It's all my master dares risk to give you.'

I felt sorry that I had compared him to a rabbit, if only in my mind. I grasped his shoulder and squeezed it, to show we were friends. 'Please thank him again. I'm most grateful.' He was a lad not much younger than Tomma and so I thought to ask if he'd heard of a boy who'd been brought to the palace.

He shook his head, no he hadn't. 'But ask my master, he might know.'

I would, if I could get him alone; an incident that took place but a moment later, when he came with stealthy tread, to see if Cesare had completed his mission.

I now had the chance to thank him myself. Then I told him about Tomma; that he was my apprentice and had gone missing.

Carpini looked at me, appalled. He had felt sorry for me, set as I'd been upon a mission I had no means of completing. Now I could see his mind was at work. Couldn't the lad have run away?

And so I added, 'I fear for him greatly.'

Seeing my evident distress, his expression changed. 'No signore, I haven't, but I pray that you find him.' And with that they set off across the campo. I went back indoors, where I took myself off to a corner; I say corner, but the room being circular, there was no such thing. Let me correct myself then, I sat upon the floor, furthest away from di Fassa as was possible to be and spread Carpini's gifts before me

They were small squares, but an eighth of the size of his, a tenth of di Fassa's, but a ruby is small, is it not, and a dewdrop, a fly's wing? Upon them I set to ensnare my idea.

It being well after noon, I had little time to win what

was set to be the contest of my life. I couldn't lose, for if I did I'd have no hope of finding Tomma. Or, to put it another way, I was fighting to win a battle to paint a turd of a wall in a piddling church that no one would ever care to look at... and should I lose I'd be back in that dungeon and I would never see him again. If this were not the next circle of Hell, then God was teaching me a lesson.

Though in short supply of time, I counted down each excruciating moment till darkness fell. And so it was, at dead of night, the first portion of that day's ordeal behind me, I stepped back through the palace doors. By now the sentries knew me to be amongst those competing for the fresco, and so didn't stop me. I made my way along the passage and followed the smells, changing from beeswax to dankness, to shit, from corridor to passage, at the end of which were the stairs I had been led up, wearing my hermit's shift. I steadied myself and stepped back into my nightmare.

In all such places, the damp hits you first and it doesn't take long for it to seep into your bones. The sounds are ever the same; dripping or trickling of water, squeaking of rats, rustle of cockroaches... and echoes vibrating in the silence. These bowels of hell are not filled with moaning and screaming as you might expect, for the souls imprisoned within them are depleted of energy even to whisper.

From cell to cell I went, drawing back the wooden slats affixed to the doors and calling 'Tomma' just loudly enough that if he were in one he would hear me.

I had tried six or so, when there came a drift of burning tallow. A flickering light and a withered shape loomed out of the darkness, holding a smouldering torch. Before he saw me, which I presumed would be in a flash, I lunged forward and grabbed his shirt, pulling him up until his feet dangled. He should be quiet, I informed him, or I would break his *cazzo* neck. On the other hand, if he did as I said, he would have a gold florin. His eyes bulged at the notion. He ceased his struggling and I set him back onto the ground.

Relieving him of his torch, I held it at arms-length. He peered up at me through the smoke; it was clear that he knew who I was. I took the recently returned coin from my jerkin and informed him, in a low voice, 'It's yours if you tell me the truth. If you don't, you'll know all about it.'

He managed a kind of strangled reply, which I took to be, 'Yes, signore.'

'Do you have a boy here?'

'What kind of boy?'

'Small, thin. With a crippled body.' I hated using this word for Tomma.

'No, signore.'

'You haven't seen him then?'

'No signore.'

'You're sure?'

'Yes, signore.'

'If you're lying, I'll be back. And I promise...'

'I'm not, signore.'

I held out the coin. 'If you hear anything – and I mean anything – you'll find me in the church and you never know, depending on the news you bring me, I might let you have it.'

I was desperate now. Most men would be disinclined to believe dark mortals such as he, but I had met enough in my life to know when they were lying. Or telling the truth, as it happened. Tomma wasn't in the dungeon; a fact that, though it shouldn't have, caused me very deep anguish.

I would have fallen into a fit of madness, but there was no time. I'd find him if there was but one chance in a million. To do so, however, I'd have to tread carefully, do nothing to raise suspicion. I would, for the next space of time, be the model contestant. I'd lull them into believing that turding wall was the finest that ever I'd seen... to paint it my heart's ambition.

I had no fears about my skill in the art of lying, having had a lifetime's practice. I wouldn't leave this bastard of a place until Tomma was with me again.

It was then the thought struck me... if he wasn't in the dungeon...

CHAPTER TWENTY-TWO

The top of the steps, along the passage, the stink of shit receding behind. Past the guard. Through the door. The courtyard. The temple. The sentries on the gate. Across the moonlit campo, heading down through the warren of alleys, planning what I'd do when I got to the Favoni house. How to get in without being seen? The attic first... pray *Dio* he would be in it.

If, compared to my escapade in the dungeon, I'd imagined this part of my venture would be fairly straightforward, I was in for a disappointment. To begin with, it was in total darkness. Odd, as during my nightly sojourns, at least a few windows had been lit.

I crept round to the stable yard and climbed the wall, with some difficulty I might add on account of my shoulder. I'd thought to get in by way of the kitchen, but now had a better idea and crept along the path leading up to the back of the house. The moon was waning but bright enough to let me see that, as I had hoped, the attic shutters were open. I picked up a pebble and aimed as close to the window as was safe. It hit the roof and rattled down it.

I held my breath. Moments passed. I was on the point of throwing another when... *Sangue di Dio*. It was large by the sound of it and coming fast at me. I would have run had my feet propelled themselves into action, but they stayed where they were as if nailed to the ground. Luckily, however, my arms seemed disposed to act as required, stretching out in a futile bid to halt the monstrous shape leaping from the the shadows towards me. But they turned out to be of little use as what I perceived to be a rabid wolf crashed me to the ground. My feet, too late unnailed from the ground, hovered somewhere atop my body. How quickly instincts do return. I managed, don't ask me how, to grab a rock from the side of the path and smash it into the monster's head. Blind desperation got me up off my knees, but now came the sound of feet performing contrarily to mine, in other words running most quickly. They belonged to a gentleman, large as I. I could see he was holding a chain. He lashed it out at me, smashing it into my face. I reeled backwards. Starbursts exploded in front of my eyes. And then rage took over. Not the blind sort but the cold, measured state that overpowers me at times such as these, and there have been many I can tell you. Even through my hot and stinging vision, I could see he wasn't a practised fighter. I sidestepped. He flailed out again. But chains are heavy and prone to unbalance their handler, which is why they're seldom used as weapons. On the upward rise of his arm, I kicked his balls. He crumpled and fell... and now it was his turn for the rock. I cannot say if I killed him, and getting to my feet somehow, this time they obeyed me, '*Madonna Grazie*'. I ran as fast as I was able, taking my arm into account, and had almost made the wall when a light appeared at one of the windows, then a face. I peered up at it, and through my blurred and stinging eyes saw it was the old signore.

A guard below him shouted, 'Don't worry, the dogs will get him, my lord.'

Suddenly, perfectly sound of hearing, the old man shouted back, 'Bring him to me when they do.'

I stood, incredulous, my mind in turmoil.

And now the guard was pointing somewhere in my general direction. His voice boomed through the darkness, 'There he is... Over there.'

The pumping energy that comes with shock launched me back over that wall. I half stumbled, half ran up through the pitch-dark alleys as fast as my legs, or should I say my suddenly cooperative feet, would carry me.

I don't know why I found myself in the church – the unlikeliest of places. Bewildered and shaken, I slumped beneath the Baptist. The dog... the chain. But worse than those, the old man at the window, the gift of hearing miraculously restored. I seemed to remember an observation on Tomma's part: 'There's something I don't understand, sire. If Signor Donato's father is deaf, how did he hear her out in the passage?'

My life until then had been that of a painter, drinking, carousing, with the odd brawl thrown in for good measure. Oh, I had plotted, of course, but my conspiracies, the one regarding the Buonarroti boy being a fair example, had led to nothing but disaster. Now came the painful realisation that I had been used by Donato Favoni, a man far cleverer than I. His almost absurd good nature... how he had masked his true intent. Francesca had tried to tell us. And I had sent Tomma back into the arms of his servant, one Signor Giacomo Baldassare.

Now I was certain. Tomma was there, in the house. I'd go back... no, not now... tomorrow. I'd think of a plan. 'The dogs will get him, my lord.' Dogs, not dog. How many were there? I set upon devising means of silencing them. Fantastical ideas rose up in my mind – chunks of meat... but where would I get them?

I could think no more; my mind wouldn't work. Exhausted, drained of all understanding, my shoulder paining me beyond reason, face numb and bleeding, I looked down at my hands and saw they were shaking.

This was the point I should have started to pray, I was in a church, after all. But I couldn't conjure the words. My head fell forward, my eyes refused to stay open. I must have blacked out. I woke in a pale pewter light. Memory trickled back into my mind. And as it did I heard a faint tinkling. An eerie feeling crept upon me, the hairs on the back of my neck seemed to rise. Someone was watching me; I can't say how I knew it.

I stood up as slowly, as calmly as I was able, forcing my legs to carry me out of the door. Onto the campo. I was losing my mind... if I hadn't lost it already. Now I knew why mad men laugh, why they howl and scream.

A very great cold had invaded my body. My shoulder ached like the very Devil, my head pounded, I could barely see a yard in front of me. I shuffled onwards, past the sentries on the gate, into the courtyard before they could ask what the hell I'd been up to, and made my way to the kitchen steps, descending downwards through levels of increasing heat. The place was empty; the only sign it was not abandoned being the logs ablaze beneath the great cauldrons.

I pulled out a bench and managed to place myself upon it. And then I slumped forward upon one of the tables and let sleep wash over me.

I have no idea how long I remained in this state; the next thing I knew was the word 'Signore' coming from somewhere above me. I swam up through layers of oblivion and, squinting between my swollen eyelids, could only just make out the black-haired beauty staring down at me in horror.

'Sweet *Gesu*,' she spun in and out of focus, 'what have you done to your face?'

I couldn't think of an answer.

'Did someone attack you?'

Had they? I no longer knew.

'Look,' she took a silver plate from the table, rubbed it with her sleeve and held it before me.

A sorry state of a face grimaced back; one of its eyes was split and half closed, the other swollen, its nose all crusted with blood, its lip bulging as if stung by a hornet.

She dampened the edge of her apron and held it against the worst of my wounds. 'Was it someone here in the palace?'

Two options entered my befuddled brain, fob her off with a story... or tell her the truth. Or, at least, a version of it. The latter I judged the better choice for then I could ask about Tomma.

'No, on the road. He was after my purse. He came up behind me.'

But what were you doing out there at night? Plainly this was what she was thinking.

'I was looking for my apprentice,' I said before she had

the chance to ask. 'I've lost him, you see.'

Her face softened.

'He's sixteen, but small for his age… And crooked…'
Ye gods, here I was again describing a weakling. He was
anything but that.

'Poor boy. Oh poor boy. I'm so sorry.'

'His name is Tomma. If you should hear anything.'

'Don't worry, I'll tell you, signore.'

'Benno,' I said.' I am Benno.'

'And I'm Anna. Are you hungry? You could eat could
you not?'

She didn't wait for an answer; pans rattled behind me.
By now the cooks' boys had arrived and were scuttling
about, glancing at me as they passed; no doubt my sorry
state was due to a night of hard drinking.

Eggs fried in bacon fat and pancakes were put down
beside me, a jug of light beer.

I shovelled them into my mouth and after I had wiped
my platter clean, a thought occurred to me, did she know
of Donato Favoni? If he was in cahoots with Volsini, surely
he'd be in the palace a lot.

'Oh yes, he's famous for his silk… and his beautiful
wife.'

Had she seen him here of late? And in case she asked
why, 'He wanted me to paint a portrait. I might have missed
him.'

'No. But I did see his servant.'

This threw me, I can tell you.

'When?'

She thought for a moment. 'Maybe a week or so ago,
walking across the courtyard. He was carrying something,

if I remember.'

    'Was anyone with him?'

    'No,' she said, 'he was alone.'

CHAPTER TWENTY-THREE

It took five days to clear the branches, starting at dawn and working till Vespers, stopping only for prayers in between. First collecting the smallest branches strewn all over the ground and tying them into bundles for firewood. Then the large ones, which had to be cut into logs. We took it in turns with the axe, for after only the fewest of moments our arms would ache too much to continue. And all the time I thought of Francesca; my blood stirred at her heartbreak, for is not passion a burning emotion unlike the inconsequential woes we were forced to suffer each day in the convent? And I thought of the Christ figure too, but I would have to stop calling him this. He had a name. Simone da Benno. Why were the Duke's men after him? Where was he now? Would he ever return? And if he did, what would it mean for Francesca? But perhaps it was better to burn in a fire than freeze in a waste of nothing.

So exhausted were we at the end of these days, we slept as soon as we lay down on our pallets. Which was good for it stopped me thinking about her... or about our strange visitor. The novices had forced me to tell them over and over what he had said in the cloister.

First his name: Tomma Trovatello.

'It's a foundling's name, Trovatello,' Novice Sister Catherine sought to inform us, as if we didn't know it already.

Novice Sister Perpetua screwed up her face. 'And he doesn't know why he's here?'

'Of course he knows. It's just that he wasn't going to tell me.'

'But it might have been the truth,' said Novice Sister Marta.

'What might have been?'

'Losing his memory.'

I didn't think so.

The longed-for morning came at last. When prayers were over, Sister Agata would collect her medicine box and we would set off for the Villa Favoni. Yet I feared greatly what we might find there. Every day I had begged our dear Santa Chiara to protect her, and now I'd find out if my prayers had been heard. But I should have known not to be so hopeful; we had not even finished the Ave Maria when we heard a fluttering sound above us. We stopped and looked up. A poor little sparrow had flown through one of the windows broken in the storm. It swooped and flapped about us, and when, at last, we managed to persuade it to fly back out of it again, precious time had been lost. Which meant it was late when we stepped out of the chapel, and had only reached the cookhouse path when we heard a familiar voice shouting loudly.

'It hasn't just melted into thin air. Someone has taken it. And when I find out who that someone is...'

Sister Agata stopped. I pulled her arm. 'Come on, keep going.'

141

But it was too late. Canoness Sister Veronica loomed in front of us, her face more furious than ever.

'Don't think for a moment that anyone's leaving.'

She signalled that we should follow her into the chapter house where the Sisters stood in silent dread. All were prepared for her tirade which, this time, was about Novice Sister Cecilia. Or, should I say, about her habit, which it seemed had disappeared. And until such time as the thief brought it back, we would all be punished. I should explain here that it wasn't just any old habit but a special one laid out ready for tomorrow when she was to take her final vows. The Canoness Sister's voice reached crescendo pitch. I found myself consumed with the overwhelming impulse to get away now, to run up the hill to Francesca; I could not bear it here one moment longer.

Canoness Sister Veronica closed her eyes for better effect and stretched her arms heavenward. 'Dear Lord, we beg you to punish our sinner...'

It was enough. I took a step back. Then another, and was out through the house door before she opened them again. Back across the cloister, along the path. I reached the gate, but it was locked. 'Think Sofia. Think.'

And now I know that God hadn't been listening to Canoness Sister Veronica, for if he had, my life would have gone on in its old settled way. I would have stayed in the convent forever, would not have encountered the wondrous things... and places... and people... waiting for me out in the world.

'Get over the wall,' I said to myself. The graveyard wall, to be precise, the one Francesca and I had peered over to watch Donato's strange procession.

I picked up my skirts and off I sped, but halfway across the grass I stopped in my tracks for what did I see but Sister Cecilia in her pristine new robe trying to climb over it too. Perhaps if she had been using both hands, but she was holding a bundle in one.

It is said that nuns are wont to go mad, but surely... I stared at her, blankly, watching her struggle. And then I walked slowly towards her.

She glanced round when she heard me, but it wasn't Novice Sister Cecilia's face peering down from the rim of her wimple.

I stood in utter confusion, gaping up at him.

'I'm trying to get over the wall,' he said, as if the fact had escaped me.

'Why?' was all I could think to ask.

He paused for a moment. 'I'm sorry but I can't tell you.'

Which put me off my track, but only for a moment. There was no time to ask more. 'It doesn't matter,' I heard myself say, 'I want to get over it too. I'll help you, if you help me.'

He smiled as if he considered this a reasonable bargain, and without enquiring why, he clambered down.' I'll push you up, then I'll come after you.'

It was then I remembered Corvo's box. God was surely on our side, for it was still in its hiding place. I pulled it out, rolled it to the wall, and placed it in position. Tomma Trovatello stepped upon it and gave me his hand. It was warm and strong and rougher even than mine; a workman's hand, not a prince's. This was the first time that ever I had touched a man. Such sins were forbidden, but contrary to all the warnings I didn't turn to stone. He gripped mine tightly and pulled me up, and I was kneeling close beside him. The box wobbled; he put his arm round my waist. I felt a strange tingle flow through me.

'I'll go first,' he said. 'And then you slide down. I'll catch you.'

He threw his bundle over the wall and pulled himself after it. It was a long drop. There was a thump. Now it was my turn. I looked down; he was holding his arms wide to catch me. I stretched my leg up, but at that very moment came the clinking of keys and the rustle of over-starched linen.

It was clear he thought me afraid to jump. 'Come on,' he smiled up at me.

'I can't.'

He saw my terror.

'Go… Now.' I half shouted, 'Someone's coming!'

With that he said, 'I'm sorry,' and picked up his bundle. He took a few steps backwards, still gazing at me. And when it was clear I wouldn't change my mind, he turned and off he scrambled, up the hill, Novice Sister Cecilia's habit flapping about him in the wind.

I stepped down from the box. Canoness Sister Veronica loomed above me. No need to describe her expression.

CHAPTER TWENTY-FOUR

I made my way across the courtyard. A chill was settling upon the mountains, matching the one in my heart.

It was still early but the temple was empty. All sign of Carpini and di Fassa, their portfolios, skeins of paper, chalks and charcoal all gone. I heard the door swing open and turned to see Ivan Kovac standing behind me.

He looked at me, alarmed. 'What happened to you, signore?'

'I fell.' He would have to be very stupid indeed to think I wasn't lying, but he chose not to press the subject. 'And what of your shoulder?'

'I thank you, it's fine.'

'If you are sure.' And with what I would describe as a quarter smile, he handed me a document sealed with wax and tied round with a ribbon.

I tore it open; this is what I read:

Il Gentile Signor Simone da Benno is herewith notified that he has been commissioned to undertake the painting of a fresco depicting The Coronation of the Virgin, on the north-facing wall of the church of Santa Maria del Monte. For this work he will be paid a sum yet to be agreed.

Dated this second day of November in the year of our Lord 1488

Ambrogio Boniface Teodoro Volsini.

It took a moment for this to sink in. Ivan Kovac saw my confusion.

'You left your drawing on the table. I took it to Fra Bartolomeo.' So that was the *stronzo's* name. 'He had no choice but to hand it over to those who were judging. You've won the commission, signore.'

This shocked me, though not perhaps greatly. 'But it wasn't finished. I meant to do that today. We had until noon, or so I was told.'

'You've won. That's all you need know.' Again, a flicker of a smile.

I would have asked him then if this were all real; if I were inhabiting not the true world but some other realm in which night was day, day night, up down, bad good. But I thought better of it.

'So, this will be your home for the present.'

I was too dumbfounded to reply.

'You're to begin right away, signore.'

Why the rush? But I shouldn't be questioning things, should I? My little drawing had won me time, which was of the essence; I'd use it wisely. I would find Tomma, and we'd be gone.

'Stall him, Benno,' I said to myself.

'But I have no materials… no painting tower…' The few brushes and pigments required for Francesca's portrait were nothing when compared to what was needed now. All

I could think was, the more the better.

'Then we shall provide them. Where might we get you supplies?'

'The Brothers Pieri. But they are in Florence.' Even better when it came to holding up proceedings.

I heard my father's voice. Settling debts had been his doctrine, and as I think I may have mentioned, was a lesson that stuck with me; the only one, I might add.

'Where exactly?'

'The Borgo di Ognisanti.'

'Ah well, I'll send someone there. Let me know what's required.'

But I was beyond making lists; he only need ask to be supplied with what's needed for Simone da Benno to paint a wall.

'Will this be sufficient explanation?'

I assured him it would and turned to look at the empty room. 'So they've gone?'

'They intended to leave with first light, but I believe there has been some delay.'

I excused myself from his company and limped across the courtyard, past the sentries at the gate.

Three horses stood by the edge of the campo, three figures upon them. Di Fassa saw me. He kneed his horse and off he galloped down the alley. Carpini and young Cesare followed, but turned when I shouted. Di Fassa kept going.

'*Santa Madonna,* what have you done to yourself?' Seeing my face, Carpini stopped smiling.

'Oh it's nothing. I fell.'

He seemed to accept this. 'I'm sorry.'

'I thank you, but don't be. I'm fine.'

He looked at me, doubtfully, but it being clear that I didn't wish to dwell on the subject, he smiled again. 'Oh well, if you're sure. Now all I have to do is congratulate you, Signor Benno. You deserved to win.'

'I can't think that that little drawing was enough.' Was this me speaking?

'Better you have than him. When it was only the two of us he told me there was no doubt that he would, but I shouldn't worry for he would hire me. He'd draw out the plan he wanted, and I would paint it for him. He'd pay me well, and though the very thought repelled me, I must admit I was tempted. I'm not like you, Benno, I'm a jobbing painter and men like me must take work where we find it. And there is Cesare to think of. I know now it would have been my ruin. But you have thwarted him, and I applaud you. I can but hope you don't have to struggle too much with that wall,' he said, kindly.

I told him that this was a certainty, and asked where he thought to go now.

'Oh, I'm sure to find somewhere. I can't lose heart.'

'Should you pass by way of Verona, go to the Duke Scalieri and tell him you came across Simone da Benno. That I commend you to him. He is sure to employ you; he is a fierce man, but fair.'

It was well into morning by now. I dragged myself across the campo. My shoulder pained me, my face throbbed, my brain pounded inside my skull. The next time I saw Ivan Kovac I'd beg him for one of his phials.

A little nun stood by the church door. She stepped towards me. I stopped in my tracks as she pulled off her

wimple and peered through my swollen eyelids.
'*Brutto figlio di Puttana.*'

CHAPTER TWENTY-FIVE

Once my reeling mind had settled, I tried to find my voice, but he beat me to it. 'What have you done to your face, sire?'

I looked down upon him and didn't know whether to laugh or to cry. In response to his question I had one of my own. 'What, *Santo Cristo,* is that you're wearing?'

'A disguise.'

A sensation rose up from my belly; first came a smile, then a laugh so loud as to rouse the fat friar from his slumber. 'A disguise, is it? For a moment I thought you'd joined holy orders.'

And though I knew he greatly disliked shows of emotion, I grabbed him and hugged him to me, caring not what passers-by were bound to surmise; a scruffy lout with a face black and blue, grasping a nun to his bosom. And outside the church, if you please.

This wasn't the place for conversation. 'Come,' I said, releasing him from my embrace. I led him back across the campo, past the sentries and through the courtyard. Tucked in its corner, the temple came into view. I pushed the door and we were inside.

He stood, looking round him. 'What is this place?'

'Home... in the meantime.'

His eyes now rested upon the table where a platter of meats had been set. And bread, a jug of wine and one of water. I could but assume it was my breakfast.

'Sit down and tell me... and then I'll tell you.'

The food was his main concern, however. 'I have to eat first, sire.'

I positioned myself on the furs beside him and watched as he did. How fast can misery turn to joy. And when he was finished, I said, 'Where to start then?'

'At the beginning, but you go first, sire.'

'No you.' My mind was still reeling.

'At least you can tell me about your face.'

But I chose not to, just for the moment. 'It's nothing new is it? There's many a time you've seen it like this, is there not? But I've never seen you wearing a dress.'

'It's not a dress,' said he, 'it's a habit.'

A mere six days parted from his exacting mind. How could I have forgotten?

'Let me get out of it first.' He proceeded to peel it off, then opened the bundle he'd been carrying, withdrew from it the now familiar breeches. He pulled them on, knotting them at his waist. Next came the tunic. When returned to the old Tomma, he sighed, 'I'll never look at a nun again without feeling sorry for her. These are bad enough,' he picked up the discarded clothing and stuffed them under one of the furs, 'but that wimple,' it sat upright on the table, 'it's a torture, I can tell you.'

I didn't want to hear about wimples. 'Come on, then.'

'Well sire. When I left you, I got to the house with no trouble. Baldassare was in the stable yard. Of course he was shocked to see me. Before I could explain what had happened, he pulled me into one of the stalls. I told him about the Duke's men, how they had come for us, the storm and the horses, the cave, that you were still there, that your arm was troubling you, that you had lost your boot in the mud. I asked if he could let you have another pair and another horse too, one would do for us both. He didn't seem to be listening. He said I was in danger. That I couldn't be seen there.'

I thought of the shuttered windows, the dogs. The old man, suddenly able to hear.

'He told me the Duke's men were still searching for us, that he'd take me somewhere to hide, and on the way we would go to the cave and take you there as well. He led me down through the gate tower. He seemed anxious when passing the guards, then down the hill path. We got to the cave; you weren't there, sire. I knew they had got you... I was desperate with worry, but I had no choice. I had to go with him. After some time, we came to a building set off the road. It was a convent. He left me there. I was in hiding, he told me. That I had to stay with the nuns. That he would come back for me. That he had told the Mother Superior I was a friend's son who needed to hide there for some days. That he had paid her well for her silence. He made me promise not to talk about Signor Donato or the house. And not to tell anyone we had been there.'

'*Gesu*, Tomma.'

'I had to get away, of course... I had to find you. I knew you'd be here; where else would they take you? But the nuns wouldn't let me out of their sight. I thought I was going to be trapped there forever. And so I caught a sparrow and set it free in the chapel when they were at prayers.'

'*Gesu*,' I heard myself say again.

'And when they were all rushing about trying to persuade it back out through the window, in other words, sire, when they were distracted, I took these,' he pointed at his wimple, 'and got over a wall.'

One thing was true above all others; as long as he was here in this world he would never cease to astonish, not only me but everyone else who came into his company.

'If I had half your wits, my dear Tomma.'

'Now you, sire.'

And so I related my story, about being dragged up the hill, locked in that hellhole. 'I tell you...'

'But you aren't locked up anymore,' which indeed was a fair observation.

'They freed me. Or someone did... I don't know who, apart from the fact that it wasn't Volsini.'

I told him then about the man Ivan Kovac. His austere, rich black clothes and beard cut into a point.

'A strange name. Where is he from?'

'How should I know?'

'Did you not think to ask him?'

That familiar flood of exasperation. What did it matter. It wasn't even vaguely relevant. 'No, dear Tomma, it might surprise you, I had other things on my mind. Are you going to let me get on with the story? May I continue?'

He nodded.

'When I came to, I found this round my neck. I pulled the eye-bead from my tunic.'

I expected him to remark upon its strangeness. But all he said was, 'Oh.'

I looked at him, baffled.

'They're much worn in Naples.'

Still I looked.

'To protect against the evil eye. And you don't have any idea who freed you?'

I shook my head.

'There's your answer then, sire.'

And, as ever, he'd lost me.

'It was a woman.'

'It's women who give these things then?'

'More often than not, and let's be honest, you don't have much luck with men.' Which was a fair observation. 'So, why did they free you?'

'Are you sitting tight my little friend?'

He might have nodded, I cannot say.

'To paint the fresco.'

He waited for me to laugh; surely I was joking.

'It's true, Tomma. Believe me.'

He said nothing for a moment. Pigeons cro-crooed outside in the courtyard.

'I don't understand, sire.'

I ceded that neither did I. 'They had two candidates already, a good guy and one of these fashionable bastards, variegated hose and a ruddy great pearl dangling from his ear. But wait, there's something a tad more important.' I now told how I'd gone searching for him at the house. About the dog. That it wasn't of a breed like the flop-eared boar-chasers we had encountered after our leap from the window, 'but a great savage brute that looked as if it could polish off two or three of them for breakfast.'

No 'Oh, sire, how awful' for Tomma. Only 'That

explains your face'. Then, 'And what happened next?'

'I killed it.'

He didn't look surprised.

'What I needed was a couple of chunks of meat to distract it.'

I now proceeded to tell about the old man at the window, miraculously able to hear. Despite his previous observation about how he had managed to know that Francesca was in the corridor, I allow he looked shocked. About Volsini's claim that Donato was the one who'd betrayed us. How Anna had seen Baldassare crossing the campo, carrying something.

'Whatever they're up to, they're in it together. The old man. Baldassare. Volsini. And, though it pained me to say it, 'Donato.'

He furrowed his brow, I could see he was thinking. 'But what about Francesca, do you think she's still there?'

This was too much for me to set my mind to, just at that moment. 'I don't know Tomma. Pray God she's safe.'

We sat in silence for a moment, I tried to smile. 'Tell me about this convent then.'

'It was a convent,' said he, 'with nuns in it.'

'Nothing juicy to recount.' I was thinking of the ones I knew like Sant'Angelo di Contorta, closed now, more's the pity, when some *stronzo* found out its real business, this being a whorehouse.

He shook his head, and knowing I would progress no further on the subject, changed it.

'We'll leave tomorrow. When we're rested.'

'It's too late to go anywhere, sire, there's only six weeks left.'

What was he talking about?

He stared at me, blankly. 'The design...' and when he got no response, 'for the Novella. We're here now. We should stay. Get on with this fresco?'

'No.' The answer propelled itself from my mouth with little effort.

'Why?'

What had they done to his brain in that nunnery? 'Apart from the obvious,' and though the dungeon was a good starting point I did not want to go back to that subject, '... it's a shit of a wall. I'm not giving it a moment's thought.'

'But you must, sire, it's your only hope. You can't let them beat you... after all you've been through.'

'We Tomma...What... we've... been through.'

'Stay here. Think on your altarpiece. Finish the design. Your reputation depends upon it. It's the only thing that will get you back to Florence.'

I informed him of the fact that I no longer cared about *cazzo* designs. Was that all I'd had to worry about back in August? A new plan was forming in my mind. 'No Tomma, we'll get to the coast, find us that boat for Naples.'

'What's there?' His exasperation seemed to be rising. I chose to ignore it.

I forced a cheery voice, 'A cornucopia of delights. Palaces... and new-built villas.' Specifically my lady Rizziola's. 'And all with walls to be painted.' If we were cast out, it wouldn't be into the wilderness.

'But we can't leave Francesca.'

Why did he always set himself up as guardian of my conscience? 'I can't speak any more Tomma, I have to sleep.' It occurred to me that I had been awake for two days now, not counting the time in the cell. And Tomma looked beyond exhausted.

We lay down on our mattresses, wrapping ourselves in the furs. But, despite my deep weariness and the fact that I was freed from anguish for my lost Tomma, I couldn't sleep for my mind was buzzing with tormented thoughts, this time of Francesca.

CHAPTER TWENTY-SIX

Though our Mother Superior was the gentle one, and Canoness Sister Veronica fierce and unbending, both were equally outraged by my sinful behaviour.

'The boy was placed in our care. I gave my word that we would protect him. And you helped him escape... in Sister Cecilia's robe. What were you thinking? What were you thinking?' I had never heard her so angry.

'You will do penance, Maria Assunta. You will go back to the orchard and chop the logs into firewood. Yes, every last one of them. It will be your job and your job alone.'

'And,' added Canoness Sister Veronica, 'when you have finished, there's plenty more work to be done.'

I wasn't foolish enough to ask if I might still visit Francesca.

The fallen trees had been hewn into slices, but still it would take great effort to chop them, wheel them in the barrow to the warming house. And then I would have to set about filling and flattening the holes that were left in the ground. I did not know how I would manage to do it.

But at least I'd be alone with my thoughts, which were not of Francesca, may God forgive my confession, but Tomma Trovatello.

CHAPTER TWENTY-SEVEN

I rose when darkness lifted. My shoulder pained me and my face felt as if it had been flayed, but just to see Tomma asleep on his mattress, mouth open, dead to the world, was worth all the pain I could suffer. Employing Carpini's chalk for the purpose, I marked out a note on the floor beside him.

'If you wake before I get back, go to the kitchen.'

I drew a circle denoting our temple with a square for the courtyard and an arrow pointing across it, lines for the steps.

'And ask for a woman called Anna. Tell her who you are. She'll feed you.'

I pulled on my boots. A bleak opal dawn was only just seeping into the sky and there was a chill in the air. I made my way to the gate, past the sentries and onto the campo. A few hardy souls were about, wrapped up against the wind, and who was amongst them but Anna, scurrying along, grasping her cloak tight around her.

She looked happy to see me. 'Come,' she said, 'I'll make you breakfast.'

The kitchen had not been part of my plan; but show me a man capable of resisting the promise of food and the company of a woman. Or, I should put that the other way round. I followed her back past the sentries, down the steps and into the kitchen. Its inhabitants were getting used to me now. They bade their 'good mornings' but winked at each other, not caring to hide what was in their minds.

As she dolloped a ladle of steaming polenta, thick with mushrooms and lardons of pork, into my bowl, I told her that Tomma was back.

'Oh, I'm so glad. Where was he?'

'It was a misunderstanding.' I composed the lie as I went along. 'He left a note to say he had gone to Florence to get materials. The Fra... forgot... to give it to me.'

She gave me a knowing look. But we couldn't disparage men of the church in front of the under-cook who was listening whilst trying his best not to stare at my black and blue face.

And so she said, 'You've got what you need then?'

I nodded.

'So when do you start on the painting?'

Lying about Tomma was one thing but cruel deception, well that was another. 'I don't know... there are problems.'

'Ah problems,' the under-cook said, 'we know all about them, do we not Beppe?'

Belly full, I left the kitchen, passed the sentries for the third time, and set off down through the warren of alleys towards the Villa Favoni. We were leaving the city at nightfall but I wanted to have one last look. See if the old man's thugs were still there, and the dogs. I had no idea what good it would do. None, I supposed, but the compulsion to settle these questions was by far stronger than I.

By now it was light and approaching the house I saw

a cart drawn up by the stable yard, reined to a black and white pony. I hunkered down in the cover of bushes a little way off. I had a clear view from my hiding place, and I had patience. I'd wait there all day if I had to.

It was quiet in those bushes. Not a sound came from the house; its windows seemed like dead eyes staring, unseeing, out at the world. There was no sign of dogs, or the thugs, but that didn't mean they weren't there. Time passed, a weak sun appeared from the clouds, and disappeared behind them.

The wind blew about me. The busy day began. People passed by on the alley, making their way to the campo; groups of young girls, old women wheezing as they struggled upwards, a laundry-maid, washing stacked in her basket. A lad herding geese.

Still I waited. It was when a fat ginger cat appeared by my side and rubbed against me, that something started to happen. A scuffling sound came from the stable yard gate. It opened. A man of middle years appeared. He took the pony's reins and guided it backwards. I picked a thick and heavy stick from the ground and skirted my way round the wall, keeping to the shadows. The cart had reached the gate when there came a crunching behind me. I tightened my grasp on the stick, and turned quickly round. '*Deo fa.*' And when I got my breath back, 'Do you want to kill me with shock?'

'I thought you'd be here sire,' Tomma whispered.

'Oh you did?' But I was happy to see him.

'I went to the kitchen. That woman... Anna...'

And knowing what was in his mind, 'It's not like that. We're just friends.' Was there any point trying to convince him?

'It doesn't matter, sire. She said you'd just left. I went to the church but it was empty. There was only one other place you could be.'

'I wanted to have a look.' I omitted to add, 'before we go.'

'Have you seen anything?'

'Only that...' I was about to say 'cart', when the stable gate opened and through it came Baldassare with, stacked in his arms, *Sangue di Cristo,* the same drum-like boxes he'd been carrying that night in the corridor. His companion reappeared now, with more.

Tomma prodded me in the ribs. 'Those boxes.'

'Yes... they're the ones I told you about.'

But he didn't seem to be listening. 'They're the same as the one in the graveyard.'

'What graveyard?'

'In the convent. I used it to stand on.'

He was making no sense, unusual for Tomma.

'To get over the wall.'

'*Santa Madonna.*' I took a moment to adjust my brain, then thought to ask what was in it.

At this he gave me one of his looks. 'I don't know, I was escaping. I didn't take time to find out.' Then 'Sire,' he pointed. A figure moved at a window. A blink of a moment and she was gone. But that blink was enough.

We stared upwards. No need for either of us to state the fact. She was there in the house, but more importantly she was alive.

'We have to get her out, sire.' And now we had seen her, I knew he was right. But how? We were leaving; I didn't wish to repeat the fact. But luckily there was a distraction, namely what was going on in front of our eyes. I could but be glad of the fact. And as we stood watching, a plan began to form itself in my mind, but of course, I didn't tell him.

Moments passed as the cart was loaded. The other man climbed into it, tugged the reins and the pony set off. Onto the path and down the hill it rumbled. We followed it to the gate tower. One of the guards waved it through.

'We should go after it.'

My thought exactly, but we were thwarted. The bigger and, it therefore follows, more menacing of the guards, looked me up and down. 'You can't pass, signore, we have orders.'

Tomma dragged me away from the crowd of good folks streaming through it. 'I'll go. I can dodge them.'

'You're going nowhere,' I informed him, 'unless it's with me.'

And so we trudged back up to the campo. 'What's in them, that's the question?' But it was one with no answer.

'We have to stay now, we don't have a choice.'

'No Tomma,' I stopped amidst the flow of traffic and held up my hand. 'We're leaving,' I thought to soften the blow, 'just as soon as we can. That's all there is to it.'

'But how will we get through the gate tower? The guards have orders.' Which suited his endeavours to stay.

'Oh don't you worry on that score, I've escaped enough places to make me a master of the sport.'

We reached the campo. The wind gusted up from the valley. My shoulder was paining me greatly. I'd get Tomma to bind it again.

But he wasn't thinking about shoulders. 'Take me to see this wall, sire, so I know what you're talking about.' He meant, of course, the poxing one in the church.

This I considered a mistake in extremis for he would be sure to find something praiseworthy about it. And having found something praiseworthy he'd use it against me. Or, to put it another way, use it to try to persuade me to stay.

But I wouldn't be persuaded, so what was the danger? Nonetheless, I thought to distract him. 'Let's see where the cart is now.'

He followed me to the wall by the bell tower where we stood, looking down at the road twisting out towards the horizon. But it was nowhere to be seen. I would have turned away, had not that hallowed god of lost causes forced me to stay where I was, for now we could make out a line of horsemen plodding slowly up the path, their pack horses strung out behind them, panniers straining to bursting point. They neared the gate tower, and now we could see them more clearly.

I turned to Tomma, mouth open wide.

He said the words for me. 'Look… it's the boys.'

Disregarding the pain in my shoulder, now greatly worsened by the fact we were running at speed, we made it down through the alleyways in time to watch as they came through it; three horses with riders, four laden behind them. And as the last of them loomed into view, two figures astride it, we made out Guido's stocky frame and, clinging to it as if for dear life, Celestino, skinny as ever.

It was almost too much for me, and for Tomma too. We ran towards them. When they saw us their grins were so wide, I feared their faces would split.

'We came sire. With your supplies,' said Guido, sliding down from their steaming mount. 'We thought you would need us.'

I threw my arms round them. And for once Tomma smiled. Guido slapped him on the back. Celestino took his hand. Then he gaped up at me. 'Sire... your face?'

'It's nothing, a little scuffle, that's all.'

Across the campo we led them, past the sentries at the palace gate and through the courtyard to our temple. Guido whistled through his teeth when we stepped inside. Someone had rekindled the fire; it flared and crackled, giving a homely air to the place. The smell of feet imbued the smoky atmosphere as boots were pulled off.

'I've never been on a horse so long,' said Celestino. 'I can't feel my legs.'

'They're there, still, I assure you. But come on boys, tell us...'

And sprawled in front of the fire, they did. Or should I say Celestino did for where Guido was a boy of few words, he was exuberant of speech, talking at a rate often hard to keep up with, in a great and exuberant flow. This had its disadvantages, as might be imagined, but if a deal of information was to be relayed and less than a minute in which to impart it, he was the one for you.

'The Pieri Brothers sent for us, sire, when those men came to get your supplies... they knew we'd want to speak to them and find out what you were doing. When we got there we told them... not the Pieris sire, the men... we told them we were apprenticed to you, that we were waiting for you to send for us. We asked if they would take us with them and while they were loading up your stuff I ran back to Master Sandro. I told him what had happened. And then we went. And then we got here.'

All this he said without stopping for breath.

'Thank God you did boys,' was all I could manage. 'I'm sorry I left you all this while. We've had many problems. Have we not Tomma?' I hadn't the will to list them just at that moment.

'Yes,' he affirmed. 'Major ones.'

'What, sire?' I wouldn't be let off so easily 'We … I mean I… got into a dispute.'

They glanced at each other; were not 'disputes' but a routine feature of my life?

'Let us talk of it later. Tell us what's happening back in the city.'

Indeed it was as I had fervently prayed. Sandro had taken Celestino into his workshop, and despite my gross betrayal of the man who had once called me friend, Ghirlandaio had taken Guido.

Ghirlandaio had been good to him, but his apprentices had made his life hell. 'Oh, and the Buonarroti boy left him.'

Just as Tomma had predicted. Ye gods, how fate turns round to bite us sharply in the *cullo*.

And what about Sandro?

Master Botticelli's boys were kind, but they had much work. 'Too much, in fact,' said Celestino. 'It's good to be back with you.' his cheeks reddened. 'Not just because of the work… I …'

Where before, for amusement, I'd have let him stumble on, digging himself deeper into his hole, I cuffed him gently.

'Yes,' I could but agree, 'indeed it is good.'

'He had painted a tondo, sire,' he continued, it's called The Madonna of the Pomegranate, with the Christ Child holding one. He's added me in beside some of his boys. I'm the second on the left. I hope you see it.'

If I could ever love a man it would be Sandro. Even the thought of it all made me smile.

'And the giraffe...' he continued.

This, perhaps I should explain, was an animal gifted to the court, not so strange, or so you may think. But if I were to tell you that he was larger than the largest horse, with a neck twice as tall as his body, I'm sure you wouldn't believe me, for even had I informed myself of this bizarre fact, I wouldn't have believed myself either. He was the talk of the city right up till the moment we had departed it, ambling along the streets and poking his head through windows left open for this very purpose. The people had loved him.

'...poor thing, he died. They built him a house, but he got his head stuck in the rafters.'

No time to recover from this news, for now it was Guido's turn. Somehow he managed to add to the tale, 'Master Ghirlandaio made sketches of it. It's to be the star in his Nativity.'

I looked forward to seeing it, and felt a slight tinge. I hadn't thought about Florence till now.

There was something they had omitted to tell me, however; I knew them better than I knew myself.

'What else, lads?'

Celestiono glanced at Guido, who said, 'All the masters, sire...'

'Yes.'

'Well...'

'Come on, spit it out.'

'They want to have you banished. They've drawn up a petition.'

I could but laugh very loudly at this. 'Banished? Have me banished? And who's going to do the banishing, if I may enquire? No, don't worry boys, it won't happen. Escaping a bunch of fuckheads is one thing, but they're not going to send their best painter off to enhance the glory of some other lord...' And I went on like this for a while.

When I had finished, Celestino felt the need to add, 'I said all the masters, but that isn't right, Master Sandro wouldn't put his name to it. Nor Master Ghirlandaio. And the Friars were dismayed when they heard you had gone; they don't want anyone else for their altarpiece.'

'And until I hear otherwise, I'm still the one who's going to do it.'

Of course, they were overjoyed to hear this. And as if in celebration of my announcement, Guido stood up and drew from their pack a whopping great flask of grappa. 'Before we left, we went back and took it from the workshop.'

Other boys might have rescued my lapis, but not them, good lads that they were.

When we had each, apart from Tomma, glugged down several mouthfuls, Celestino piped up, 'But what of this wall, sire? When we told Master Sandro why we were leaving he said, "All Florence will be talking about the great and wondrous work he's creating." Well, you know how he speaks...' He meant in a flamboyant way.

'I'm not doing it boys.'

They stared at me, agog.

'No. We're leaving. We've had problems, have we not Tomma? And the wall is a bastard. There's not sufficient money in Christendom to persuade me otherwise.'

I looked at Tomma for support, but I wasn't going to

get it. 'I can't agree with you, sire, until I have seen it.'

All this time and he hadn't seen it?

'You tell them, Tomma.'

So he did, starting with the day we arrived, our leap from the window, Donato, my shoulder, the fever, Francesca's portrait, our escape from the Duke's men, the cave, his stay in the nunnery, mine in the dungeon, my release, his escape. Wise as ever, he said nothing about the locked room, the symbols, dead crows or boxes. Or my little incident in the garden.

Guido blew through his teeth, then sat silently for a moment. 'But sire,' he looked baffled. 'Why did they lock you up in a dungeon if they wanted you to paint it? Why not just give you the job in the first place?'

'Be sure, dear Guido, when I find out you'll be the first to know.'

Now it was Celestino's turn. 'But you can't leave. Master Sandro is right. Now that the Duke Umberto's men came to get your supplies, all Florence will be talking about it. You have to do it sire, you can't let them think that you've failed.'

I saw the glint in Tomma's eyes; to have such boys who ganged up against you.

'We'll talk it over, but now you must eat.'

As I said, I knew my lads better than even I did myself, and above all else that they would be famished, and so I sent them to the kitchen. 'Tomma will take you.'

They returned carrying pies and cheese and bread and wine, and fell upon the feast like starving beasts. Strangely, I found I wasn't hungry.

I watched as they ate. Not for one moment since they'd

come into my employ could I have thought myself glad to see them stuffing their faces and rubbing their mouths on their sleeves, though Tomma, as always, with less gusto. Guido and Celestino would be painters one day in their glorious futures; their histories, of course, including the words 'Apprentice to Simone da Benno'.

A different fate awaited Tomma, I knew not what it would be; a planner of plans, devisor of strategy, a solver of problems, and as I sat watching him caught up in his silent thoughts as he ate, I fell to pondering upon his strangeness, his wisdom. I had become complacent, had allowed myself to forget one simple fact; he was but a lad of sixteen though I thought of him now as my protector.

'Well,' said he when they'd finished, 'let us go and look at this wall.'

I couldn't bear to cast my eyes upon that turd of a thing; I was happy and wished to remain so, at least for tonight.

'We'll go tomorrow.'

'No sire,' he said in a tone that brooked no argument, 'we're going now.'

Thus we found ourselves in the church, our torches lighting the space before us. Jerome hadn't moved from his grotto; the Baptist appeared mad as ever.

Celestino and Guido gaped at them in horror. '*Gesu* sire, but you're right.'

'Who could have painted such things in the first place?'

Guido laughed, 'Are they meant to be some kind of joke?'

Tomma stood silent. Suffice to say he shared their judgement, and though he wouldn't have put it this way, the wall was indeed a bastard. He rubbed a finger along

Jerome's grimy surface, then came his pronouncement, 'We could always paint them over.'

I couldn't ignore the fact that, rather than master and apprentice, we had a partnership here, Tomma being in possession of brains and I of the now less significant talent.

I allowed the proposition time to sink in.

'Give them an ultimatum. They can keep those decrepits or have a work by a man who can paint.'

'I can't, Tomma. I've developed an odious hatred of it. It's too much of a challenge.'

'But you like challenges, sire, do you not? Besides, look around you, the church has a simple kind of beauty, it's only these... things... that stand in your way. And if they don't agree to your terms, well, we can still leave, can't we?' But I knew this was the last thing he wanted.

'It's a good wall though, sire. If you have it to yourself. I can see wild colours painted upon it.' This was Guido.

'You're softening me lads. I have a notion to give it a try.' For wasn't Tomma right as always? Time was passing; it was too late, too cold, too impossible to go tramping out on that balls-aching road again. And there were four of us now, not only two.

And so the task transpired. I had trained my boys well, and they were young and had passion. Here would be our place of work for the next space of time. Here we would set out our drawings, chalk the wall, prepare gesso, mix pigment. Here we would labour, eat and often would sleep. Tomorrow a blank wall, in some weeks a glowing mass of movement. And between now and then, elation, frustration, setbacks, disasters, unsolvable problems to be, as ever, solved in the end. Aching arms, stiff fingers, ribaldry, pranks; though I exclude Tomma as far as those last two categories of behaviour are concerned.

Paint over the wall then, make finished drawings from my sketches, during which time the boys would set to constructing our tower. And we would start.

Celestino pointed, 'Look sire.' Stacked at the side of the altar were the piles of cargo from the good Pieris. But we could do nothing about them just then, a very great exhaustion having fallen upon us.

'Come,' I said, 'we need to sleep.'

Back in the comfort of our temple, I stretched out on my furs and, despite the agony of my shoulder, fell into a slumber so deep not even the gods or thoughts of Francesca could have roused me.

CHAPTER TWENTY-EIGHT

When I woke it was light. Memory trickled into my mind; my boys were with me again. If emotions were shades, my blackest of black was now burnished to gold. And the pain in my shoulder had eased, *Dio grazie*.

I may have told you that cold comes fast to the mountains, and that morning there was a keener chill in the air. This I knew to be but naught when compared to what would follow up here in the mountains. If the boys thought winters in Florence were bad, this would be a shock to their systems.

As if by their own volition, my feet took me to the end of the courtyard, past the sentries, across the campo to the spot by the bell tower where – was it only yesterday? – Tomma and I had looked down on the hill path and beheld the boys' arrival. And there I stood for I know not how long, for cast before me was a scene of such splendour as to make my heart leap. Dawn was spilling into the sky. The foot of the rocky summit on which I was perched swept away to the distant mountains. Beneath, the city tumbled downward, clinging to its rocks. But as the frozen mist dissolved, revealing the roof of the Villa Favoni, serenity left me. I saw the dog again, the chain whipping out towards me, the old man as he listened to the thug shouting up at him, Francesca in the stable yard the last time we'd been together. The glimpse of her at the widow. We had run away and left her in that hellish place.

Turning my back on my conscience, I made my way towards the kitchen and down its steps, noting as I went that no warm smells wafted upwards. At the door I saw why. Anna was crouched by one of the fires, pumping a pair of bellows, vainly trying to tempt it back into life. Apart from her the place was empty.

Where was everyone?

'Down by the gate tower.' And before I was able to ask the next question, 'Unloading provisions.'

'Give them here.' I took the bellows.

She looked up at me, cheeks redder than ever, and I thought she might cry with relief. She bent over me adding a few sticks of tinder, then a dribble of oil from a jug as I pumped the bitching things, pain biting into my shoulder.

'I should have reset it, but I am so tired and there was still a glow, so I thought...'

She stopped and held her breath as a lick of flame leapt up from the kindling.

When I stood, pleased with my handiwork, she put her arms round me, and for the first time since leaving Florence I felt that most exquisite of sensations, the soft cushion of breasts pressing against me.

At another time, in another place, I would have pursued her for she had that quality of careless merriment I love in a woman. I can't say what stopped me for I knew that she, like most other members of her gender bored with the strutting peacocks around them, found my unadorned self

174

extraordinarily strange and enticing. But though I had done it so often I couldn't have counted the times, please believe me when I tell you I didn't like breaking hearts. Or perhaps there's something about the words, 'It's not a good idea, sire,' that tends to stall idle pleasure.

My shoulder was a sound enough reason to release her before I found myself doing something I knew I'd regret.

She pushed her hair from her face and smiled. 'Well, that deserves a good breakfast.'

As she scuttled about clanking pans and spoons, I said, 'So you met my boys.'

'Yes, first the one who was lost. Such a poor little soul, and so serious. Now I know why you were worried.'

Was this Tomma she was talking about? True, he was small and his body twisted but his mind was a shining beacon. 'Yes he is serious, but he has the quickest wits I have known. He'll be a king one day, or Pope. Or ambassador in some foreign court. Just wait, you'll see.'

No need to tell me to sit for I was doing that already. She laid a platter of pork and cornbread before me. I dug into them for my appetite had returned with a vengeance, and when I was finished, I thought to ask, 'That day you saw Signor Favoni's servant, you said he was carrying something. What size was it, would you say?'

She held her hands about half an arm-span apart. 'It was round,' she said. The same as the boxes.

If I had been senselessly hanging onto some last vestige of hope that Volsini had lied, it was now smashed to pieces. I forced my mind onwards, for there was another question to ask. 'The man called Ivan Kovac... tell me about him.'

She looked at me, puzzled. It was clear she had no idea

who I was talking about.

'He has a beard cut to a point?'

'There's no one like that I can think of.' She stopped for a moment. 'But… wait… perhaps. A stranger arrived a short while ago. We've never seen him, but they say he has an unusual appearance. They suppose he's waiting for the Duke to return.'

'So the Duke's not here then?' It occurred to me that I hadn't given him so much as a thought until now.

'No, he's in Ferrara. And Amerigo has gone to Milan.'

Who was Amerigo?

'His son.' She said this with loathing.

'You don't like him I take it?'

'No one does. We're safe while his father's still alive. But he's old. The day he dies, I'll leave the city… and so will all other sensible people.'

'And,' I stopped myself saying the shithead, 'the one called Volsini?'

'He's the Duke's Chamberlain. We hate him as much.'

'The man… the stranger… what is his link to the Duke?'

'It's only gossip, but they say it's something to do with his wife.'

She had lost me now.

'Amerigo's wife. She brought a dowry large enough to pay off all his debts. And he had many, I can tell you. It's the only reason he married her. They say she's a monster.'

'They deserve each other, then.'

Her cheeks reddened even more when I said this. 'No, I don't mean a monster in that way. I mean she's a monster. Like a gorgon. They say no other man in the world would have her. That she wears a veil to hide her great ugliness.

Poor lady, to be fit only for marrying off to someone like him. It is said that he treats her most cruelly. And to be so far away from her home.'

I would have asked where that was, where she came from... and Ivan Kovac too, but just at that moment Guido appeared at the door.

'You must come, sire, Tomma is saying it's late.'

But 'late' is a subjective word, is it not? In Florence our days would start at five, or often as early as four in the morning for this is a time of silence, there being no scuttling of servants or patrons arriving to inspect your work as it progresses. Today was different, however. I had told them to sleep longer, but it seemed they'd ignored me.

And I was right. Tomma and Celestino were crouched by the altar, not praying, which would have been somewhat unsettling, but setting our materials out on the floor.

I greeted them with a 'By *Gesu,* you're early'.

Celestino looked round. 'It's not really, sire.'

Considering our customary habits, I could but suppose he was right.

'We thought to get started.'

And they surely had; all was laid out in neat rows before them.

Brushes. These being most important of all.

Gum Arabic.

Parcels of pigment, marked for quick identification: the usual ochres and umbers, encompassing shades of yellow, brown and red. Terra Bianco, a very bright white, Verdaccio, the green I'd have used for Francesca's robe had Baldassare been able to find it. Sinopia, a red required for sketching images onto the first layer of plaster, Ultramarine, ground from lapis, and so costly most artists confine themselves to restricting its use to their Virgin's cloaks. I say most painters, not me.

Rolls of paper
Ink of various hues
Drawing charcoal
Red chalk
Mixing knives
Compasses
A square
Measuring sticks and plumb line

Happily, such commonplace items as chalk plaster required for gesso, or timber with which to construct painting towers are to be found anywhere.

'And look at that sire,' he pointed to a notice pinned on the door.

Until forthcoming work is completed, all prayers and masses will be held in the church of San Cristoforo.

'I asked about it, sire. Its halfway down towards the gate tower.'

'Rejoice boys!' I shouted. 'The place is ours. No one to disturb us.'

Better still if the Fra went there too.

I sent them off to the kitchen. I should have gone with them but I started pondering on what Anna had told me. First about Ivan Kovac – why had he saved me? My mind then wandered to Baldassare... the box. Why was he taking it to Volsini? What the shitting hell was in it? 'Stop Benno.

Stop. What can you do about it? Nothing. Whatever they're up to, let them get on with it. You have a wall to paint, an altarpiece to think of. Your boys are back with you. You're happy...' I spoke sternly to myself, and hoped I was listening. But I wasn't.

They came back to find me sitting by the altar, my eyes fixed upon it.

'Are you all right, sire?' asked Celestino.

I lurched to my feet a little too quickly. 'Yes. Yes. I was thinking.'

Tomma knew differently, however. He caught my eye, but there wasn't the chance to take me aside, ask what was troubling me, for at that very moment the door banged open and the Fra shuffled through it. Clearly he hadn't read the notice.

Signally ignoring the state of my face, 'Ah, Master da Benno,' he said with tired resignation, as if to convey the fact that he wished that either di Fassa or Carpini was there in front of him now. 'I believe I must congratulate you.'

He must do nothing save pay attention to what I was about to tell him. 'I need to limewash the wall.'

'I don't follow your words, signore.'

'Then listen more carefully...' Tomma's foot kicked mine '...if you'd be so kind.' I curved my lips into what might have been construed as a smile. 'The wall which I am to paint is occupied by two other works.'

'Indeed you are right. St Jerome and...' Even he didn't know who the crazy one was.

'...The Baptist,' I ventured.

'Ah yes,' said the Fra.

I'd have told him that I wouldn't suffer those pieces of

piss anywhere near my fresco. But for the sake of concord, said, instead, that I would not paint between them.

He pondered my words. 'Pray why, signore?'

I had no answer, except, 'They're eyesores' and would have said it. But Tomma was quick.

'It is not theosophically accepted, most honourable father.'

What he meant by this was beyond me, but his words had a weighty ring.

He went on, 'The Virgin, being of higher order than the saints, must be afforded a space of her own.'

'It's the only one there is.' As if to signal the end of our conversation, he sat down at his lectern, picked up his quill and started scratching upon the ledger propped in front of him.

I barged in at this point, trampling upon Tomma's careful groundwork. 'I'm going ahead.'

It was clear this meant nothing to him.

'I'm painting them over.'

Impossible, said his expression. His words did not reflect his thoughts. 'I shall speak to the Chamberlain.'

'When?'

'I believe I may see him on Friday.'

'Speak to him now, or we saddle our horses.' Which was but to enter the realms of fantasy, having no horses to saddle.

He returned to scratching with his quill. 'Then saddle them, signore, I won't hold you back.'

I felt a great violence surge up inside me, and a hunger to throttle his holy neck. As I strode out onto the campo, Tomma close on my heels, he didn't so much as turn his head.

'Who is he sire?' This was Tomma.

'*Un cretino enorme*. One day... I promise...' I'd have gone on but for the fact that there was something a deal more important to tell him. I pulled him into the shadow of the door. 'I was in the kitchen this morning, with Anna.'

'Yes,' he said.

'I wanted to know the size of the thing Baldassare was carrying the day she saw him.'

'And?'

'It was the same as the boxes. It's all linked. Him and that sodding bastard Volsini.'

But I could say no more, for Celestino appeared just at that moment. He looked at us, puzzled. Why were we huddled there, whispering?

'We're thinking about the painting tower.' Amazing how fast my brain can work when required to do so. 'We have to get our hands on some timber.'

Which was a fact indeed; we'd need a good lot, and so I'd send him to find it. But what to do for payment; there was only Francesca's florin, which was far too much to hand over for a few planks of wood. But perhaps he could negotiate, after all was he not champion of the sport?

But 'Oh no sire' said he, 'we still have almost all the money you gave us.' He scrabbled about in his jerkin, coming up with a handful of silver coins and some soldi.

Did I not tell you that they were good boys?

'I'll leave it to you then.' And when he had found what was required they could get a move on and start with the limewash.

'You're a hard taskmaster, sire,' said Guido, who had joined us by now, 'but it's good to be with you again.'

A statement that heartened me greatly.

Whilst Celestino was out bartering with the wood merchants, or charming them should I say, for with his golden curls and sweet expression he could cast a spell on the very Devil himself, Tomma and Guido set to work. They found a table upon which they set out the brushes and knives and mixing bowls, then unpacked the parcels of pigment and laid them in order, alongside the charcoal and chalk. And all the while I sat there, silent, until our stomachs informed us of the fact that it was time to fill them again. Not a moment too soon, Celestino returned triumphant. It had not taken much for him to win over some poor unwary fellow, namely the first one he'd come across, and had found exactly what was needed. It would be with us by evening. But as we stepped out onto the campo, heading for the kitchen, Tomma held me back. 'Go boys,' I told the other two. 'We'll be there in a minute.'

'Sire, I've been thinking, should we not go back to the house?'

The last thing I'd hoped he would say, though of course I'd been thinking the same thing myself. But in the singular. My life was one thing, Tomma's another. But how to put him off the scent?

'And what, pray, could we possibly do there?'

'More watching. Perhaps we'd see something.'

'No, Tomma,' I adopted a serious tone and, just as I had told myself before I'd had my crisis of conscience, 'We're finished with the Favoni, with their locked doors and their thugs and dogs and deaf fathers, miraculously cured. And we're finished with those sodding boxes.'

'But what about Francesca?'

There he had me. 'I worry about her too, my little friend. But we have more to think about now; the altarpiece to start with. Time is slipping out of our hands.'

*

Said timber duly delivered early that evening, we worked through the rest of it, building the tower. Or should I say, the boys did; I was unable to help them as I would have before, for though, where walls are concerned boys work and masters paint, this had never been my way. All masters were apprenticed once, and the art of nailing struts to beams never leaves you. The first time Guido had witnessed me labouring thus, he seemed astounded at my mastery of awl and hammer. This time, however, my shoulder forced me to leave them to it, though I admit to having suffered a dent to my ego, seeing how well they could manage without me. A few hours of shouting needless instructions as it grew higher and higher, and the crucial point came. Tomma astride Guido's shoulders, atop the all but finished construction, placed the standing platform onto its beams.

By nightfall the wall was a blinding white. It had taken all of three coats to cover Jerome and his lunatic neighbour. The boys were admiring their handiwork when arrived the Fra, trundling along on his oversized legs, a truculent look on his face. He made great play at peering up at the blanked-out wall, tutting and shaking his head.

'You have an objection?' I challenged.

Tomma grasped my elbow. 'There's no point, sire,' he whispered.

'The only point needed is a sharp one stuck up his

priestly arse.' I didn't bother with whispers.

'I don't like to think what the Duke will say,' pronounced our tormentor, as if the day of reckoning was poised to fall upon us.

'Oh please do not vex yourself, Father,' came a familiar voice from behind us. 'He will be most happy, I assure you.'

Our heads turned in unison. Ivan Kovac stood close to the altarpiece. I did not think then to ask myself how he had got there without passing us.

The Fra changed his tone. 'Oh, my lord, indeed you are right. And when he looks upon the wondrous fresco yet to be painted upon it he will be happier still.'

In a bid to display his newfound interest, he stood on his tiptoes, gazing upwards again. 'How high will the painting be when finished, Signor da Benno?' He had missed his vocation in life, no, not of an actor but a clown.

'To the ceiling.'

'To the ceiling, my, that will cause great effect. And how wide?'

'From one end of the wall to the other.'

'A vast undertaking.'

His heels now firmly returned to the ground, he bade his farewells and left with a swiftness I'd never had chance to witness, even by a card-shark under the *ponte* when one of the Street Constables came into view.

I turned to thank Ivan Kovac, but he was nowhere to be seen. We stood bewildered. He'd vanished...

'Who was that?' enquired Celestino, 'and where has he gone?'

But I didn't answer, for just at that moment I heard it, the faintest tinkle, as if from a bell. It was of some consolation to observe that Tomma did too.

'That was him.' We were making our way across the campo, Celestino and Guido enough in front to be sure they were out of earshot.

'I thought so, sire, by his beard.'

'You saw how he's dressed.'

'You're right, he's wealthy.'

'And his accent. Where is he from? And how did he vanish like that? He didn't go out of the door?'

He said nothing by way of reply, and so I continued. 'His phials of liquid... The eye-bead,' I was, preposterously perhaps, linking these with thoughts of symbols and quicksilver. 'Could he be involved in some kind of magic?'

'No, sire.'

'How did he do it then?'

'I don't know, but there will be a rational explanation.'

'And you heard that tinkling?'

He nodded.

We had reached the palace gate by now; the boys were waiting. It was clear that one of the sentries had taken a shine to Celestino, as men were often wont to do.

'Cold night,' he remarked.

Ever the friendly one, Celestino replied. Something about the poor men themselves, standing there frozen. Their conversation continued, giving Tomma the chance to say, 'It was like a greyhound's, sire.'

I didn't quite follow him.

'You know, those little bells clipped to their collars.'

Ye gods, he was right.

And the sentry was too; it was cold. So cold that our breath escaped from our mouths as if it were steam from a boiling pot. You can imagine what it did to my shoulder. And stepping into the church the next morning was like entering an icehouse.

'We must get us a brazier, Tomma.' I looked at the boys in their flimsy breeches. 'And the thickest cloaks we can lay our hands on.'

But they didn't seem to be listening. Tomma looked deep in thought, the other two had something better to think about, namely Anna who was standing in front of the wall, staring up at its dazzling whiteness. She smiled when she saw us. 'This is where you're going to paint?'

I affirmed that it was.

She turned to me, mystified. 'How will you do it?'

And so I set about explaining how it would be plastered, marked out in sinopia, coloured one section at a time, how each of these sections is called a g*iornata*, the quantity of lime plaster applied to them being enough for a daytime's work only.

'And while this is happening, the pigments are mixed. Then I paint onto each section of gesso while it's still wet.'

I didn't feel the need to add that this depends upon how quickly it might take to dry. In cool weather, quite slowly, which means that a larger section can be prepared, in very cold weather you might have the space from dawn to dusk, so it can be larger still. But during the heat of summer, a morning is all you can hope for, which forces you to work on a far smaller portion.

Nor did I feel it important to tell her that when we had found us a brazier and painting began, it would have to be moved far enough away to ensure that the gesso would not be allowed to dry out too quickly; we wouldn't do without it completely, it being crucial for the warming of hands when they grew so numb we could no longer feel them.

I supposed that I shouldn't protest too much about the cold, for working in heat is far more of a nightmarish task.

'I'll come every day and watch you.' She touched my face as she said this.

*

How many blank walls had I coaxed into life? I took measure of this new one and, as I studied it the old feeling returned... and I knew why I had chosen the life of a painter, uncertain as such are, for each step forward two must be taken in retreat. I contemplated the journey set out before me. There is the map, with the destination marked upon it. Were it simply a case of closing your eyes in order to arrive there, as if by the speed of thought. But it is not, for many a river will have to be crossed, mountain climbed, hostile cities conquered till you get there. Set out before me was my journey, my task to transform it from a mere stretch of plaster into a wonder for all to behold.

And as I stood seeking to work out a route, it came to me, the wall was not the problem, but rather the subject to be painted upon it. I loathed Coronations of Virgins with a vengeance, but rebuked myself nonetheless. '*Forza*, Benno, get on with it.' I forced my mind back to the sketch on Carpini's square of paper. 'Embroider upon it. Anything will do.'

But would 'anything' come to me? My mind remained empty as the wall. I paced awhile, ever a signal to my boys that all is not well.

After a good stretch of doing this, clouds floated into it, as sketched on Carpini's square of paper, the Virgin below them, the angels above, as if being sucked up to Heaven. I took a piece of chalk and knelt on the floor. I would start with the clouds as a kind of divider between the upper reaches and the lower. But my hand had other ideas.

It drew a figure swooping downwards. One leg bent, arms stretched out like wings. I omitted the pool of water beneath him.

'But Benno', I sought to remind myself, he was to be kept for my altarpiece.

I thought again; what if I used the wall as a template. And when it was finished, transfer the image to the drawings to take to my Lord de'Medici. Work from large to small, instead of the other way round. No one had done it before. I, Simone da Benno, would lead the way forward. I gave thanks to the muse of inspiration for choosing to strike when she did. The halves of the circle, I call it. One half is a void, the other flooded with light. One moment your mind inhabits the dark side, the next a bright radiance glows all around it.

Guido appeared beside me and looked down at my tumbling figure. 'How did he come to you?' he asked, an uncommon passion in his voice.

Alerted by my silence, Tomma and Celestino appeared and stood beside him. 'In a dream?'

'Yes, sort of,' which wasn't completely a lie.

'It's…'

'Well?'

No response for some time, then Tomma, ever the practical, ventured, 'Who is he?'

'Our angel.'

'Which one, sire?' for were there not veritable multitudes when it came to Coronations of Virgins?

'I'm changing the subject, lads. We're doing an Annunciation instead.'

A moment's silence, then Tomma again, 'But that's the subject for your altarpiece.'

I confirmed that it was.

'They won't want a copy of something you've done already, which it will be if you paint it here first.'

'But what if I planned it out on the wall. And when I've sketched the whole thing, transfer it to paper. And, at that stage, you boys can take it to Florence. Perhaps I'll come with you.'

Celestino looked doubtful. 'Don't you think that, perhaps sire, it might be too... unconventional... for here? It's a small church, in a small city. They may not be prepared for the...' he stopped for a moment, '...shock.'

As Guido and Celestino studied the sketch, carving it up, in their minds, into its constituent sections, Tomma pulled me out of earshot.

'Sire,' he said, 'I was thinking.'

'No, Tomma, it's my wall and I don't want a balls-aching Coronation. Who cares if it upsets their sensitivities... all the better! We can't paint the same things over and over; we must move forward or the world will stand still.' And on I went, like this, for a fair stretch of time.

He let me finish.

'No sire,' he said, 'I was going to say, what if I went back to the convent, got into the graveyard? If that box is still there I could...'

I stopped him before he was able to add 'look inside it'. 'You're not going near any graveyard, and that's an order. Losing you the first time was a hell I don't want to inhabit again. A second time, well, it would kill me.'

I spent the next part of the morning transferring my angel from the floor to the bottom right-hand corner of the wall, turning him from the few lines of the sketch into a full-blown image. This is how I always work. Paper smudges and tears, and by the time your lads have picked it up a thousand times to look again at an angle of an arm or placing of foot, it's in tatters and you'll be required to make another one, two, three, four, versions. Take a portion of wall that in the end will be covered by paint and draw your image upon it. You can use whatever you want for this; I prefer charcoal. But charcoal can be rubbed away, and so I cover it with size.

I felt breath on my neck as I rose from the task.

'What do you think then?'

When I turned, Celestino was standing, mouth open. Not a word did he say.

Alerted by the silence, Guido came over and stood beside him.

There being no response, I ploughed on. 'We'll have him swooping down from the top left-hand section and...'

Guido interrupted. 'Sire, you are truly a genius.'

Rich and noble men might applaud me, cardinals and kings, captains in possession of castles upon Garda's shore, painters of a lifetime's standing, but nothing compared to praise from my boys.

'Tomma must see it.' They ran to get him, but when they returned, worried looks on their faces, I felt I knew what was going to come next.

'We looked everywhere, but we can't find him.'

'Where can he be, sire?'

I managed to shrug.

*

I stood at the gate tower, staring down towards the valley. Here was a time when I needed a cloak. When we needed cloaks. It was bitter.

The guards beckoned me over. 'Come, signore, and sit by our fire.'

And though sitting was the last thing I wished to think about doing, I accepted his offer, which gave me the chance to ask if a small, crooked boy had passed through that morning.

'Yes,' said a fellow wearing a badge inscribed with an eagle emblem. 'He's not hard to miss.'

The wind wailed around us; the fire crackled and sparked. A stretch of time passed. Cloak-clad people passed through the gate, which was good for it kept the guards busy and there was no time for conversation.

Warmed now, I left my new companions and started pacing, back and forth. I put my hand to my breast and curled my fingers round the eye-bead. '*Dio* Tomma, where the hell are you?' when I saw him; no more than a dot on the hill path, but it was him alright, drawing nearer, arms round one of the of the *cazzo* boxes. Close to the gate now, he saw me. I would have thrown my arms round him as he walked through it, but stopped myself and said, 'Are you mad?'

'No, sire,' he replied, 'Just curious.'

'And what if they'd caught you?'

'But they didn't.'

He followed me to the corner where I'd been standing. 'Come on then, don't keep me waiting. What's in it?' I all but grabbed the box from his hands.

'Nothing sire, apart from a feather.'

Had I heard him correctly?

'A feather. You know, from a bird.' He held the box out towards me; I lifted its lid. The feather was long, grey and mildewed. An acrid stink wafted up from it, which, for some odd reason, seemed familiar. But this was no place to stand, smelling boxes. 'It's that crazy one who was hugging the nun. Now look what he's doing. Someone should call the city inspector.'

No longer moving, the cold had hit him by now. I took off my jerkin and wrapped it round his shoulders.

'We'll talk when we're back.' But words are easy, are they not. As we climbed up through the alleys, I started my tirade; he shouldn't have so much as stepped out of the gate, did he know what such escapades did to my heart. Then I got down to practical matters; how had he got into the place?

'Oh that was easy. Getting out was the problem. I couldn't climb the wall and hold on to the box at the same time. I had to throw it over, after I'd looked inside it of course. Which meant I had nothing to stand on. There was a cracked headstone. I broke part of it off.'

'*Sangue di Dio*, Tomma.' Desecrating gravestones was a criminal offence.

And now came the stretch of alley leading up to the Favoni house. We quickened our pace as we passed it; bad enough that we should be seen, never mind what I was carrying.

It was late in the day and the boys stood by the church door, clearly keen to get off to the kitchen.

'What's that?' Celestino wanted to know.

'A box.' Better to state the obvious. 'We thought it might come in useful.'

'What for?'

'Oh this and that. This and that.'

He turned to Tomma. 'Where have you been all this time?'

'Oh, nowhere interesting,' he answered, untruthfully for once.

'Get yourselves to the kitchen then. I want to run through a few things with Tomma.'

'Why him and not us?' their looks said.

'We have to go over some bills.' This was nonsense, of course, there being no bills to look over, but even mention of the word sent them racing off across the campo.

Thanking God that the friar was nowhere to be seen, I set the box upon the table and took off its lid. With no frigid wind to blow it away, the smell was overwhelming. And now I remembered.

'It was on her skin.'

'Whose skin, sire?'

'Francesca's. That night in the garden.'

He didn't waste time asking if I was certain, but leaned over the box and took a great sniff. 'And as it's in the box, too.' I could see his mind working. 'It tells us...'

'What? What did it tell us?'

'That it's linked to them both in some way... And to the feather.'

I took it from him and even before I got it to my nose, I started coughing.

And so, that night, the first part of my half-thought-out plan. I left the boys under their furs, bellies full of dumplings and marrowbone, sunk deep in the sleep of the dead, and made my way across the courtyard, past the sentries, along the now familiar passage from the smell of beeswax into the stink of shit. Down the stairs, at the foot of which I gave the door a mighty kick.

A shuffling came from behind it. The clanking of keys, and there he was, holding his lantern out before him.

'Ah, signore,' he blinked up at me. And then in a tremulous voice, 'Aint 'eard nothin' bout no boy.'

'I'm not here for that.'

He blinked again.

'What do you know of the Villa Favoni?'

He drew the lantern to his side; shadows leapt on the wall. He took a moment to say, 'Only that strange things is happening there.'

'What kind of things?'

I took a step towards him.

'Magic they says. And stuff of the Devil.'

'Go on.'

'The place... well, they say it's been took over.'

'By whom?'

He winced, 'Dunno, signore.'

I had enough experience of men like him to know if not exactly telling the truth, neither was he lying.

'If you don't know that then tell me what you do.'

'Only what I've 'eard.'

'And?'

'Word's going around that he's holding his wife there. Locked up, like. Don Favoni, I means. And there's great hulking dogs in the garden. Take a man's neck out before he knew what had 'it him.'

I turned to leave him in his shithole. He held his lantern up. 'That boy you was looking for?'

But as far as his florin was concerned, I had disappointing news. 'Oh, don't worry on that score, I found him.'

Back in our temple, my shoulder eased by the warmth of the fire, I unlaced my tunic and felt again, against my chest, the cool glassy roundness of the eye-bead.

CHAPTER TWENTY-NINE

I do not know how much time had passed ~ each day a trial beyond endurance. Not for my back, pained from bending to chop the logs into firewood, or my hands cut and bruised from wheeling them up to the wood pile, but from thoughts of Tomma Trovatello for he had stirred a very great force inside me. I could not get him out of my mind. But even now I am not being honest; I did not want to get him out of it. I feared that one day when I woke, his face would be gone. You might ask me to describe it more fully, but I do not have the gift to do so. To say it was strong and slightly forbidding, that his eyes were dark and wide set, his nose straight, his hair long, his mouth turned slightly downwards. That when he smiled it was as if my soul had been bathed in warmth and light...

His hand holding mine as he pulled me up onto the wall. His arm round me...

Such exquisite feelings; I would never let them go.

CHAPTER THIRTY

When we stepped into the church next morning, what did we see set close to our tower but a brazier, lit and glowing. Beside it lay a bundle of cloaks, four in all, plus a new pair of hose – of the correct length – a pile of undershirts and a crimson doublet, fine enough to have graced the back of any of the Medici clan, which, clearly, by its dimensions, was for me.

'Who sent them, sire?' Celestino looked up at me, puzzled.

I could but suppose it was Ivan Kovac.

Guido stood on the tower beside me. I was grateful to have him; his talent was such it would open the gates of destiny for him. I only hoped that I would still be of this world when it happened. We were drawing our angel then shading his form. For this we use sinopia, that dull red dust mixed with turpentine that fills the air around you and covers everything, even your teeth.

Only when working thus, could I escape my worries. We'd often talked about this strange occurrence, Sandro and I; so fixed does your concentration become that all else flies from your mind. A morning passes as if in a moment, whilst outside your closed little world bankers bank, silversmiths hammer, market stalls stir with bustle and when evening falls on the city they are cleared away. Schoolboys learn their daily lessons, dairy maids make cheeses, and you have painted but a hand, or the cuff of a sleeve, or portion of a face or three jewels upon a sceptre. Or if it's a lucky day, a complete figure. And all around you is silence, save for the creaking of the ladder when one of the lads brings more umber, or the scratching of the spoon against the bowl as pigments are mixed under your painting tower. Afraid to risk so much as a whisper, apprentices communicate with signs they have devised for the purpose.

And now there it was; the outline of our angel tumbling down towards us.

Feet firmly planted back on hard marble, we strained our necks to look at him.

'He's a marvel sire, he moves.'

'Moves? Moves?' Guido gave Celestino a scathing look 'He flies.'

'No, flying is gentle. He dives.'

'Whatever he's doing, he's not like any other angel.'

And Anna confirmed when she came to see how our work progressed, jumping back as if to get out of his way before he crashed down upon her.

A reaction that pleased me greatly.

'It's Gabriel,' I informed her. 'And now I'll block in the Virgin.' And I found myself explaining, again, about wet plaster and *giornate*, and the mixing of colours. And then we set off for the kitchen.

As we walked across the campo, something cold pricked my face; a tiny flake fell down from the sky, then another. The boys stopped.

Guido and Celestino's jubilant cries; no doubt their thoughts had turned to last year when the Arno froze over and too much of their time had been spent skating upon it.

As Tomma and I walked behind them, 'I went to the dungeon to talk with the gaoler,' I informed him. Stop Benno. What was I doing?

But he knew me too well to be perplexed at this statement, and certainly wasn't going to let me off the hook. 'What about, sire?'

I altered the truth just a little. 'The Favoni. And Francesca. We've struck up a friendship, he and I. I thought he might know something useful.'

'And did he?'

'No.'

'You've tried, there's nothing more you can do, at least for the moment,' which should have been enough to alert me to the fact that he knew I was lying. Or stretching the truth should I say. 'Let me think on it awhile, you need to focus on your Virgin.'

How could we have known how ill-fated this last simple sentence would turn out to be, how my Virgin would take on the form of a harlot and lead me into temptation. But that is less than half a truth, for by now you must be aware of the fact that when temptation beckoned, I did not hesitate for a moment.

The snow fell all night, and in the morning it was as if the noise of the world had been blocked from our ears.

Three days had passed since we'd given birth to our angel and a very great panic was rising inside me. By now his Virgin should have taken her place beneath him. But this was a problem for I hadn't yet started to devise her; the section of wall inhabited by Jerome before his rude eviction remained as white as the campo.

A battle raged in my mind, the Virgin, Francesca. Francesca, the Virgin. Francesca was winning. As were the boxes – the smell, not to mention the garden, the dogs, the old man suddenly able to hear. And topping it all, the fact that there was less than one month and a week until my lord de'Medici's birthday.

'Time's slipping, sire.'

Which was certainly true, but I couldn't propel my brain into action.

The snow was still falling. Celestino and Guido were out on the campo, whooping and yelling at their icy games. I needn't tell you that Tomma had chosen to stay where he was; we sat by the brazier whilst I strove to return my mind to the matter at hand.

'*Cazzo di merda…*' But this is as far as I got for that was the moment we heard a great shouting. Tomma ran out to see what was happening and came back to tell me. Travellers had been seen on the road; nothing so strange about that but for the fact they carried a pilgrim's banner. The townsfolk were rushing down to the gate tower to watch them making their way up the hill.

Thus unfolds the tale I told at the start of my story, of the Abbess, the man called Mortimer, the string of pack mules… my out and out folly. You may remember that upon hearing the word 'English' murmured through the crowd, I offered my services, for though they had a guide with them he looked a rough sort.

And you may remember, too, that the man called Mortimer had explained they were on their way to Assisi, which seemed utter lunacy for they had been travelling north, not south.

'We landed two days ago,' he continued, 'at the port of Livorno.'

I led them up to the campo. Just as we got there, the Fra came running towards us, as fast as his fat legs would carry him. Volsini's guards were not far behind, pushing their way through the crowd. And now the shithead came into view, striding along as if he were the very Duke himself. Not trusting my behaviour in his company, I turned to go. But not fast enough. He saw me and signalled me forward. I could not but discern he looked somewhat unnerved.

'My, you are a dark one da Benno, but it would seem you are useful for something... if only their language.' He wished, of course, to speak with this Mortimer, and gestured for me to translate his words.

They're on their way to Assisi, I told him.

'How long shall we have the pleasure of your company?' he spoke to the Englishman, not me.

I put their reply into Italian. 'Until it stops snowing; a few days, they pray. The gentleman says that time is against them, they aim to be in Rome by Advent. It will take them some time.'

A flicker in Volsini's eyes. 'But you've come the wrong way, signore, you should have travelled further south before turning inland.'

As I translated, Mortimer looked somewhat unnerved. His next words told me he knew nothing of this. 'It's what we have planned.'

'I charge you signore, you can't go that way. You must change your route. Turn west when you leave here and go by the coast road.'

'These are not the directions we were given.'

Volsini sneered. Was this man as much of a fool as he sounded?

'The Livornese, signore.' He gave me a look that said, 'Put it into your own words, da Benno...'

'...know little of pilgrims' routes,' I said for brevity's sake.

'We'll talk of it later. We welcome you in the meantime, signore. Stay with us until the snow stops. It may be some months,' he warned.

Mortimer looked at him, alarmed. 'But we have to be in Rome.' He repeated, '...for Advent.'

'You may not be there until Easter.'

As the company made their into the courtyard, by way of the gate, the Fra turned to me. 'Don't venture far, da Benno. You may be required to act as translator.'

By *Gesu*, was I mad? Why did I open my mouth? If I could have turned back time, walked again out into the snow, watched again as they rode through the gate tower...

'Don't you think it strange, sire?'

'I find I'm getting used to these words.'

'I mean, Volsini's expression.'

He had lost me.

'When he heard you speak in the pilgrims' language.'

I shook my head. Just tell me Tomma.

'It was filled with alarm. But just for a second. Then he fixed his mask on again.'

'If I can do anything to alarm that *figlio di puttana,* I am a happy man.'

'But, sire...'

'No Tomma. We cannot ponder upon his unbalanced mood swings. Time is slipping.' The greatest understatement I'd ever heard come out of my mouth. I could see it shrunk into nothing; as long as the buggering snow lasted I'd be forced to take up the role of interpreter, in attendance morning till night. December would pass, the wall abandoned, my altarpiece gone... I was in his pocket. He had me now.

It was late in the day; darkness was falling, as was the snow. We turned towards the kitchen. The boys were mightily impressed.

'You spoke in their language, sire.'

'They said it's called English.' He meant the folks in the crowd. 'What did they mean?'

Reluctant to prolong this strain of conversation, for I could not force the same cheery tone. 'That they're from England.'

But if I had thought this would suffice, 'England? What's England?' Celestino asked.

'I've heard of it, sire.' Guido cut in before I was forced to expand on the subject, 'It's an island set on the edge of the world.'

'It doesn't have an edge.' This was Tomma, of course. 'Don't you know your Pythagoras?'

Clearly he didn't, and neither did I. But to put an end to the discussion, I realised now, would but seem churlish. I steeled myself to explain, but there was no chance for just then we heard someone shouting behind us, 'Signore.' We stopped. A boy came panting towards us. 'Signore,' he said again. He held out a small roll of parchment.

'It looks like a letter,' pronounced Celestino. And, sure enough, my name, in small neat writing, attested to the fact he was right.

'Please signore,' the boy said now, looking up at me with embarrassment. 'The lord Volsini instructed me to tell you that it arrived yesterday.' I gestured that he should continue. 'He gave me orders to tell you exactly these words...' He turned his eyes downward and said in a whisper, '...that you should consider yourself fortunate that he permits you to have it, for he had no need to do so.'

I stood for a moment; what could I say?

'I'm sorry,' he added, these being his own words, and darted off before I could ask him I don't know what...

I looked down at the writing. It was familiar.

The seal had been broken, no surprise there, and as snow blanked the campo around us, I unrolled it, and read:

Dearest Benno,

We hope this will reach you; we have sent it with one of our merchants travelling north.

We trust the materials sent with your boys will meet your requirements, but if there is anything lacking please send us word and we shall deliver it to you.

The main purpose of this letter, however, is to give you some information we feel you should know. There is no gentle way of breaking the news that in your absence you have been banished from Florence. This is a most unfortunate turn of events and the city's loss, indeed. We wish to let you know of it before word reaches the Lord Umberto.

May we say, dear friend, that we are certain your design would have merited the greatest acclaim and that we are distraught to know that you will no longer be with us here in the Borgo. It is Florence's loss, not yours.

You must not be downhearted; your life is ahead of you and many altarpieces await.

Niccolo and Giovanni Pieri

Beside their signatures was sketched a phoenix rising from flames.

I stood with the snow heaping up on my shoulders, blotching the ink.

The boys gaped up at me. 'What is it?' asked Guido.

He took it from me and after a while I heard him say, 'Come, sire, we'll think of something... or Tomma will think of it, you'll see.'

'I need to be alone boys, I won't be good company for a while.'

I set off back to the church.

Tomma ran after me. 'I'm coming with you.'

'No,' I told him, 'stay with the others. I only need time.'

'But, sire...'

'I don't want them to see me like this.'

'But...'

'I mean it, Tomma. Go back to the boys. It's been a long day.'

He took off his new cloak and, stretching upwards, wrapped it around my shoulders over my own, as I had wrapped my jerkin around his that day at the gate tower, and I knew he would stand watching until I had passed the sentries, crossed the campo to the church, pushed the door open, and stepped inside.

I climbed to the top of the painting tower and slumped upon it, there to wallow in my anguish. This state of misery quickly ascended into wild fury. It rose up inside me like a tidal swell, or perhaps like a phoenix. I cursed myself, I cursed those sons of whores, I cursed the little shit Michelangelo and his bastarding father.

I pulled my cloak, and Tomma's, around me, and tried to cheer myself with the words, 'Your life is ahead of you, many altarpieces await.'

I was unsuccessful, however. Cold seeped into my bones. But it ignored my shoulder which, now reignited, burned like the gaoler's blazing torch. I fell into a tortured sleep; I am in a vast and mysterious space, which I know to be the Novella. As I approach the sacristy, through the dim light, I catch a glimpse of my altarpiece. But there is no image painted upon it, only a ground of gesso. My brushes and bowls of pigment are set out before it. I know I must reach it but I cannot move. The friars stand waiting, in silence. A figure steps forward. They seem strangely transfixed as he picks up my brush.

And when he turns, I see it's the Buonarroti boy.

CHAPTER THIRTY-ONE

Yes, all this while my mind was besieged by thoughts of Tomma Trovatello. Surely they had been sent by God, for they eased my fright about Francesca, about her very great distress when Signor Baldassare had dragged her away from us and bundled her into the carriage... how I had promised I'd go to her. She would not know I had tried my best, even clambering on to the wall with Tomma Trovatello... and that for this sin I was forced to stay here in the orchard. Every day, I prayed I would hear the sound of her carriage pulling up at the gate and see Dosolina shuffling through it, for though I was not free to take her note from its hiding place under the cobblestone, I could call to her from my side of the wall. And then she would know what had happened. And then she would tell Francesca... But all this time had passed and she hadn't come.

We had not even reached the end of November, yet a great snow had fallen, and this was what saved me for it was impossible to work out of doors. So bitter was the cold that the warming house fire had been lit where the Sisters gathered between times of prayer and of work.

On the first evening of my release from the orchard, the Reverent Mother sent for me. What would my new punishment be?

I was prepared for the worst but she spoke in a different voice. 'Maria Assunta, the dear Lord in his wisdom has sent you the chance to atone for your sins.'

Which was the very greatest surprise.

'Pilgrims have arrived in the city. You will go there and help them.'

You might imagine my joy at this revelation; pilgrims were in the city. And so was Francesca. For the first night in such a long time, I did not fall into weary sleep the moment the candles were snuffed, but lay awake waiting.

It wasn't yet dawn. Stars crackled above us. Sister Monica drove the mule cart up through the snow. We reached the gate tower. The guards sitting by their fire waved us through. Up the steep and winding lanes, closer and closer and closer to Francesca's house. It stood, white and frigid; the trees in its garden seemed moulded from ice. I asked Sister Monica if we might stop for a moment, but she feigned not to hear, and it was behind us.

We reached the campo close to the time for prayers. 'Go to the church,' Sister Monica said, for the pilgrims were sure to be there. I slid down into the snow and as she tugged poor Bella's reins and turned the cart, a great swell of happiness filled my heart; I was free, at least for the moment. I stood, collecting my thoughts. What would the pilgrims be like? Were they poor people, come to give thanks to our Blessed Maria? Or were they rich, wishing only to show how much they were prepared to suffer in her name, thereby wreathing themselves in glory?

I didn't care, one way or the other.

The church loomed out of the darkness before me, its

bell tower stretching heavenward. I waded through the snow towards it. Its door was so enormous, so heavy, I had to press my whole body against it in order to push it open.

Still the dawn had not yet broken; all was dark and silent but for a glow and a hissing of charcoal which came from a brazier set beneath what looked like a tall wooden structure. I hurried towards the beacon of warmth, my clogs tap-tapping on the stone floor. And when, in the flickering light I saw it, I gasped.

It may be impious to say that my loathing for our convent was tempered not by the Gospels, but by the painted images on the walls of our chapel. I would not think of God when I knelt to pray but of the mortals who had made them. How had they done it? The little donkey upon which Mary sits, Joseph leading their way into Egypt, though I knew not where that land might be. Adam and Eve expelled from the garden, holding their hands to their eyes, the animals looking on in sorrow.

I can't say how much time passed as I stood gazing up at him, arms spread wide beneath his wings, in the shape of the crucified Peter, upside down... only moving... moving.

A sound... a shifting atop the tower. The spell was broken. I stepped back and peered up. Some kind of creature was staring down at me.

He swore very loudly, a fact that proclaimed him as human.

But I knew what tone must be employed when talking to poor lunatics, for Sister Agata had trained me well.

I steadied myself and told him, as calmly as I was able, that he had nothing to fear from me; I was only looking for the pilgrims.

CHAPTER THIRTY-TWO

From somewhere beyond the edge of my dream came a clattering sound. By *Gesù*, I almost jumped out of my skin. I got to my feet and peered down.

A nun stood beneath me. My memory is of asking if I could help her, whilst she maintains the first words she heard come from my mouth were charmless, uncouth, boorish... I'd go on with the list had I time to expand.

It seemed she was looking for the pilgrims. I confess to being confused, for this she told me in my own language. Why had they dragged me in to translate for them when all the time they had her?

How *in nome di cazzo* would I know where they were...?

CHAPTER THIRTY-THREE

At that very moment the door crashed open and a figure came scuttling through it. I held my breath, but it was only Brother Bartolomeo. He ran towards me, seeming in great agitation.

'Don't speak to him, Sister.' He pulled me away.

I didn't much like Brother Bartolomeo, may the Good Lord forgive me for saying so; I'd never thought he was to be trusted.

'Who is he, and what is he doing up there?'

'Supposed to be doing, Holy Sister. Supposed to be doing. He's supposed to be painting a fresco, but he has other plans. He is the very Devil incarnate. I pray the Good Lord will rid us of him.'

Just then the Angelus started to toll. When it stopped its clanging, he asked, 'But what brings you here? Is the Reverend Mother with you?'

I told him she wasn't, that I was alone, which seemed to disappoint him. I had come to help the pilgrims. I'd thought to find them here, this being the hour for prayer.

He spread his fingers and chuckled, and as if he were describing mischievous children said, 'Oh these foreigners, they have different ways.'

What did he mean by foreigners?

'*Don't you know, Sister, they come from England.*'

I felt foolish for asking. Was it a city?

'*Yes,*' *he said,* '*set upon an island some way to the east of Milan.*'

Dawn was seeping into the sky as I stepped back onto the campo. I should have gone straight to the palace for Brother Bartolomeo had told me the pilgrims were there. But though I was frozen through to my bones, I stood for a moment, just thinking. First of the angel. I could not conceive of such a being; not meek, like others I had seen, but strong and terrifying, his arms spread wide beneath his wings like a great bird of prey, as he flew down from paradise. Then of what Brother Bartolomeo had said about the poor madman on top of the tower. But he'd been wrong; he could not be the Devil incarnate for only one touched by God's genius could possess the powers to create such a wonder.

'*Can I help you, Sister?*' *A figure loomed out of the purplish mist. A guard stood before me.*

I took a moment to gather my thoughts, but when I told him that I had come to help the pilgrims, that Brother Bartolomeo had said I would find them in the palace, he gave me a worried look.

'*Are you alone?*'

I told him I was.

'*And you're certain you're to go to them?*'

Again, I said I was.

He seemed reluctant but then he said, '*Come then, Sister. I know where they are.*'

CHAPTER THIRTY-FOUR

First the nun; now a sodding bell started clanging.

The next sound was of feet on the ladder. I thanked the Lord and all His saints when Tomma's head popped over the struts. He looked at me anxiously.

'Don't worry, I've not done away with myself. I'm still here, as you can see.'

I made space for him; he sat beside me and handed me a piece of bread wrapped around a sausage.

'I'm not hungry.'

'Eat, sire,' he said sternly. Easier to obey. I bit into the sausage, its greasy juices ran down my chin, enough to persuade me to repeat the action.

'It's a setback, sire.'

Is that what he called it?

'Yes,' and he went on. 'But every problem has a solution. It's just a case of finding it.'

He thought it so simple?

'You've been banished.'

I hadn't forgotten.

'So you have to un-banish yourself, that's all. The altarpiece will do it. When the Medici see your design they'll want you back. In fact, they'll beg you.'

I grasped his arm and would have kissed him had he been Celestino or Guido.

'Go get the boys.' I was standing now; had cast off my misery.

'No,' he said, 'you need to sleep. One day won't matter.'

And, as if I had conjured up their very essence, we heard feet upon the ladder.

Guido's head appeared now, he squinted up at me in pity. 'You don't look well, sire.'

Celestino's now, 'No, sire, you don't,' he added, for good measure.

Thus it was that I let them lead me back to the temple where they unfolded me from my cloaks, pulled off my boots, and tucked me under a pile of furs as if I were a child.

I took a glug from the flask of grappa and fell into a fitful doze, vaguely aware of sounds in the background, Celestino setting the fire... Whisperings next. A light flaring up... Good boys. And in a while, the crackling of logs.

CHAPTER THIRTY-FIVE

It was clear that the guard disliked the pilgrims, but I couldn't think about that. I could only think about Francesca.

He led me back across the campo, through the palace gate, the sentries nodding to him as we went, past a small, circular, building with pillars ringed around it and came to a door, even more massive than the church's. The guard held up his lantern and, between its metal studs, I could see trees and birds carved upon it. I followed him through it into a vast hall and along a labyrinth of passages, leading one from the other.

I had never been in the palace before. Or any palace for that matter, but I felt I knew it if only a little for Francesca had often described it to me; its floors of white marble, its walls inlaid with precious woods, its tapestries, even its staircases, wide enough for men to clatter up on horseback.

My life for so much time had been the convent, and though we did go out into the world it was to poor places, as I have said. The only extravagances that ever I'd seen were those in the Villa Favoni, which was in stark contrast to Francesca's old house, where I had lived as a child. But even the gaudy decoration lavished on her new one could not have prepared me for the excesses my eyes were forced to look upon now. I thought of our sweet Santa Chiara and the world she had rejected.

After some time of walking, turning one way, then another, we came to a wide passage, and had proceeded but a few steps along it when loud yelling broke through the silence. First a woman's voice, then a man's. I stopped in my tracks and looked up at the guard.

'It's been like this since they arrived,' he spoke loudly so I might hear him above the noise of the quarrel. 'They fight like cat and dog. And to make it worse, no one has a clue what it's about.'

'Surely if they listened.'

'Were it so simple, but the thing is they don't speak Italian.'

Until that moment I had thought all the people of the world spoke the same language, which of course was ours, but here was a new one. Perhaps it was only in its shouted state that it sounded harsh and ugly.

He gave me a wary look. 'There's still time to turn back.'

I shook my head.

And when he saw I was determined, 'Then you have to be careful, Sister, especially of the Abbess.'

Did he mean they were nuns?

'Oh yes,' he replied, 'but not as we know them.'

Which shocked me even more than the shouting. That those from holy orders should behave in such a manner.

'I counsel you, Sister. Change your mind before it's too late. Let me take you back to your convent.'

But that was the last place I wanted to be. He was kind; I did not wish him to think that I chose to disregard *his advice, and so I smiled, 'Our Reverend Mother has sent me,' which was the truth. 'I can't disobey her.'*

'Ah well, but if you should need help you must promise to send for me. Just ask for Captain Orlando.'

I told him I would and thanked him, and followed him to the door behind which the battle was raging. He waited for a lull in the shouting and knocked. A moment passed. He knocked again, and was raising his fist for the third time when it opened and I stepped into the strangest world that ever I could have imagined.

CHAPTER THIRTY-SIX

'Sire. Sire.' Hands were shaking me.

'*Per l'amore di Dio*' I had only just lain myself down.

'Wake up. We have something to tell you.'

Whatever it was I had not will to hear it.

'There's another letter sire.'

Celestino smoothed it out and held it close to my vision, but I couldn't get my eyes to function.

'You read it.'

So he did.

You are hereby summoned to act as interpreter at a banquet to be held this night in honour of our English guests.

It was signed by the shithead Volsini.

I cursed very loudly; something along the lines of not caring a tinker's cuss about the sodding English.

CHAPTER THIRTY-SEVEN

A man and a woman stood in the centre of a large and opulent room; they turned when they saw us, not seeming the slightest ashamed to have been caught behaving in such a manner.

The man was tall. He wore a blue doublet and striped hose. His hair was shorn behind one ear; a large white pearl dangled from it.

The woman, whom I took to be the Abbess, was dressed in a strange type of habit. Where our Reverend Mother's wimple was white and starched, and made it seem as if her head had wings, hers framed her face in the shape of a heart. And where our Mother's habit was stiff and straight, hers was copious and flowing. Where our Reverend Mother's robe said 'austere', hers said... perhaps the word is 'alluring'.

Chaos surrounded them. Panniers lay open, their contents spilling out over the floor with garments and shoes strewn everywhere. Half-eaten food littered the table. And now three nuns and another two men appeared, gaping at me as if I were an oddity.

I spoke in a clear voice. 'I am Novice Sister Maria Assunta. I have been sent from our convent to help you.'

For a moment, I thought the man with the earring understood what I had said, and waited for him to reply. But he didn't, and so I repeated my words but this time in Latin. They did not look pleased to hear what I'd told them, in fact I would say that the man seemed upset. He stood for a moment, then he stomped past me out of the door.

I sat on a stool in a corner for the rest of that day. No one spoke to me and nothing happened. The nuns sprawled back on their couches, the men – one with a beard that looked much like a bush sprouting out from his chin and the other a swollen, mottled nose – sat playing cards. Piles of coins were stacked up beside them. The Abbess took to her room.

Time, then, to gather my thoughts... not of Francesca or even Tomma Trovatello, but of the angel plunging down towards me. I was glad the pilgrims did not seem to care if I were with them or not for it meant I was free. I would go to the church tomorrow to look at him again. And then I would go to the Villa Favoni.

The midday bell rang, but no one stirred for prayers. Brother Bartolomeo was right after all; they had different ways.

Every so often, servants came with trays of food. A woman with cheeks red as apples gave me a bowl of stew. It was rich and delicious, unlike the simple fare we were used to, and I realised how hungry I was.

When I thanked her, she said, 'Oh... you're not foreign.'

She smiled when I told her I wasn't. 'I'm from the convent of Santa Chiara. I've been sent to help the pilgrims. I only arrived this morning. My name is Maria Assunta.'

'That's why I haven't seen you before. Do you know

anything about them?' she whispered.

I shook my head.

'Be careful of them, Sister,' she said, just like Captain Orlando.

She turned to go, and then she turned back. 'Oh, and I'm Anna.' She looked at me with great concern. 'Come to the kitchen if you need me.'

The evening Angelus had tolled. The men, their game long over, sprawled back upon cushions, mouths opened like the dried cod fish hanging in our convent larder. The Abbess shouted from her chamber. The nuns ran to help her. I could not but be shocked when she appeared, for now she wore a rich habit of lustrous black silk. A large cross hung from the jewelled girdle buckled around her waist. Her wimple, heart-shaped as before, was pulled back from her forehead revealing a band of yellow hair.

With the mottled-nosed man and he of the beard close behind her, she swept out of the door, one of her nuns following at a distance.

It seemed the English did attend prayers, but only at this time of evening.

'No, Sister,' Anna said when I asked her about their strange customs. She had come to the room just after they'd left. 'They've gone to a feast being held in their honour. We've been cooking all day. So much effort, and all will be guzzled in no time.' She pointed at my little bundle set on the floor beside me. 'But where are you sleeping?'

'I don't know.'

She looked at me, horrified. 'But you can't sit there all night.'

She opened a door beside me and I saw a small

storeroom filled with a jumble of broken chairs and tables, birdcages, flower bowls. And then she brought blankets and spread them out on the floor.

I was touched by her kindness.

'It's the least I can do,' she smiled, and striking her flint lit a candle. Not the old tallow type we used in the convent, but of beeswax, which made me think of the Villa Favoni. But it was too late, and too dark, to go there now.

'What do you make of them, Sister?'

'They're from England,' was all I could think to tell her.

'Where's that?'

I wasn't about to say an island some way to the east of Milan, for I didn't believe Brother Bartolomeo. And so I was honest. 'I don't know.'

'Wherever it is,' she crinkled her nose, 'I never want to go there.'

CHAPTER THIRTY-EIGHT

To say I hated feasts, least those that are held in great houses rather than taverns or such like places, would be an understatement of considerable proportions. Naught to do with food but with the balls-aching job of making genteel conversation. And this time I'd have to do it in Sir Richard's language.

I looked at my face in the glass. The purple bruises had faded to blue. The gash on my cheek would settle into the type of scar I'd picked out for di Fassa. I might have been uncaring of my appearance but never before had I let myself run to this. Those joyless weeks of sleepless nights had changed me greatly; my appearance now being comparable to one of Donato's staff-carrying bumpkins. Yet that's to be unfair to them.

I ran my hand across my stubble. 'Leave it, or shave it off? What do you think, boys, shall I look like a hard man or one of principle?'

'Shave sire,' said Celestino.

'You do it then.' He had a surer hand.

Job finished, I put on one of Ivan Kovac's fresh under-shirts and my crimson doublet, as you will know this was the first chance I'd had to wear it. Its silk was soft and shone like garnet. Tomma laced it for me; my fingers were shot. Two days gripping that shitting sinopia brush and they refused to function.

'How do I look?'

'You scrub up well, sire.'

And so it was that, washed and polished, off I set across the courtyard. A path had been cut through the snow and the icy heavens were spread out above me like a cloak scattered with diamonds. I entered the hall; the sergeant at arms led me forward. Flames leaped and crackled in the hearths at either end of the hall, but did little to ward off the cold, nor did the tapestries hanging from ceiling to floor, or the stout shutters.

A table, set with silver and glass, ran the length of the space. A hundred candles burned in their sconces.

This night, Volsisni's cap stood up from his head in folds of yellow. And though he should have seemed the teensiest bit grateful that he had some poor bastard to translate his words, he peered down his long nose at me as if I were a dog about to shit at his feet. He didn't remark upon my face, which now he was close enough to see. No doubt the Fra had informed him about it.

Stirred by accelerated loathing, I felt my temper rise. 'Let's get through with this night,' I said. 'I'm here to explain what the good pilgrims say, naught else,' and with that I strode off after one of the servants who had come to show me to my place.

The company of six was reduced, now, to two, a man with a beard and the other called Mortimer. I was vaguely aware of an attendant nun, but young, old, fat, thin, pretty or otherwise, I couldn't have cared. All others present, the fuckhead Chamberlain apart, were strangers to me.

Mortimer, visibly wincing at my appearance, which before had been masked by the snowstorm, managed to bid me good evening.

'Sir,' I replied, 'Volsini,' omitting to preface his name with lord, 'has asked that I act as translator.'

'Ah,' he said, 'so that's your profession.'

I might have washed and put on a fresh shirt, but did I look like a scholar?

'No,' I informed him, 'I'm a painter, late of the Medici Court...' I could go on to tell him whatever I wished, could I not, for no one present could discern any lie '...where I designed,' as I would have by now, were it not for the little shit Michelangelo's sodding bastard of a father, 'a great altarpiece for the Medici. And now I'm here to here to paint a fresco for the Lord Umberto.'

'What's that you say?'

I looked at him, puzzled. Clearly my English was worse than I'd thought.

'This... thing... you talk about.'

'What thing, sir?'

'The thing you're painting.'

I said again, pronouncing my words clearly, as if to a child, 'A f r e s c o, sir.' And when I saw that still he did not understand, I took it one step further. 'A picture. Painted on a wall.'

'So that's what you call it. And where are you painting it?'

'The church.'

'Ah yes... and your name, sir? I don't believe you have told me.'

'Simone da Benno.'

He didn't react to this, or indeed to the subject of painting, which wasn't altogether a blow for hadn't Sir Richard said, 'We're not artists, Benno. The wonders I've seen in this land vastly outshine those in England.' And I had thought he was simply being polite.

A rustle of skirts put paid to my incredulity: a woman appeared at the doorway, and I was struck as if by a thunderbolt.

How to describe her? Impossible, yet I shall try. Perhaps it was how she carried herself, head held high, poised, self-assured; she might have been an empress, all she lacked was a crown. These were the kind of women I loved, for they tested me. And though she was as far removed from those usual fearful, half-starved, bloodless nun creatures as was possible, I could but assume she was the Abbess.

The company got to its feet, and though many might think me a ruffian, I can bow as well as any gentleman.

I watched like a ravenous wolf as she was led to her place beside Volsini. I hadn't felt such lusty cravings since first I'd seen Anna in the kitchen.

Having so recently sat himself down, he of the yellow hat rose again, signalling to me that I should do likewise.'

'Most Reverent Mother.' He launched into a speech so convoluted in language that naught but a don would have wit to interpret. But even had I been unfortunate enough to belong to that species, my heart wasn't in it. This was tedious stuff; I cared not for sermons composed of words meaning nothing. Had I fallen thus low that trifles like these were to sully my life from now till the Lord de'Medici's birthday?

I replied in one sentence, 'Volsini welcomes you to the City of the Old Mountain.' I didn't then know that cities keep their names when translated.

I assumed that one of her men would reply. But, no, she did, lolling back in her chair as if she were half feline.

'I am the Abbess Elinor of the Convent of,' again came the name of some saint of a gate with no Bishop, 'as my lord Mortimer has explained.'

The fact that her accent was greatly dissimilar to that of Sir Richard's forced me to concentrate more on her words than her lips, as I'd have preferred. Here is a rough translation of what she said.

'We are pilgrims, as he' – not as the Lord Volsini, or as our eminent host, but as 'he' – 'explained. We travel from London to Rome, by way of Assisi.' Had not Mortimer told me already?

To speak so clearly, so vigorously, to appear so composed after spending a great part of yesterday in the saddle... and added to that, in a snowstorm. She was no delicate flower. 'We arrived two days ago, at the Port of Livorno.' Again, as Mortimer had informed us. 'I have a letter from the Lord Lieutenant of London.'

She drew it from her sleeve and held it towards me. I took time to stand and walked slowly towards her. She paused a little too long before releasing it into my hand. 'I'm a match for you, or any man,' her gaze had the power to tell me. And what of that gaze, through half-closed eyes? It had taken till now to understand, for though Sir Richard had omitted to inform me of the fact, it was clear the English had them too. This convent with a gate without a Bishop was a type of establishment long familiar to me for had I not fucked my way through many a Venetian whorehouse masquerading as a convent; I might have mentioned Sant'Angelo da Contorta as being the best.

No, she couldn't fool me; they were set for somewhere in that blizzard, but it wasn't Assisi.

The flicker was there; the game almost started. How long was it now since I'd lain with a woman? I strove to remember. I handed the letter to Volsini. He broke the seal and read it. This time his words were unembellished. Keeping its contents to himself, saying only by way of reply, 'We greet you, Holy Mother. We are honoured to have you here in our city.'

We ate boar. And though, after that morning's sausage my appetite had returned, it was difficult to chew, swallow and turn my language to English and English back to my language, with all the time my eyes upon her, Volsini watching me like a hawk.

'Reverent Mother,' pronounced Mortimer, when his plate was scraped clean, 'it may be of interest to you to know that Master da Benno is painting something he calls a…' He turned to me.

I told him, again. 'Fresco.'

After imparting this information, he turned again. 'And where are you painting it, sir?'

Again I told him, 'The church.'

At this the Abbess feigned to stifle a yawn. She then proceeded to select an olive from a plate set before her, and pushed it, slowly, into her mouth.

Oh, she was good.

As courses were served, talk continued. Tedious stories of shrines visited, relics touched. I avoided large portions when translating.

Candied fruits and coloured almonds were served, for now we were nearing the end of the evening. With them came young boys with recorders, and for a moment I was transported back to the corridor, being led along it in chains.

Till then all faces, save that of the Abbess, had been turned towards me, all forced to listen whether they wished to or not. But now they looked at the little orchestra as their music took effect.

Mortimer turned to me again, 'So this...?'

Ye gods... not again. 'Fresco... sir.'

'May we see it?'

'Yes, if you'd like.'

'What do you think, my Lady Abbess?' he turned to her, 'Shall we go and look at it tomorrow?'

As she opened her mouth to answer, I feigned to stifle a yawn. I then took an olive from her plate and pushed it, slowly, into my mouth.

CHAPTER THIRTY-NINE

The morning Angelus had tolled. I peeped through a crack in my little door. The room beyond was empty. Here was my chance. I was halfway across it when the men appeared from their sleeping chambers pulling on their cloaks, as if readying themselves for an outing. And I was right, for now the Abbess stepped from her room, her nuns in tow. Unlike our Holy Mother's modest, threadbare cloak, hers was of velvet. And when she turned, I saw it was lined with white fur.

I stood aside to let them pass, only praying they would hurry in order that I could sneak out of the palace and down the lanes to the Villa Favoni. Things didn't turn out like that however; the man with the mottled nose prodded me and gave a brusque sign that he wished me to follow them. I calmed myself... it was still early; the angel couldn't fly away. And Francesca had waited all this time. Surely one more morning...

CHAPTER FORTY

Tomma was shaking me. A greyish light seeped through the window.

I pushed him away.

'But sire.'

'*Porco miserie.*' I forced my eyes open and peered up at him.

'They're on their way to the church.'

Still I peered.

'They... The English... To look at the fresco.' Memory trickled back into my brain.

I stood and peed long and hard into the piss pot.

Tomma helped me into my clothes; no time for tunics or lacing of doublets. We pulled our cloaks around us and waded out across the snow, past the sentries and onto the campo. A market was in full flow and, despite the cold, all kinds of labour were being enacted; we jostled our way through the crowd of goose-sellers, women with baskets of apples or cheeses, boys roasting chestnuts...

CHAPTER FORTY-ONE

He led us through the labyrinth; that someone newly come to the palace should seem familiar with the course of winding passages didn't then strike me as odd. We reached the great door with its carvings of trees and birds. The guard pulled it open and we stepped out into the snow. I followed them across the courtyard, past the sentries at the palace gate, and we were out on the campo. The smell of roasting chestnuts hung in the air; it was market day. The cold had done nothing to discourage the stallholders who stood with their trays of apples and cheeses, or holding up geese strung through with twine. Crowds gathered round them and there was much noise.

The man with the mottled nose turned and addressed me in words I could not understand. Seeing my consternation, he repeated them, slowly, and it stuck me, he was speaking in an odd sounding Latin; he wanted to know where the church was, which again seemed most strange for a pilgrim.

I pointed.

'Take us there,' he ordered, with no please or thank you.

We are told we must swallow our pride along with our passions, that we are all equal in the eyes of Our Lord, that

232

we must love each other as He loves us. But as I looked at his nose and his purple-veined cheeks I knew that never in my life would I learn to love the English, with their rudeness, their cards and their money, dozing Sisters and conceited Abbesses. If not for Francesca, I'd have done as Sergeant Orlando had said; I'd have left them, gone back to the convent, told the Reverend Mother that they had no need of me, and they would never have seen me again.

The men elbowed their way through the crowd, making a passage for the Abbess, caring nothing for the townspeople as they thrust them aside. She followed, looking neither to left nor to right. The nuns scampered after her. I pulled my hood down over my face, for I was ashamed to be seen in their company. The bell tower emerged from the half-light, then the church; the great circle of its window looked down upon us like an all-seeing eye. The bearded man pushed the door open. A servant woman was sweeping the floor. Behind her, Brother Bartolomeo sat by a lectern, his feet upon a warming pan. He jumped from his chair when he saw us approaching.

The mottled-nosed man spoke in his version of Latin. 'We are looking for the man who is painting... that thing... you know... on the wall.'

Such a surge of excitement rose up inside me then. I thought of his angel, and then of his face looking down from the tower.

After a moment working out what he had said, Brother Bartolomeo hunched his shoulders and rubbed his hands together, feigning to seem less knowledgeable than his better. 'Ah, you might mean the fresco, my lord. It is a most peculiar word. It has nothing to do with painting. I can see why you struggled.'

I hated the English so much by this time I could not help but feel pride in our friar's perfect use of the sacred language.

But the bearded one didn't care about language. 'Where is he then?'

Brother Bartolomeo turned to the little sweeping woman and told her to go and summon the painter.

'Where is he Father?' She looked at him, flustered.

My pride in him fled with his reply, 'Don't you have a shred of wit? The guards will know. Ask them.'

The friar drew up his chair and plumped its cushion; the Abbess deigned to sit upon it. Less than a moment passed before, making it clear that she was bored with such waiting, she got to her feet and glared down upon him. I could almost see him tremble. What she next said was translated into his form of Latin by the man with the mottled nose. 'Where is this painting, Sir Priest?'

He pointed at the well of darkness behind us and, tutting in irritation, she turned from him and led her company forward.

The tower loomed before us. The friar struck his flint and touched a taper to the lamps set upon the floor about it. Light guttered upwards, slowly, slowly. A glimpse of arms spread wide beneath his wings, and the vision of wonder came to life, crashing down upon us.

The English stepped back, as if struck by lightning.

But I stepped forward and pulled back my hood.

And at that very moment, as if a miracle was being enacted, a cold light broke through the circle of window and now that I could see him clearly, I was overwhelmed.

234

It was as if that plummeting angel had put me under a spell. And what of the creature who'd painted him; what Brother Bartolomeo had said? He might be the Devil incarnate, but I didn't care. In the days that followed, or even the weeks, I would steal every moment I could to come here and stand beneath his platform, and watch his mad genius unfold.

From somewhere beyond the edge of my mind came the sound of the door crashing open. I forced my eyes away from the angel and turned... and my heart seemed to stop. He'd changed greatly since the day we had watched him stumbling along the path by the graveyard. His hair, which had been short and standing up from his head, was longer now and there was a wild look about him. Gone was Christ being led to his crucifixion, now he was closing in on the money lenders.

A jolt of something that never I had felt before pierced right through me.

He stopped at the font and dipped his fingers into the water. And dabbing it onto his forehead, chest, left and right shoulders, tracing the sign of the cross, ambled towards us, his tunic unlaced under his cloak, his uncombed hair almost reaching his shoulders, unaware, or uncaring, as to what lay ahead.

But if seeing Simone da Benno was like a thunderbolt, what do you think I felt next, for who was walking beside the main performer in the unfolding spectacle...

CHAPTER FORTY-TWO

I wasn't in the fairest of moods, by the time we reached the church. Tomma tried to cheer me. 'Remember, sire, they're from England. They're bound to talk about your great talent when they return to their land. Who knows, they might invite you...'

But even this could not raise my spirits.

I crashed the door open. They stood by the wall. All heads but the Abbess's turned. I dipped my finger into the holy font, tapping water onto my face, left shoulder and right, making great show of my godly devotion, and strode towards them, Tomma beside me.

'Ah, Master da Benno,' exclaimed Mortimer.

I bowed.

'We're admiring your... frenshco.'

My angel tumbled down towards them, arms stretched wide like wings, as he had for all the long days since we had started upon him.

I kept my mouth shut.

'But what is he?' enquired the Abbess. This day she wore a cloak lined with ermine.

'Gabriel, madam.'

'How odd he seems. But where is the Virgin?'

'Still trapped in my mind, Holy Mother.'

Only now did she turn her gaze upon me.

Last night by candlelight she had seemed younger; close to her now I saw lines on her brow. Her eyes were deep green, her lips plump, her cap pulled a fingertip from her hair, which wasn't dark, as her eyebrows, but the colour of honey.

'Pray why, sir?'

I didn't choose to answer.

'Are men of more interest to you than women?'

Mortimer shuffled his feet. A little nun in their company seemed unaware of what had just been said, her attention caught up with staring at Tomma. The others feigned to look up at the wall as if impervious to her discourtesy.

But I didn't care; there was many a man I'd rather have lain with than some of the women pressed upon me.

'Ah ha!' she laughed, and with the artistry of the courtesan she most certainly was, crouched against the wall, holding an arm out as if in fear, and, half turning, gazed up at the angel.

And as she did so her cloak furrowed around her, gathering into folds and pleats, its fabric transformed from a Spartan black into rivulets of jet and pewter. This, it now hit me, was where I'd gone wrong; I'd been thinking of Virgins, not robes. Yet it was this that would save me. Crinkling and creasing and bunching around her, it would fill her section of wall with energy equal to that of my angel. And another thought struck me; I wouldn't paint it in blue as convention required but would use its dark and luminous shades as contrast to her angel's robe, which I could now see would be the colour of oranges.

'Stay there, my Lady,' I shouted. I rushed to take up my charcoal, and sketched her shape on the edge of my wall.

A moment only, but enough to get it down before she moved. 'If you are good, Master da Benno, I'll offer myself as your Virgin.'

I held her gaze. This was a game; who would win? She opened her mouth slightly and touched the tip of her tongue to her lip.

Mortimer coughed; the company seemed somewhat flustered, but needless to tell you she looked away first. She wasn't to be defeated, however, for next she stepped towards me. My tunic was unlaced, as I've said, such had been our rush. She lifted her hand and placed a finger on the eye-bead.

'And pray, what is this?'

I replied as I had to Tomma before he had enlightened me of its purpose. I shrugged, 'I don't know.'

'Where did you get it?'

Was she one of the Grand Inquisitors? 'Oh... I found it one morning.'

'I've seen such a thing before,' and with what might have been mistaken for a smile, 'I hope it won't disturb you to know it was nailed to a corpse's neck.'

A corpse's neck was it... she'd have to do better than that. I laughed, which didn't seem to please her. And so, as if to stir up some other reaction, she drew herself closer and pressed her body against mine, an action which, in normal circumstances, would have been appreciated most gratefully, but the bulk of her cloak did the great disservice of preventing me have any sense of what was beneath it.

'Do you suppose it has given me hellish powers?' I

whispered into her ear.

I'd thought to win this battle of words, but I was mistaken for what did she whisper back as she turned to go but, 'I hope so.'

I looked round at Tomma, expecting the usual frown of disapproval followed by his caution about it not being a good idea. Surely he could forgive my behaviour; we had us our Virgin and that's all that mattered. But his mind was elsewhere, for now came the strangest sight that ever I had been caused to witness. As the company made their way towards the door, one of the little nuns in the company glanced back at him with such a strange look it shocked me, I can tell you. And even more perturbing, he stood gazing after her.

Tomma smitten. The world had surely turned upside down.

Had he been Guido, I'd have made some bawdy remark. But this was Tomma. I kept my mouth shut.

Moments passed.

'Tomma,' I said his name gently.

He looked away, flustered; the first time I'd seen him like that.

'Is anything wrong?'

'I don't know, sire,' he managed. 'I'll tell you when I've had the chance to decide.'

CHAPTER FORTY-THREE

I managed to stumble after the English out into the snow; there is no need to say that my mind was in turmoil. And I think his was too for when he saw me, he had stopped and stood as if frozen to the spot, and we had stared at each other.

What was he doing here? What was he doing with the man called Simone da Benno?

A great excitement filled my breast. But, no, that isn't exactly right; exhilaration, elation... I can't find the word. But perhaps that's because there is none to describe the thrill surging through me. I felt I might cry, but not with sorrow. Now, more than ever, I had to get to Francesca. I had to tell her. Simone da Benno hadn't gone... he was here. And so was Tomma Trovatello.

We reached the palace gate. I waited until the English were safely behind it, and then I turned and set off back across the campo.

CHAPTER FORTY-FOUR

How we had struggled, but God had rewarded us. And though I could not think he had time for harlots dressed in nuns' clothing, we had witnessed a miracle for he had given us our Virgin. All we had to do now was take stock of her, and her angel; the energy formed from the crashing figure and the crumpled robe.

I left Tomma with his thoughts and went to find the boys. They were out on the campo, throwing snowballs at each other, their antics rewarded by adoring looks from the young servant girls who stood watching.

'Come on,' I waved at them. 'We're starting.'

The girls were forgotten for here were lads desperate to get on with the next stage of work, which, unlike the building of towers or limewashing of walls, was the real one. But first we would go to the kitchen for my stomach had begun to rumble.

Celestino glanced around. Where was Tomma?

'I'll go and find him,' said Guido.

'I don't think he's hungry,' I said with as much conviction as I could muster. 'He'll come when he's ready.'

Are not warmth and food comfort for the body or, in Tomma's case, a means to divert lovestruck hearts, at least for the shortest duration? If he'd been with us, but he wasn't. And so in the meantime we sat without him, before a blazing fire consuming great platters of roasted meats, flatbreads covered with anchovies, mushrooms and polenta, frittata spread with cheese and herbs, barley broth. Apart from easing our present condition, this was good practice, for when we started on the gesso, the brazier would be placed on a spot far away enough from where we were working. We'd have to fuel ourselves instead. Now was the time to build up good coverings of fat.

Comfort for the body or lovestruck hearts. Or those filled with lust for an Abbess. When would I bed her? Tomorrow, with luck; I could not wait longer. And, knowing such women, neither could she. But, belly full, feet toasted as kippers, my mind floated backwards. How to set about saving Francesca? 'Come Benno, think.'

CHAPTER FORTY-FIVE

In my trembling state of elation, all caution left me; I did not care if I should fall and slide all the way down the frozen alley. But my clogs were sturdy and somehow, though slipping and slithering, I managed to stay on my feet and at last the Villa Favoni rose up before me, dark against the silver sky. I half ran, half skidded towards the gate and pulled the bell. It clanged into the silence. But no one appeared to open it for me. I pulled again, it clanged more loudly, and as it did, a huge skulking shape crept out from the shadows. It slunk towards me, stretching its jaws. I saw pointed fangs and felt the blood drain from my face. I tried to run, but my legs wouldn't work; I could do naught but stand in mortified silence and watch. Closer... closer... it reached the gate, and, flattening its ears, its lips trembling, let out a low growl and started to scrabble up the railings. It would have got over them in a heartbeat, but now came a yell and what I could perceive in my agonised terror to be a man, came running towards it, lashing out at it with a chain. It slid to the ground and cowered there, yelping.

'Go Sister!' he shouted, 'it isn't safe here.'

The blood so recently drained from my face pumped through my veins as I stumbled and slid my way back onto the alley, where I stood, shoulders hunched, gulping for breath.

'Are you all right?'

I felt a soft hand touching mine, and turned to see a girl with a bundle of firewood strapped to her back staring down at me. I had not strength to reply.

'Was it those dogs?'

That thing was a dog?

'It's wicked, what's happening in there.'

I stared at her, blankly.

'Haven't you heard?' But no, I wouldn't have, would I, locked away down there in my convent? 'They say it's all to do with the mad-man.'

And when still I stared, 'Haven't you seen him yet, Sister? He lives in a tower inside the church. They say he's a servant of Satan. That them dogs are there to protect the Lady Favoni from him getting at her. They say he wants to steal her baby.'

I gaped up at her in absolute horror, at which she gave me a worried look. 'I'm going down the hill. I'll help you as far as Santa Chiara. We can wait a bit until you feel better.'

Somehow I found voice to thank her... but I wasn't going to the convent. I was going up to the campo.

'Then I'll come with you. It's no trouble.'

I thanked her again. There was no need; I felt better now.

'Ah well, if you're sure. But take care on that ice,' and she stood watching as I set off up the slope in a daze. I still do not know how I got to the top. But somehow I did. Snow had started falling again. I pulled up my hood and stood in a daze.

I do not know how much time passed, a moment, or two, or ten. A voice I seemed to know from somewhere, 'Come Sister, you'll freeze.' Captain Orlando towered above me. He smiled; it was clear that he thought to help me into the palace. But the last thing I wanted was to be back in there with the English.

'It's most kind of you,' I tried my best to smile, 'but I have to go to the church.'

'Then let me get you there in one piece.'

I set off beside him. 'How are they behaving? I see you've survived.'

'Yes,' I said, 'but it's hard.'

'I don't doubt it. The sooner the snow clears and they're gone, the better for everyone.'

The few remaining stallholders were clearing away their honey and cheeses, and the crowds had lessened.

The church was still there at the end of the campo, though by now all things were so confused in my mind, I thought it might not be. He pushed the door open. There was the angel, swooping down from his wall. And there was the tower beside him.

I do not know if I thanked the kind captain; I was too overcome.

'Remember, send for me if you need me.' He raised his hand in a little salute, and I was alone.

I pulled my cloak around me and stood in a daze of absolute horror. The house. The gate. That creature scrabbling up it. Dear God in Heaven.

They do say that shock does strange things to your mind, and they are right for I imagined I felt something touch my shoulder. I could have fallen down in dread, but forced myself to look round.

'I prayed you'd come back,' said Tomma Trovatello.

A radiant numbness crept up inside me.

'I thought I would never see you again. And then, there you were.'

He stood staring at me; I had forgotten how dark his eyes were.

'What are you doing here?' I managed, but in a voice so low I did not think he had heard me.

He smiled. 'It would take too long to tell you right at this moment. Can we meet later?'

I felt my heart soar. I nodded.

'Here. At midnight. After the bell?'

Just then, the door creaked open. We turned as one of the sentries stomped through it, beating snow from his cloak. 'Ah, there you are, Sister. I just met the captain. He wants me to help you back to the palace... when you're finished, that is.'

He started towards me, but stopped in his tracks when he saw that I wasn't alone.

Tomma squeezed my hand, made his way to the door, and in the blink of an eye he was gone.

The sentry gave me a quizzical look; a nun, alone... with a man. 'Was he troubling you, Sister?'

I smiled back while I thought of an answer. 'Oh no, I know him. He stayed for a while at the convent.'

Ah that was it... the infirmary. 'Poor boy,' he said, 'it must be hard when you're a cripple.'

CHAPTER FORTY-SIX

We had all but finished eating when Tomma appeared. I saw the look on his face and would have asked what was troubling him, but something stopped me.

Stomachs full, excepting for Tomma's for he hadn't eaten a crumb, we got ourselves back to our Virgin, and by the time light faded to darkness her image was set in its place, crouching, perhaps in terror, perhaps in awe, as our angel swooped down towards her.

CHAPTER FORTY-SEVEN

I followed the sentry across the campo. Through the gate, past the little temple with its columns, to the door where he left me to make my way through the labyrinth, taking careful note of its twists and turns for, joy of all that was joyful, I would be making my way back along it at midnight.

I reached the chamber. All was as it had been before. The nuns lolled on their couches, eyes shut, mouths open. The men sat at the table, their cards replaced by a scroll of some sort. They poked their fingers at points upon it and scratched their heads. I supposed the Abbess was abed. Not one so much as gave me a glance as I walked quickly past them.

I shut my door and falling onto my pile of blankets, curled myself into a ball. I should have been thinking about the house... the monster dog scrabbling onto the gate, closer to me and closer. What the girl with the firewood had said. But I could only think about Tomma.

And though it seemed that time had stood still, the midnight bell clanged through the silence. A surge of joy swelled up inside me. I peeped through the crack in the door. The room was empty, the Abbess's door ajar. I wrapped my cloak around me, tiptoed to it and looked inside; her bed was strewn with garments, and the table beside it with bottles and boxes. And then I crept out and into the passage. I made a few false turns and had to retrace my steps, but God was with me and I reached the entrance hall. The guard at the door looked shocked that any soul should be about at that hour, and so, thinking quickly, I told him I was late for prayers, that Brother Bartolomeo was taking my confession. It was a foolish thing to say for confessions are not taken at such a time, but a nun can say anything she wants, can she not, and no one will doubt her.

'Ah, yes, Sister,' he said, 'but be careful out there.'

I waded through the snow, past the temple, the poor sentries still guarding the palace gate, and out across the campo.

The church was even darker than it had been the night I arrived, for then, at least there had been the brazier's glow. But now so deep was the blackness, I felt myself blind. I started to panic. He wasn't here. He wasn't coming. But just as these thoughts flew into my head a wavering flame came floating towards me, shedding light upon the silhouette behind it. A nun's to be precise. My panic turned to dread; it could only be one of the English. Too late to turn back, but, after all, I was in the church, so would it not follow that I'd come to pray.

Closer, closer, I could but stand, panic striking deeper. In front of me now, she held out the skirt of her habit. 'It's been most useful,' she said in Tomma Trovatello's voice. And in the flickering light of his candle, I saw he was smiling. Before I was able to gather my thoughts, he put his hand on my arm and turned me towards the tower looming behind me. A ladder was balanced against it. 'Let's get ourselves up there where no one can see us.'

We wobbled up it, I after him, and at last, reaching the top he held out his hand. I took it and, just as before, I did not turn to stone. And when I was safely on the platform, he stuck his candle into a well of wax in its centre, cleared a space from the jumble of pots and bowls strewn about, and we sat with it guttering between us.

Not wishing to let him see my fluster, I thought to speak first. 'That man, Simone da Benno, why were you with him?'

His face was in shadow but I could tell that my words had shocked him most deeply. There was such a long silence, I thought he wasn't going to answer. But then he did. 'He's my master.' A moment passed. 'How do you know his name?'

'Francesca told me.'

The candle flickered, he stared at me in confusion. I took the drawing from the folds of my habit. And though it was smudged, I could still see the beauty of its lines, the curve of her face glancing over her shoulder.

I handed it to him. He took it and held it out to the flame, studying it for a very long moment. Then he said, 'Where did you get this?' I felt he was judging me, as I was about to judge him.

'She gave it to me.'

'I don't understand.'

And so I told him that she was my friend... no not my friend, almost my sister... about our life together when we were young, why I had been forced into holy orders.

When I had finished, he leaned towards me, and in the guttering candlelight I saw the tender look in his eyes.

A great feeling engulfed me but I forced myself on. 'And I know that your master painted her portrait.' 'Yes he did.'

I would have plunged right in, told him what the girl with the firewood had said about him being the servant of Satan. That he wanted to steal her baby. And Brother Bartolomeo, about him being the Devil incarnate. But I had to tread carefully, so I said nothing.

He smiled. 'Now it's my turn to tell you my story.' He reached out and took my hand in his, winding his fingers around mine. And though many years have passed since that night of awakening I only need close my eyes to relive the moment, feel that delicious, heart pumping sensation as he started on the strangest of tales; of how they had come to the city to paint a fresco. Of an argument with Don Volsini. I had never seen him, but I knew he was the Duke's Chamberlain. A leap from a window. Their rescue by Francesca's husband; this being upon the day we saw Donato leading his strange procession. How the old signore had asked him to paint her portrait. Of how they had become friends. How Donato had betrayed them. How she had helped them escape. How he had fallen from his horse in the storm and they had hidden in a cave. How he'd gone back to the house to make sure that Francesca was safe. How he'd been caught before he could see her. How Signor Baldassare had taken him to the convent.

'What puzzles me is why take me there? Why not simply turn me in? But anyway, before he did, we went back to the cave to find my master, but he was gone. It was clear they had caught him.' He pulled up the hem of his habit. Or should I say Novice Sister Cecilia's. 'That's why I stole this.

If there was any hope of finding him, I had to get me some kind of disguise, for they were sure to be after me too. Well now you know all about it.'

So he had rescued him, then.

'No. I got back that day and found he'd been freed. For some reason known only to them, they'd changed their minds. They wanted him to paint the fresco; we can't explain it. You've seen that we've started.'

The angel crashing down towards me. 'He's the most wondrous thing I could ever imagine.'

'I know, he's good, even by my master's standards. Thank you for helping me get over the wall,' he said now.

But I hadn't; if anything I had taken so long to clamber onto it I could have ended up getting him caught.

He gave a little half smile. 'There's more than one way of helping.' We sat for a moment, then he asked cautiously, as if not wishing to give me bad news, 'And Francesca, when did you last see her?'

I had always thought myself a strong person. Strong, and sensible. That I could weather any storm. Sorrow, till then, had barely touched me. The day papa had taken me to the convent, was the last time I had cried. Then something seemed to close my soul. But this was the moment it opened again; a great feeling welled up inside me, I felt my lips trembling.

He put his arms around me. They weren't like women's. Instead, they were hard with muscles, and strong, and his hair smelt of plaster dust, I remember, and was thick against my face. And I cried, for the second time in my life. He didn't try to stop me.

When the worst of my sobbing was over, I said, 'Not

since the day after you left.'

He smoothed my face. *'You have a lot to tell me, I think.' he smiled a sad little smile and placed his finger on my lips.*

So I did; of how Francesca had come to the convent the day after the storm, when they'd escaped from the Duke's men, of her stupor, her frenzy. How, as punishment, after being caught with him on the wall, I'd been forbidden to leave the convent. How, as atonement for my sins, the Reverend Mother had sent me to help the pilgrims. How, after I'd seen him in the church, I had gone down to the Villa Favoni *'There was a great snarling... beast... of some kind. A man with a chain.'*

He stopped me. *'I know...'*

And now it was my turn to stare at him.

'My master went back there one night. He hoped to get into the house, find Francesca. The gate was locked. But things like gates don't stop him; he got over it. One of those dogs was prowling around.'

There were more than one?

'It attacked him, but he's a good fighter. He killed it. Then a guard appeared; he doesn't know if he killed him too, but he thinks he might have.'

I tried my best not to show my horror and he continued as though this kind of thing was nothing special as far as his master was concerned.

'But something else happened that night; he saw Donato's father at a window, talking to another guard. Or, to be more specific, listening to him.'

Which shook me out of my shock; that couldn't be right. *'But he's deaf.'*

'*That's what he wants the world to think, but it's as much a disguise as this habit. I don't know what he's up to. Him and his son, and that weasel Baldassare.*'

'*You know about him?*'

He nodded. '*And about the book with symbols. Francesca told us.*'

'*And the silver slime that she couldn't put back in its bottle?*'

'*It's called quicksilver.*'

So he knew of such things? '*She thought they used it for magic, along with the spells in the book.*'

'*It is used for that by some misguided souls. But it's not why they had it. I think it was for some kind of experiment.*' *He gave me a gentle smile.* '*And whatever that was, it had nothing to do with Francesca. Or not until after she found it, along with the books. That's why they asked my master to paint her, to keep her out of their way. But one night he found her in the garden, staggering about in a daze.*'

Just as she'd told me.

'*He wanted to take her to Baldassare, this was back at a time before we knew about books or symbols or strange goings-on; we simply thought he was a physician. But her servant begged him not to. Now we know why. So he carried her back to her chamber. Her servant said she had taken too much poppy. And there was no reason to disbelieve her.*'

I sat for a moment, unable to speak, then I said, '*The last time she came to convent, just after you escaped, she could barely stand. She was shaking. There were blue marks on her face. Sister Agata wanted to keep her with us, look after her. But Signor Baldassare arrived and took her away.*'

'*Why would he do that?*'

'I know. It's a mystery. Oh and there was a smell about her. Sister Agata...'

He stopped me. 'That box, in the graveyard; the one we stood on...'

The box in the graveyard? Why did he care about boxes in graveyards? And then it hit me. The box. Yes the box. That's where I had smelt it. But not exactly on the box. On Corvo's feathers. An image crashed into my mind; I saw him again, stretched stiff inside it.

The first time I saw Simone da Benno, we were digging a grave, as I've told you. But I might not have mentioned it was for a crow.

'It's not the only box, you know,' he said now. 'There are piles of them in the house. I opened a couple; they were empty and had a completely different smell, like honey. I was curious and so I went back to the graveyard to see if I could find the one we stood on, but more importantly to try to find you. I didn't want to you lose you from my life.'

He leaned towards me. I caught a glimpse of his face in the still guttering light of the candle and felt a great urge to touch it.

'As for the box, I had to see what might be in it.' This was when I began to suppose that he wasn't like other, ordinary, mortals, 'I took it back with me and opened it... there was that smell. Apart from that, there was nothing except for a feather.'

'Yes, it was empty by then. But Corvo was in it before that. He was her crow. Her husband killed him.'

I felt I was making no sense at all, but 'I know,' he said. 'She told us.'

'We buried him in the graveyard. That's why the box

was there. She brought him in it.'

'Ah, he said, 'that explains the feather.'

By now the candle had burned halfway down, tallow smoke floated thick around us.

'But why would he want to kill her crow?'

'She thought it was some kind of warning.' I chose not to mention my wild thoughts about sacrifice.

He looked at me earnestly. 'Let's keep this between us. I can't tell my master... not yet at least. He has enough on his mind as it is – there's the fresco to finish, and he hasn't much time. His future... our futures... depend upon it. He can't be distracted. I'll have to get into the house without him knowing what I'm up to. I need to think how to get her out of there.' The candle sputtered. 'But I want to hear about you. You said you were sent here to help them?' He meant the English.

'Yes. Well... No.' I couldn't stop thinking about the box. I mumbled something about the fact that it had been a mistake. That they didn't need helping at all. He'd told me so much, and this was all I could think to say? So I added, 'I only stayed because I thought it a way to get to the house, and Francesca. But, you've seen how they are, they don't behave like holy people.'

'That's because they're not.'

This was too much for me.

'Pilgrimages aren't made at this time of year. And why come north when Assisi is south?'

I gaped at him, mouth wide. He was right. I would have to sharpen my wits if I hoped to keep up with him.

'What does your friend say about them?' he asked.

'What friend?'

'The nun.'

'What nun?'

'The one in the church. She was standing beside you.'

'She's not with me. She's one of the English.'

'But,' he replied, 'she was there at the convent. I saw her.'

I would have told him that he was mistaken, but there was no time for next came a shuffling sound. We held our breaths and looked down. Brother Bartolomeo staggered across the floor beneath us, a candle in one hand, a flagon grasped to his belly. He burst into song, 'Good... night... sig... norina, I bid you g g g good niiiight,' and crashing down on his chair, slumped across his lectern.

We made our silent way down the ladder and onto the campo. A bitter wind whipped around us, cutting into our bones. A guard swung his lantern, and came towards us through the snow.

'Ah Sisters, it's late to be out.'

'We've been praying for the English pilgrims,' Tomma declared in a high-pitched, wavery voice.

'Let me help you back to the palace.'

'Tomorrow night,' Tomma whispered as we reached the gate.

I nodded.

He pulled me back, 'But wait. All this time and I don't know your name.'

'Maria Assunta. But my real one's Sofia.'

'Ah,' he said, 'perfect.'

'Was it? Why?'

'It's Greek,' he said. 'It means wisdom.'

CHAPTER FORTY-EIGHT

I rose early next morning. In Florence I'd have thrown some object or other to wake first Celestino, then Guido. There was never a need to wake Tomma, for as I'm sure I have said he was always first up; in winter the brazier would be lit, in summer the shutters opened. This I called my grunting time, it being the only sound I was able to muster by way of communication. But it was also my time for thinking. Great visions would swarm into my mind; the colour that yesterday had caused such torture would appear in front of my eyes. Now I would know that a red or purple was needed, or that a figure had to be changed or taken away altogether, or a sword removed from a battling soldier to be replaced by a pennant.

But, strangely, this morning, somewhere under his pile of furs Tomma lay still and silent. I was thankful for I wanted to be alone. Two subjects inhabited my mind; my altarpiece and Francesca. Or was it the other way round?

As far as the first was concerned, all was in place. This was the day I'd set about recovering our lives; when the boys came we'd measure out the paper, fasten it down and the job would begin. January, and I'd be back in Florence. But what of Francesca? Where the wall was my triumph, she was my failure. What had become of me? I, Simone da Benno, who'd ruled the streets of that city, yet here had been defeated by a dog. I tried to conjure up a new plan. Thoughts of the gaoler sprung into my mind. He was violent enough for the job... and he seemed to have liked my gold Florin. I started to work on a plan of sorts, but wasn't about to tell Tomma. I had dragged him into trouble enough to last him a lifetime. This was my problem now. Mine alone. I'd have to think how to solve it.

Hope returned, I pulled on my clothes, left my boys to their slumber and made my way across the campo, through the freshly fallen snow, my footsteps spoiling its pristine perfection, up the church steps, and hauled the door open. Inside was colder than outside. I'd light the brazier, surprise the boys. Tomma had rekindled it the night before, and I was grateful for this. I took my flint and was about to strike it above the oily rags set in the charcoal when I felt my flesh tighten. Someone was watching me. I held my breath, and then came a sound so faint that had the brazier started its hissing I wouldn't have heard it; an all but inaudible tinkling. I'd have thought I was going insane, but for Tomma. He'd heard it the last time, '...like a greyhound's bell, sire... you know the little ones clipped to their collars.'

Yes, he'd been right.

I took the few steps to the wall. Something – or someone – was behind it.

Instinct made me reach for my dagger, but it was still back there in the attic, under my mattress. All I had was my voice, so I shouted, 'Who are you?'

The tinkling stopped.

'Tell me!' I shouted again. 'I know you're there.'

Silence closed in, the cold grew colder.

And now came another sound, this time from behind.

I turned and would have struck out at it. Thank the Lord I was too slow, for there was Anna, holding a platter. She wrinkled her brow. *Gesu Cristo,* what would she think of me, talking to walls? I struck a nonchalant air. 'I thought I heard something. It must have been the heat from the brazier, shrinking the plaster.'

I could see her looking over my shoulder. 'But it isn't lit.'

I shut my eyes. Sift your brain, Benno. Find something to say.

She held up her candle; it dazzled my eyes. 'Don't worry,' she smiled, 'this cold, it does strange things to our minds. Let's light it now.'

She handed me the platter and touched her candle to the rags. Light flooded about us and it was as if the red-traced figure crouching above us came to life. She stood, mouth open.

'It's the Virgin. I've started her,' I said, as if explanation were needed. Still she stood, gazing upwards and didn't even turn her head when Tomma appeared beside us.

'Why are you standing there, sire?' He looked at the platter. 'You should eat that chop before it gets cold.'

When I had followed his instructions, and the empty platter, and Anna were gone, we crouched over the now glowing charcoal, rubbing our hands.

'That sound. I heard it again.'

He took a while before he said, 'There'll be an explanation.'

Which didn't go far to reassure me... but what could I do about it? I had him alone; I shouldn't squander the moment. I adopted a casual, 'So, are you going to tell me?'

'About what, sire?'

'The little nun. Yesterday. In the church.'

'She helped me escape.'

I looked at him, blankly.

'She was at the convent. She helped me escape,' he said again as if repeating the words would help me understand. I unravelled my mind enough to say, 'But what was she doing there if she's English?'

'She's not English, sire.'

Better I said nothing, let him go on.

'But I managed to speak to her.'

He spoke to her? When did he speak to her? Still I kept my mouth shut.

'It turns out she's been sent from her convent to help them.'

And, with that, he went to wake the boys and left me pondering. Tomma didn't lie, not if his life depended upon it... and there was many a time that it had. But I knew he'd held back on telling me everything. And, another thing I knew, someone was there behind the wall. Sod it let them watch me whoever they were, and I tried to turn my thoughts to my Virgin; what colour and shading should be employed to infuse her with light? And her face? It should belong to a young and innocent girl, not a harlot.

A sound broke into my thoughts. Not a tinkling, but a rustle of fabric. I turned to see the Abbess striding towards me, Mortimer mincing behind her. He stood back when they reached me, giving her stage. 'Ah, my artist,' that odd English voice again, 'We have come to see what you've done.'

She sauntered, slowly, towards the wall. The light from her lantern flickered upon it. 'Ah, there are two of me now, I see. My own living self and my drawn one.'

She stood back to better regard the sinopia outline. The fur of her cloak softened her face as fur always does on a woman, though had I been employed to paint her portrait I'd have chosen sable; her skin was somewhat dulled by ermine. She clicked her fingers. Mortimer stepped forward. She passed him the lantern, instructing him to hold it up.

And her pronouncement? 'You've caught me nicely, Master da Benno. I think I approve.'

Caught her? No, I hadn't done that. Not yet. But give me time. Three months and I hadn't lain with a woman.

She turned to face me. 'Don't worry, sir Benno,' she declared in her languorous fashion, 'I shall come back and pose again for you soon.'

And, before I could tell her I thought this an excellent idea, she strolled off, Mortimer in tow.

I could but chuckle to myself; if she thought she had the upper hand she was most sadly mistaken. And when she returned, well, who could tell, perhaps perfection could be improved. I cast my contemplations aside, for now it was time for the kitchen. I'd warm myself by the fire, and then I would go to the dungeon.

CHAPTER FORTY-NINE

Celestino and Guido sat together on their bench by the table, steaming bowls of bread and milk before them, shovelling it into their mouths; a stranger would be justified in thinking they hadn't eaten for weeks. Tomma sat a little way off, his bowl untouched, his spoon beside it. I was an old hand at the game they call love, but not old enough to forget that when it comes for the first time it hits with ferocious intensity.

The kindest thing was to leave him alone, and so I told the others to stay where they were for the while. No need to start yet; I had much to think on before we moved to the next stage of proceedings.

'Aren't you eating sire?' Celestino shouted, but I was halfway up the steps. Tomma could tell them about the chop.

Now for the second part of my plan. I crossed the courtyard, round by the temple, the guards at the palace door, along the corridor. Past the smell of beeswax until I reached the one of piss. Down the steps into darkness. Freezing cold damp crept up to meet me. I reached the bottom and kicked the door. And then I kicked it again.

A shuffling sound, a hatch clunked a little way up. Eyes

peered out.

'Open the *cazzo* thing.'

A clanking of keys. A thud and a click.

I was confused for a moment, so bulky and fat was the figure before me. But as my eyes adjusted to the dim I could see it was him right enough, swathed in blankets, a cap pulled low on his head.

He stepped back.

'I want to hire you.'

Who was this? What was he saying? He took a moment to come to his senses, if he had any in the first place.

He stepped forward again.

'Aren't you going to invite me in?'

Ah now he could see. 'Yes, signore.'

I followed him to a table. His lantern was set upon it. He struck his flint and lit it. Shadows reared up on the walls. He set about dusting a stool with his sleeve, giving him time to consider his answer. He invited me to sit but I opted against it.

'The Favoni house, I need to get in there.' It was obvious what was bound to come next. 'With your help, of course.'

He screwed up his eyes. 'How... signore?'

'I don't know. I need to work it out. And I want you to think on it too. It's surrounded by a wall, as no doubt you'll know. We'll have to get over it, which would not be a problem except for the fact that 'strange things is happening', as you said, relating, no doubt, to the dogs in the garden. How to get past them, that's the question.'

He looked more than doubtful. He sure as hell wasn't going anywhere near them.

'What if I were to tell you it's a matter of life and death?'

He knew I meant his.

He adopted a fawning tone. 'I'm not much use … My back, you see… been troubling me something awful it has.'

'Oh, you mustn't concern yourself, I don't need you to do heavy lifting, only a little in the way of distracting.'

I took the florin from my jerkin and held it up, as I had before, turning it in my fingers and thanked the lamplight for making it glitter.

'What do you want me to do, signore?' Amazing how quickly he said this.

'I'll come back and tell you.' I returned the coin to the lining of my jerkin. 'And, in the meantime, I'll hold on to this. And it goes without saying, we've struck ourselves a bargain here. If you should think of crossing me.'

A clanging saved him from attesting to his dependability on this score. I looked up, following the sound to its source; a wooden grate in the ceiling above us. I could but wonder if the bellringer knew that the dungeon was down here below him, right under his feet.

CHAPTER FIFTY

I should have been thinking about the house, the dog in the garden, the old man suddenly able to hear... the pilgrims not being pilgrims... the box. But just as the night before I could only think about Tomma.

It must have been dawn before I fell into a troubled sleep which seemed to last no more than a moment before I was jolted awake by loud voices. I crouched down and peeped through the crack in the door. The English were grouped around the table, at the end of which sat the man with the earring, at the other, the Abbess, a silken shawl of bright scarlet draped around her shoulders. They seemed to be arguing. I moved a little, adjusting my vision, and at that very moment the door swung open and a man with a large, pleated cap stepped through it. Silence descended.

He looked at the one with the earring. I could but thank God for he spoke in Italian, and so I could understand, 'We are having a little... disagreement... my lord.'

'Did I not tell you?'

'I know, but it's enough to drive a sane man crazy. I'm afraid I am losing my patience.'

'You'll have all the time in the world to lose it when they are gone, my dear Matteo.'

The earring man put his hand to his head, as if trying to calm himself. 'I know, but...' at which point the man with the cap took a seat beside the Abbess. Now, now, my dear Elinor, I know of your troubles but I beg you be calm, and we shall get there.'

The man with the earring translated his words. They had an effect. She settled back in her chair. The man with the cap unrolled the scroll, smoothing it out on the table, and prodding his finger upon it turned to the man with the earring. I held my breath.

'Now let us just run through this one last time. The third on the right... and as I've said, you'll have to search carefully through it.'

He looked around the company. 'We must pull together. We're almost there. A few days and it will be over... to our satisfaction. But all the same I do understand; it's no wonder that tempers are frayed, cooped up in this room for days on end.'

The man with the earring, whose name I knew now was Matteo, put this into their language, and just as he finished the morning Angelus started to toll. The door opened. A manservant approached the table and spoke to the man with the cap in a voice too low to hear. 'Come, everyone...' the cap man stood and pushed his chair aside. 'I have organised a little diversion; I hope you will enjoy it.'

And in a moment they were gone. I got to my feet and stepped into the now empty room. Remnants of breakfast were spread on the table. The sight of it made my stomach rumble. I grabbed a pastry and was in the act of stuffing it into my mouth when there came a tap at the door.

I tried to swallow but it stuck in my throat.

A second tap, then a voice, 'Sister... Sister.'

I crept across the room and cracked it open. Anna stood before me, holding a tray. 'Oh Sister,' and seeing the empty room behind me, 'thank goodness you're alone. I was coming to clear the breakfast things and they asked me to tell you that someone's here; they wish to speak with you.'

Someone... what someone? It could only be Tomma.

'They said it's important. You have to hurry. They're waiting for you in the hall.'

She needn't have taken the trouble to tell me; I was out of the door in a flash, running through the labyrinth, down the stairway, along the chequered flags of the hall and my heart plunged. It wasn't Tomma sitting on a bench by the great carved door, but Sister Agata. She stood and rushed towards me. 'Oh, my dear,' her voice trembled. She grasped my hands. 'Something's happened.'

Now my poor heart seemed to stop.

She glanced around and lowered her voice. 'Is there somewhere we can speak alone?'

There was only the courtyard and so I led her past the guard out into the snow. She did not even wait to draw breath before she started. 'Sister Madalena came to see me.'

Sister Madalena was an apothecary, like Sister Agata. She tended the sick at the convent of Santa Lucia.

'She wanted advice about one of her patients. And after I'd helped her, I took the chance to tell her about the Lady Francesca. I had started to wonder if her symptoms had, in fact, been caused by the poppy. They were similar, that's true... but not exactly. I couldn't put my finger upon it. I described them to her. First the shaking and confusion. Both

are symptoms of that. But then there was her agitation, her despair... the poppy imparts a cool detachment or even euphoria. Her pupils were dilated, which made me think she had used belladonna. But then I began to wonder; how was she able to drop it into her eyes considering the state she was in? It requires precision, you know.'

I held my breath.

'Do you remember that very strange smell?'

I stiffened.

'Well, my dear, it held the answer. But I'm afraid I ignored it. I thought it was vinegar spilled on her clothes. Thank God I mentioned it. Sister Madalena knew what it was right away. Or what had caused it, should I say. There's a plant called witch's sage...'

I stared at her in horror.

'Oh my dear, how to tell you. It turns the mind almost to madness. It's said to be the choice of poisoners.'

A vision of Corvo, stiff and rotting, the smell on his feathers. On Francesca's skin. Her voice. 'They mean it as some kind of warning.'

I couldn't answer; I couldn't think.

'But if used in small doses, it dampens emotions, confuses or blurs the mind. Did you hear me, Assunta?'

The book. The symbols.

'If Sister Madalena is right, she's in the gravest danger. But...' she looked at me perplexed, '...who would want to poison her?'

Signor Baldassare. But how could I tell her? I felt the blood drain from my face, and seeing this, in a bid to calm me, she gave a little laugh, 'But I've talked too long in this awful cold. Go and get your things. We'll tell the Reverend

Mother all about it when we get back. She'll know what to do.'

Dear Sister Agata, how good she was. To come all this way in the snow. And though demonstrations of affection were forbidden, I put my arms around her. 'No, I thank you, it's better I stay, there's someone here who can help us.'

What on earth would she say if she knew this someone was the thief who'd run away in Novice Sister Cecilia's habit?

She looked at me doubtfully. 'Oh, I'm not sure, my dear.'

'Let me speak to him first.'

Him? Her eyes widened at the word.

'And then I'll come back. I promise.'

This seemed to placate her. 'Very well. If you think it is best. But go inside or you'll catch your death.' She smiled again, 'and I'll have to come all the way back up here to take care of you. Oh, I almost forgot,' she added, 'I brought these for you.' She held up a small package and handed it to me. 'Barley buns,' she said, 'I know how much you like them.'

I hugged her again and kissed her cheek.

'Now, get yourself inside.'

I stepped back through the door just to please her. But then I stepped out of it again and watched as she waded back through the snowy courtyard, past the sentries and onto the campo where the mule cart would be waiting. When I was sure it would be well on its way to the gate tower, I thrust the barley buns into the folds of my habit and set off in the opposite direction. I pushed the church door open and hardly had I stepped inside when I stopped in wonder. All thoughts of Francesca flew out of my head, for in the feeble daylight the once blank section of wall below the angel had burst into life and it was as if the very Abbess herself were cowering beneath him in terror, her robe bunched around her, folding and pleating in exquisite patterns. If this vision was here last night, it had been too dark to see it.

A shouting and clattering echoed around me. I dragged my eyes away, and there was Tomma pushing the wooden tower from one side of the wall to the other. Two boys came to help him, one was small with golden ringlets, the other tall and powerful, much like a blacksmith's assistant. A warmth swelled inside me as I watched. I longed to run to him, but I couldn't. 'Let's keep this between us. I can't tell my master, not yet at least.' I had given my word; hellfire might curl around my ankles but I wouldn't break it. I would wait here all night, if I had to.

I sat down in the shadow of a pillar, hidden from sight, pulled my cloak around me, and blind to the comforting scene before me, thoughts started crashing into my mind. A plant called witch's sage... turns the mind almost to madness... the choice of poisoners. 'They mean it as some kind of warning.' 'Help me Sofia, I'm frightened.' I shut my eyes and sought to thrust her words away. I must have slept. I woke in the dim light of the brazier. A loud snoring came from the direction of Brother Bartolomeo's lectern, and there was he slumped upon it.

Time passed far too slowly; I ate one of the barley buns, all the while thinking what Sister Agata had told me, until I feared my mind might explode.

When, at last, the midnight bell tolled, Brother

Bartolomeo grunted and stretched. He lit his lantern and holding it out, shuffled across the space of the church, pulled the door open and left me alone. The angel plunged out of the darkness above me. 'Please make him come soon,' I whispered. And as if he had answered my prayer, the door creaked open, the wavering light of a candle. A surge of happiness welled up inside me. 'I'm here,' I called softly. 'I'm here.'

He led me to the tower and hardly had we reached the top when I started, 'Something terrible has happened...' And, as he clambered onto the platform, 'Sister Agata came. They're poisoning Francesca.'

He put his hand on my shoulder. 'Shh Shh,' he said, 'tell me, slowly, from the beginning.'

I couldn't do the first thing he'd asked but I could the second.

And so I did. I told him about Sister Madalena, how she had come to our convent, what she had said about the smell on Francesca's skin... that it came from a plant called witch's sage. 'It's used to kill people, or drive them mad...'

Where others would have lost the thread of my babble by now, he seemed to be following what I was saying. Or what I was thinking... the box in the graveyard. Corvo's feathers.

We sat in silence and after a while he said, 'She's right. I know about that plant, and what it can do.'

'If it's called witch's sage, is it one of the things described by those symbols?'

'I don't think so. It's well documented. Why would they need to refer to symbols?'

'Do you think they've killed her, like Corvo?'

'No.' He shook his head, as if disbelieving of himself. 'Why did I not tell you before when my master and I went down to the house a few days ago – we had thought to do some spying – we saw her at the window.'

They had seen her? I closed my eyes and could but thank Gesu.

'Just a glimpse, that's all.' But I knew he was hiding something from me.

'What is it?'

'Oh, nothing.'

'I know it's not. You have to tell me.'

He looked at me sadly. 'It's just that they might want to keep her alive until the baby is born.'

A shiver ran through me; this was worse than the very worst thing I could have imagined. Now I felt able to tell him what the girl with the firewood had said, about his master's plan to wait until it was born, then to steal it, and Brother Bartolomeo about him being the Devil incarnate.

A smile crossed his face.' If my master's the Devil then all I can say is that Hell is a fun place.' His expression changed. 'I have to get her out of there.'

'But how?'

'Give me a day to think on it. I'll go tomorrow night.'

'I'm coming with you.'

'No,' he said. 'No.'

I stared into his eyes. 'I'm coming, and that's the end of it.'

'Well,' he said. 'We'll see.' And trying to deflect the conversation, 'So what of the English?'

It was almost too much for me to set my mind remembering; the morning seemed such a long time ago.

'*I didn't think to tell you, but I sleep in a little storeroom. There's a crack in the door and I can peep through it. Well, I woke when I heard their voices. They were sitting at their table. The Abbess was shouting at one of them, and he was shouting back.*'

'*He?*'

'*Yes. He's with them sometimes.*'

'*A priest.*'

'*No, just a man. And then another man appeared. I hadn't seen him before.*'

'*Describe him.*' *He leant very close to me; I wished he would lean even closer.*

'*Tall and thin. He had a large, pleated cap.*'

Tomma lurched forward. '*Cristo.*' *This was the first time I heard him swear. And then,* '*You don't know who he is?*' *a rhetorical question, it being obvious that I didn't.* '*His name is Volsini. He's the Duke's Chamberlain. The one I told you we were escaping from the day we jumped out of the palace window... Madonna Santissima,*' *this was the second time,* '*what is he doing with them?*'

He sat, lost in thought, as I sought to remember what had taken place next. '*The man... Volsini... sat down beside her. He managed to calm her. The man the Abbess had been shouting at speaks their language. He translated the man Volsini's words into English for them, and back into Italian for him.*'

Tomma shook his head. '*I don't understand. If one of them speaks English, why is my master wasting his time translating for them?*' *He leaned closer to me; I thought my heart might burst. I longed for him to touch me.* '*Can you remember what he said?*'

'Something about the third on the right... that they'll have to search carefully through it. And then they stood up and went out of the room.'

He closed his eyes, I could see he was thinking. 'The third on the right. And they'll have to search carefully through it.'

Some time passed. He opened them and gave a wry smile. 'I hate puzzles when they defeat me.' He touched my arm. It tingled. 'But look, it's late. We have to go. The last thing I want is my master to wake and find I'm not there. I need to keep him out of all this. But you know that already. And you need to get back to them. I'll come with you.'

And though I wanted him to, for it meant I would be with him longer, I told him there was no need. I was quite safe for I was of no importance to anyone.

'Ah but you are.' He gave me the gentlest of smiles and picked up the candle.

But there might be another way to have him stay with me a little longer, for, just at that moment, odd as it sounds, I remembered the barley buns. I took the rest of them from the fold of my habit and spread them before us. And when we had eaten them all he picked up the candle again.

Snow was falling again, like clumps of frozen thistledown. Our arms wrapped closely around each other we slipped and slithered across the campo. Before we got as far as the gate, he stopped and gazed at me for a moment. For so much time my life had been filled entirely with women, I knew naught of boys – or of men – or of longings or yearnings. And as I had before, I felt an urgent desire to touch his face, for him to touch mine.

'Come,' he said. 'We'll freeze if we stay here like this.'

We passed the sentries and stumbled towards the palace door.

'Could we meet earlier tomorrow? Just after the evening Angelus?'

I nodded. What could be more wonderful?

'I'll have worked out how to do it by then.'

We stood close together for a moment, and then we parted.

CHAPTER FIFTY-ONE

There are times when you ask yourself 'What if?'

What if I had stayed abed, listening to the boys' light breathing They slept late this morning, and for once, Tomma did too. But my mind was too tangled; I once entered the maze in the Marchesa's garden and though there was a way to the centre, I knew I'd never find it. But I couldn't let myself think like this. 'Get back there Benno. Get her out.' A plunging feeling in my guts… if I wasn't too late.

I pulled on my boots and cloak and stepped out of our temple into the courtyard. But instead of turning left towards the palace gate, I waded my way to its door. The guard asked my business. Unable to think of a story I told him the truth; I wanted to speak to the gaoler.

Not an answer he had expected. He stood waiting to hear why.

I smiled benevolently. 'I'm thinking to sketch his dungeon.'

He looked me up and down. My, we were odd, we painters. But he let me through.

Along the corridor smelling of beeswax until it turned to piss. Down the stairway, light disappearing behind me. He of no teeth sat by the open door of the hellhole, his head lolling forward. I kicked the leg of his stool. He leaped up and reached for his cudgel, but I was faster, unhooking his lantern from the wall and holding it close to my face so he could see me.

'Oh...' he twisted his into something that might have resembled a smile. 'It's you... Signore.'

'I've come to tell you the plan.'

He nodded and licked his lips like a cat when it's frightened.

'I'm going to the Favoni house.'

His eyes widened. 'What does you want me to do?'

'Meet me at midnight, out on the campo.'

A vicious wind howled across the courtyard, whirling the snow into spirals. I had almost reached the kitchen steps when somewhere behind me a voice called, 'Signore.'

Porco Miserie. I quickened my pace. It shouted again. There was nothing else for it, I stopped and looked around; the same boy who had delivered the Pieri's bad tidings was running towards me. 'Signore,' he said for the second time. 'Fra Bartolomeo sent me to find you.' He gave me a sympathetic look. 'He wants you to go to the church... He says it's urgent.'

This was the last balls-aching thing I needed.

'I'm to tell you that if he hasn't arrived by the time you get there, would you please wait for him.'

'Ask' and 'please' were not words I would readily think of as his, but get the sodding thing over with, Benno. I thanked him and made my way towards the gate. As I passed the sentries, one of them said. 'There's a blizzard on the way.' He looked up at the sky. 'I don't doubt it'll hit us by evening.'

I reached the church, and as I had done so many times now, pushed its door open.

The place was empty. Where was the dickhead? I paced up and down. If he didn't come soon, I'd be off and leave him fucking to it.

And then I heard it; the faintest tinkling. I froze. It stopped. I took a step towards the wall, and as I did a voice broke into the silence 'Ah, my artist.'

I turned. The Abbess stood behind me. It's easy to look back and say that I knew something was about to happen. But, as God is my witness, I did know. I did know. A sense of alarm rose up inside me. Tomma would have read it at once, but I was not in possession of wits such as his. I stood like a numbskull and watched the theatre as it unfolded in front of my eyes.

She held her hand towards me. *Dio* only knows why I took it, for as I did she opened her mouth and from it came screeching so loud, and so piercing, I felt my ears had been punctured. Till then I did not believe such a sound could come from a human.

Spent of breath, staring up at my startled face as if to say 'Haven't you guessed what I'm about, Master da Benno?' once more her mouth opened and the screech came again.

I stood in a state of utter confusion, stuck to the spot, her hand still in mine. She pulled it away and tore at the neck of her habit, ripping it open, the first time that ever I found myself unwilling to pay careful attention to the breasts of a woman, and so am afraid I cannot describe them. As all this took no more than some seconds, I forgive myself for standing there, struck dumb as a fool, as she took the grinding bowl from the table beside us and hurled it at me. It missed my face but struck my shoulder, and I was engulfed in that old searing pain.

And what if Tomma's skinny frame hadn't appeared at that very moment? 'Come sire,' he yelled as he pushed her aside, dragging me after him. He might have been small, but by God he was strong, 'Run!' he shouted. 'Run!'

If Tomma said 'Run' that's what I'd do. Or try to at least, for all I could manage was a clumping hobble. We reached the door and had progressed but a few paces beyond it when hands grabbed us and pulled us into the shadows just as a column of guards ran past. Amidst the slushing of their boots, Ivan Kovac's voice said something. I cannot report what it was; no longer could I make out words. He at one side, holding me up, Tomma at the other, willing me on, my mind a blank, he led us through an archway, down steps, up steps, down more, and into a passageway. He opened a door and pushed us through it.

CHAPTER FIFTY-TWO

I had entered a world in which there were men, not like Brother Bartolomeo but those who listened and talked to you as if you were their equal. And those men had powers enough to paint angels and climb over walls dressed as nuns. Surely the dear Lord had sent Tomma to me. I closed my eyes and felt again the turn of my heart when he touched me, his eyes which seemed to look into my soul. I'd once heard of a nun who loved a man. They made a tryst and met by a river, but the Prior trapped them and ordered boulders to be tied around their waists, and they were thrown into a river. Until now I had thought it a ludicrous story; who would break the rules of holy order simply to meet with a man? But now I understood; some things are stronger than we are ourselves. I prayed for time to pass, for it to be the Angelus hour when he would come to the church and sit close beside me on top of the tower.

I fell into a dreamless sleep and woke to the sound of a storm whipping up. I peeped through the crack in my door. The nuns lolled in their chairs, the men stretched their legs out in front of the fire. It seemed that the Abbess had stayed abed. All was exasperatingly normal until the door opened and the man with the earring stepped through it. The nuns, cheeks bulging with marzipan cake, looked somewhat unsettled to see him. He threw his cloak on the floor and frowned down upon them. And then, without seeking permission, barged right into the Abbess's chamber. After a while, they emerged together. But, far from sharing the same uneasy expression as her companions, she looked triumphant.

Roused from their torpor, the men came to the table, followed by the nuns. They clustered around the one with the earring. The man called Mortimer, spoke in his guttural voice.

The scroll was rolled out. The nun whom Tomma had thought my friend was now the centre of attention. There followed a deal of pointing and tracing of fingers across it. They seemed to be asking her questions.

It's true; time moves quickly when you wish it not to, and slowly when you do. After the man with the earring departed, the nuns returned to their comfortable chairs. The Abbess retired. The men pushed the scroll aside and opened their chessboard.

The storm rattled the shutters outside in the room. Such was its noise I might not have heard the door slamming shut. But I did and put my eye to my peephole. They had gone. I took my cloak and stepped into the room The sand in the clock marked five and a half of an hour after noon. Only one more half mark till the Angelus rang.

I took two pies from the table and thrust them into the folds of my habit, along with an apple and a marzipan cake. And though I cannot think what madness made me do it, I snatched the scroll and put it there too. The storm howled and shook the windows as I ran though the labyrinth.

The guard looked shocked when he saw me. He pointed at the window, I could see nothing through it but heard the wind gusting. 'I can't let you out in that, Sister. I've known many a blizzard before, but nothing like this.'

I didn't care about blizzards, or how bad this one might be. I only wanted to get to Tomma.

I smiled and thanked him, as if grateful for his warning, and made to turn back along the corridor. God was surely with me for I had taken but a few steps when there came a great knocking from outside. As the guard peered through his shutter to see who was there, I set my mind working. The sound of the storm battered around me, and with it streams of frigid air. The door was opened enough to let two snow-covered figures stomp through it, clapping their arms about their shoulders and stamping their feet. Here was my chance, I crept up behind them – pray, Sweet Gesu they wouldn't turn around – and slipped out into the courtyard. The wind whirled and screeched. A mound, which had once been the temple, rose out of the darkness before me. I pushed past it and reached the gate; huddling souls were stumbling through it. If the poor beggars and destitutes sought to find shelter inside it, what must it be like on the campo?

I cannot say how I managed to stand, far less walk in that storm. But is it not true that if you want something badly enough, nothing will stop you? And more than ever I could have imagined, I wanted to be with Tomma. After a few steps into the driving snow I found that if I huddled low and pushed my weight against it, I was able to stay on my feet and stumble towards the fuzzy shape of the bell tower that loomed up before me. Then the church; I heaved the door open and just as I did the Angelus tolled. Darkness closed in around me. I found Tomma's ladder and clumped up it but even before I got to the top I knew he wasn't there. I dared not light the candle. I sat down, took the scroll, the pies, the marzipan cake and the apple from the fold of my habit. I laid the scroll beside me and ate them all. And then I lay down and curled myself into a ball. The cold bit into my bones. Bats swooped above me. Time passed but there was no Tomma. Tears stung my cheeks and a very great sadness pressed down upon me.

I fell into a sleep of nightmares.

CHAPTER FIFTY-THREE

Ivan Kovac led us into a great chamber. So overwhelmed by pain was I by now, I have but a hazy recollection of how it appeared to me then; a mass of flickering candles, a fire blazing, the perfume of roses.

Sweat trickled down my back; the pitch had been spread across my shoulder again and set alight. I cannot say how much time passed before I found voice enough to whisper, 'What *Deo Santo?*'

'Don't you know, sire?' I didn't have strength to tell him that if I did I wouldn't be asking.

'You were about to rape her.'

Had something gone wrong with his mind?

'No, I mean she wanted to make the world think you did.'

I had considered myself a worldly person, deft in navigating the perilous boundaries of life, but it seemed I was mistaken for now I saw myself not as a sharp and cunning sophisticate but a dense and artless slow-witted dolt.

'She wants to get rid of you, sire.' He seemed in full control of his senses.

'I'm missing something here, Tomma.'

'Look, her plan was this, she would shout "Rape", the guards would come running and you would be back in the dungeon.'

Ivan Kovac's voice came from behind him, 'He's right, signore. You speak English. It was simply a matter of time before you found out what they're up to. By the time Volsini learned of the fact it was too late, he couldn't get rid of you. And so he decided to use your knowledge of their language as a weapon against you.'

'And what is it?' asked Tomma, thinking to add, 'that they're up to.'

'We don't know… yet. But we will, you can be sure.'

Only now did I think of Guido and Celestino. And, as if he had read my mind, Ivan Kovac said in his flat, even tone, 'Your boys are safe, you need not worry.'

He motioned for us to follow him. By now my head seemed fit to burst, but somehow I managed to do as he said. He led us out of the vast and luxurious chamber into a smaller one, every bit as lavish, with a fire burning in the corner, in front of which was a cushion-strewn couch. I slumped down upon it. I owed my life, again, to Tomma. How had he known to come and save me?

'I guessed, sire. I woke, you weren't there. I thought you must have gone to the kitchen. I was on my way there when the duty guard told me the Fra had sent for you. That you'd gone to the church. It didn't seem right so I went there to find out what was happening.'

'I thank God you did, my little friend.'

'We'll get you away from here,' Ivan Kovac said now. 'You're safe for as long as they think you've escaped. But we have to move fast; time is against us. Wait till the storm's past. We'll give you horses and take you as far on the road as we can. He touched my shoulder; such was the agony, I all but jumped out of my skin. 'I'll give you something to ease the pain, help you sleep. You'll feel better when you wake.' He walked to a cupboard, unlocked its door, and then he unlocked a small box inside it. Beside us again, he handed me one of his phials. I thanked him and downed its contents in one.

A great wind whipped at the window. A log moved in the fire.

The bastarding English, who are they *in nome di merda?*'

And this is the last thing I remember saying. I fell into a stupor; I wouldn't call it sleep. My brain was filled to overflowing; there was no space to fit in any more.

CHAPTER FIFTY-FOUR

I was drowning in an icy river. I tried to swim to its surface but my arms wouldn't move. Nor my feet. Nor any other part of me. It was as if a boulder was tied around my waist. And then warmth enfolded me, arms were holding me tight ... A voice whispered above me and my heart started beating and leapt.

'You've been here all this time?'

I would have told him that it didn't matter now I was with him. But I thought such words could not be spoken to men.

He lit the candle; it guttered, and flared up into the darkness, and then he helped me sit. My wimple had fallen onto my shoulders. Only God was permitted to see me with my head uncovered, but I didn't care.

He ran his fingers through my stubbly hair. 'I'm so sorry... but something's happened.'

I could but stare at him.

The flame lit his face. 'Look,' he said, 'it's like this, the Fra called my master to the church. But it was a trick. He wasn't there. The Abbess was, though. She started screaming. She wanted to let the world think he'd...' he seemed to be struggling to find the right word, '...attacked her.'

This was too much for me. 'But, I thought she liked him. I thought she liked him very much.'

'That's what she wanted us all to think. But it was part of some plan. She wanted him back in the dungeon. But we got away. And now we're in hiding. He's escaping the city when the storm ends.'

A fearful despair welled up inside me. They were leaving.

'But I'm not. Not until I get Francesca out of that place. They can go ahead; I'll follow.'

A wave of unbounded relief. But he was still going to leave me.

'And, while I'm at it, I'm going to find out what that nest of vipers is up to.'

And then I remembered. I picked up the scroll and placed it between us. 'I took it from their table. It might be what they were talking about with the man Volsini.'

We knelt beside each other. 'Go on,' he said, and as I unrolled it he fixed down its corners with bowls and a rule. When it was flattened, he picked up the candle and held it close to the paper. I could read and was familiar with pictures; Jonah inside the whale's belly, the burning bush, the good Samaritan stopped on the road whilst other travellers pass him by, Adam and Eve expelled from the garden, as I think I might have told you already. But the drawing I saw now meant nothing to me. It seemed but a series of lines joined together, and the words beside them were not Latin. Nor were they like Signor Baldassare's strange marks.

Tomma traced his fingers across it, just as the English had done. We sat for a moment in silence. I knew he was thinking. Then he said, 'It's the Villa Favoni.'

I didn't understand.

'Look,' he pointed, 'here's the entrance, here's the main chamber, the kitchen on the right.' The series of squares set beside it represented the second floor, five rooms on one side, windows on the other. And then, up again, to the third floor.

And as I followed his finger, a picture formed in my mind. He was right, it was Francesca's house; the garden at its front, at its end a square, with sketched beside it a little stick horse. I bent further towards it... four more squares, set out in a line. The stables... it was the stable yard.

Now he pointed at two lines set close together, drawn out in red, rather than black like the others. 'I think it's a tunnel. Look,' he drew his finger along it, 'it leads from the stables right up to the kitchen.'

Another silence then he said, 'What are they doing with this? We had one mystery, now we have two. But perhaps we don't. Perhaps they're part of the same one.'

Did he mean that the English and Signor Baldassare were linked in some way?

'The third on the right... and they'll have to search carefully through it.' He had remembered my words? I couldn't have even myself. He traced his finger back up to the squares representing the rooms set on the second floor. Along one, two, three. Then he said, 'It's where Francesca found the books.'

We stared at each other. 'It doesn't make sense.'

'But it must,' he closed his eyes as if better trying to think. 'We just don't know how yet. I have to get in there.' He opened them, and then he said, 'I'm going now.'

But he couldn't, not all by himself. I wouldn't let him. And so I said, 'I'm coming with you.'

'No Sofia.'

'I don't care what you say. There's no point in arguing.' Something in my voice must have told him I meant it. But then I had a flash of memory; that thing trying to clamber over the gate. 'But what about the dogs?'

'If the map's right, and the tunnel's close to the stable yard, we can go through it. Then it's only a little way to the kitchen.' He put his arms around me. 'I just need to get a few things.' rolled up the chart. 'But first we have to get this back to the English before they find out it's gone.'

'I'll take it now. You only need wait for me, I won't be long.'

He touched my hand. 'We'll go together.'

'No. The guards know me. It's safer if I'm alone.'

'I'm not sure.'

'Look,' I said, 'time's passing. The longer we sit here...'

At first I thought he would not be persuaded but then, 'If you're sure. But don't put yourself in any danger.' He kissed my head, 'and get out of there as fast as you can.'

The blizzard still raged as we made our way across the campo. Past the sentries and through the gate. Tomma stopped at the snow-covered mound of the temple. He struggled to shout above the wind. 'Meet me here. And Sofia,' he touched my face, 'be careful.'

The beggars and destitutes who had come into the courtyard for shelter, now sat safely inside the door. In the confusing huddle of bodies, it was easy to slip past the guards.

Through the labyrinth as fast as I could. I reached

the chamber, opened the door the tiniest bit and peeping through it into the room could but thank the Dear Lord that it was empty. I took the chart from my habit and put it back on the table, exactly where it had been before. Then I ran back all the way to the hall. The guards were too busy to notice as I pushed past the sheltering people out onto the courtyard.

The wind had died down but still had power to whip the snow into whirling spirals. Tomma's shape emerged from the blur.

'Praise God,' he said. He wrapped a cloak around my old threadbare one. It was thick and warm. 'It's Guido's. He won't be needing it just at the moment.' He pulled up its hood. 'I borrowed a couple of things from the kitchen.' He took a knife from the folds of his own cloak, and a cloth parcel.

What was it?

'Just wait,' he said. 'You'll see. I got the idea from my master.'

He put his arm around me and held me close. I felt myself shaking, but not with fright.

'Come on then,' he said. 'Let's get ourselves down there.'

We clung onto each other for balance, the campo behind us, the wind shrieking like phantoms, the cold searing into our faces. There wasn't a soul to be seen in the alley, all were snug and warm indoors. Through cracks in shutters came the glittering flicker of fires, which helped light our way. Often we'd slide out of each other's grasps, and when I fell, which was often, Tomma pulled me back onto my feet. He might have been almost as small as I, but he was strong.

We turned off the alley; through the storm the house rose up before us like an icy apparition. Keeping tight hold of each other, we reached the garden wall and began to make our way around it. If we had thought the snow deep before, now it reached above our knees; you can't imagine how hard it was to wade our way through it. An owl hooted, but apart from that all was as silent as before. At last we reached the stable gate. It was bolted. Tomma cursed and stood for a moment; I knew he was thinking, and taking his arm from its grip around my waist, he knelt down and started to scrape at the snow piled against it. It turned to ice as he dug. By now I had lost all feeling in my feet and I feared greatly for him, but he persevered, and after long moments, had cleared a space big enough to wriggle through. This required lying flat on the newly formed ice. I helped him slide under it. And then it was my turn. I stretched my hands out towards him; he took them in his and pulled me through to the other side.

The first part of our mission completed, I followed him to the end of the stable yard. A low whinnying came from one of the stalls. I could but pray that no one had heard it.

'I think it's round about here.' With that, he began to tear at the frozen ivy clinging to what seemed like a fence; it snapped and fell onto our heads. And there it was. He took a candle stub from his cloak and struck his flint, lighting a burrow-like space barely large enough to enter, and we were small. Tomma went first, I close behind him, clambering through a musty smell of tree roots and earth. We must have shuffled about a hundred paces along it before he snuffed the flame and we stepped back out into darkness. He had been right in his reckoning; we were close to the

kitchen. Grasping hands, we ran towards it, were almost there, when a shape hurled out of the darkness. I froze in utter terror, but not Tomma. Pushing himself in front of me, he took what I could but perceive as being a chunk of meat from his parcel and tossed it behind us. Only a moment's distraction, but enough to let us race to the door.

But the Saints were not with us; it was locked. He crashed his shoulder against it, it wouldn't budge. I felt my heart race as, taking the knife from the waist of his breeches, he set about the lock on the shutter. It sprung open and we scrambled through it, a blood-curling howling too close behind us.

From outside, the house had seemed deserted, but embers of a fire smouldered in the grate, food lay on the table, tattered clothes hung on a line, from which came a stench of unwashed bodies. Its glow was enough to lead us some way along the passage, my hand gripped very tightly in his. We didn't dare light the candle, and so when the feeble glimmer faded behind us, we crept along it, groping the walls to steady ourselves and had almost reached the corridor when Tomma stopped in his tracks so abruptly he all but toppled me over. Unable to see much but darkness, he must have heard something. I strained to listen, but all seemed perfectly silent to me. A moment passed before he took my hand again and led me onward, judging the number of steps to the stairway. It creaked as we climbed. We reached the first floor. A gleam of white from the snowy garden seeped through the gaps in the shutter and we could see again.

And now out of the silence came a small sound, not unlike a mewing kitten. We turned to each other not daring to hope, but there was no time for even a whisper for from the far end of the corridor came another, like the scratching of nails upon marble. Tomma grabbed me, hurtling us through the door nearest to us. He shut it behind us, as softly as the moment allowed, and we stood in darkness again, not daring to breathe. But forced to at last we were hit by a smell so sharp, so acrid, so pungent our throats seemed to shrink. We didn't dare cough or make a sound. I felt my lungs fill with the noxious vapour, and my eyes started streaming. Tomma took the candle stub from the fold of his cloak and struck the flint. Its flame danced about us, falling upon a large shape set on the floor a little way from us. One hesitant step towards it, Tomma behind me, the overpowering reek of vinegar making our heads swim. The candle flickered and died. He cursed. He found his flint and lit it again, one more step, then another. It was larger than first I had thought, and wrapped in a blanket. Tomma reached down and pulled it aside, and what did we see gaping up at us as if in blind terror, mouth open, white hair standing up from his head, but the old signore's face. We stared at each other in shock, Tomma's expression melted with disgust. In my work with Sister Agata I had seen many dead bodies crawling with maggots, but it was clear that he had not.

I dragged him away and after listening to make as sure as I could that the coast was clear, I opened the door very slowly. But we didn't get further, for without any warning a shape flew towards us. Or, to be more precise, towards Tomma. It knocked him sideways. There was a crack as his head hit the wall. He slid down it, and the beast was upon him. I stood back, able only to watch as it reared up, fangs white in the eerie light. The gate flashed into my mind, the monstrous dog climbing onto its railings, and something most peculiar happened; I felt myself fill with fury. I cannot think I possessed enough strength... but I must have. Tearing a flagpole from the wall, I lashed out, striking at it with all my might. A growling sound. I struck again, this time with such force it split in two. It let go of its grip on Tomma and turned towards me, rearing up, ready to pounce, and fuelled by what I can but describe as raging frenzy I plunged the splintered shard into its belly.

It quivered and slumped down upon Tomma. Only now did I feel myself shaking. An abject and creeping horror filled me, but I wasn't about to give up. Summoning what strength was left to me, I took hold of its legs and pulled. The slime of blood helped it slide to the floor.

Horror turned to panic; I couldn't be sure it was dead. I put my ear to Tomma's chest and thanked sweet Gesù for he was still breathing. I had to get him away, more dogs might come lurching towards us at any moment. And so I slapped him.

His eyes opened, and after a moment he mumbled something.

I rubbed his poor face, 'You're all right,' though this was more wishful thinking than fact.

'What?' his voice was stronger now.

'Remember,' I whispered, 'we're here. In the house.'

A moment more and he nodded.

'We have to get out.' I pointed at the monster stretched out beside him and helped him clamber to his feet, and holding his arm around my neck with one hand, the candle stump in the other, we stumbled together down the stairway. Through the passage into the kitchen; he seemed less confused by this time. I could but pray thanks we did not have to climb back through the window, it was simply a case of unlocking the door.

I blew out the flame and, fast as we could, we made our way to the tunnel. The stable yard now... sliding under the gate. But first I pushed the candle through it.

At the other side, I took his flint, lit it again and held it to his eyes. His pupils reacted as Sister Agata had told us they should if the patient had suffered no damage.

He stood for a moment, then, 'You saved me. God Sofia, you saved me.'

He wrapped his arms around me, and I wrapped mine around him. And we waded through the snow, out onto the alley.

I don't know how we got to the campo, but somehow we did. And there we stopped, still holding tight to each other.

The guard came towards us, his lantern a beacon in the swirling darkness. I'd never been so happy to see him.

'Thank you, signore,' I smiled up at him when the palace gates opened. 'We can manage from here.'

And now, safe inside them, Tomma took my hand, and led me forward towards the snowy mound of the temple. We had just about reached it when two figures emerged from the darkness; it was clear they were coming from the palace. We stepped into the shadows. One had a hood pulled over his face and the other... Tomma looked at me in a desperate way, 'Volsini,' he whispered.

Just then the other man's hood blew back and his earring shone out in the darkness.

A moment passed, then another. 'I think I know who he is,' said Tomma.

*He led me to the little building, knocked the snow from
the door and pulling it open, struck his flint and touched its
flame to the wick of a lamp. It flared up, lighting a circular
space with a ceiling that disappeared into blackness. Pallets
lay upon the floor with furs spread upon them. With barely
strength left, we slumped down upon one. Tomma pulled
me close to him.*

'You saved me,' he said again. Then, 'What happened?'

'That thing... attacked you. I hit it with a flagpole.'

He shook his head. '...Sofia.'

'I was so angry.'

He smiled. 'I don't think you're really a nun.'

'What am I then?'

*'A champion of the arena?' He placed a finger on my
lips. Something I might have then called emotion, but now I
know is desire, welled up inside me and I had to concentrate
hard in order to hear what he said next.*

*'The old man. Who killed him? That's what I want to
know.'*

*Why was he asking? Wasn't it clear? 'Signor Baldassare,
of course.'*

*'No, it wasn't him,' which seemed a strange thing to
say. I would have asked why he thought this, but had not
the strength. A fearful trembling had taken me over.*

*'I think we need something to calm us.' A flagon stood
on the floor beside us. He tricked some of its liquid into a
bowl and handed it to me. 'You first.'*

*I took a gulp. It burned my throat. But in a moment a
feeling of calmness flowed through me. I handed it back to
him, he did the same. And then he said, 'That whimpering
sound.' I had not dared put my thoughts into words... but*

he did. 'It was a baby...'

We sat in silence for a moment. Wild thoughts filled my head.

But his were practical. 'It has to be with her. It can't just be there on its own. Babies don't survive without care. And what wet nurse would be crazy enough to venture within a mile of that place?'

I wished I could be as sure. 'But how can she manage there, all alone?'

'She's not. Dosolina will be with her... but we'll get her out. We'll get them both out. It should be fairly straightforward; and now there's only the dogs to contend with, the guards have gone. Something made them leave... very quickly. That meal on the table, the clothes hanging up.'

We sat for a moment, then he said, 'Drink some more.' He placed the bowl back into my hands. 'It'll help you.'

And as I gulped another fiery mouthful, 'There's something else, Sofia... back there in the house. When I stopped in the passage. It was because I remembered. That woman... that nun... the one I thought was your friend. Now I know where I saw her. It wasn't the convent. It was there, in the house.' I could but stare at him. What was he saying? 'I caught her listening at our door. She was wearing a black shift and she had a white cap on her head. That's what confused me.' And as if this were not enough, 'That man we saw in the courtyard. The one with Volsini. I think his name is di Fassa. There's no time to tell you why. Have you seen him before?'

I took a deep breath; he was the one I had told him about, who translated their words for the Chamberlain.

He thought a little more. 'One thing's for sure, you're

not going back to them. Ever again. Stay here, you'll be safe... and I'll come tomorrow.'

He put his arms around me again. Something stirred inside me. I longed for him to hold me closer, and he did. He pulled me down, and we lay together on the furs. He undid my wimple and smoothed my stubbly hair. 'You are so beautiful,' he said.

I couldn't believe him; Francesca was beautiful, not I.

He looked at me with great tenderness, then he pressed his lips against mine. His mouth was warm and strong. A great emotion filled me; I felt that I wanted to cry.

And then he said words I had never heard spoken before. 'I love you, Sofia.'

My heart seemed to stop. He looked deep into my eyes. 'I have since the first time I saw you. That day in the convent,' he gave a little smile. 'I thank God for all that happened before then, for it led me to you. And I have only one thing to ask. Will you come with me when we leave?'

He was asking me to come with him.

'I don't know what's going to happen, where we'll end up. But wherever it is, we'll be together. It's all that matters...'

So overwhelmed was I, I couldn't find voice to answer.

'...At least to me.'

He touched my tears. 'Please say these mean yes.'

When he had gone, I put my finger to my lips and tried to feel his kiss again. The thought that soon he'd be gone had been too much of a deep hurt to suffer.

But he was taking me with him.

CHAPTER FIFTY-FIVE

I woke to the sound of crackling logs. A fire glowed in the pewter light. What was this place? Memory slowly seeped into my brain; the church, the Abbess, her wide, screaming mouth, Tomma, Ivan Kovac. My agony. But now all pain had left me. I lay, summoning strength to wake Tomma, though only now do I know that I wouldn't have found him, for one simple reason – he wasn't there.

The storm battered and ebbed at the window, then would come silence, then screeching again. And it was in one of those soundless lulls I heard it, the faintest tinkling.

Forget about summoning strength, I was on my feet in a moment, trying to follow the sound when the storm calmed enough to let it be heard. Judging it to come from the end of the room, I crept towards it, hardly daring to breathe. Past a small table, a cluster of chairs and there, by the light of the fire, I saw a door. By now you'll know me to be an impetuous fellow, which, if Tomma had chosen to tell me, would have said lay at the feet of my troubles. I pushed it. It opened, and I found myself in a narrow corridor with burning sconces set on its wall. And here, sealed off from the storm, plunged into an even more heady scent of roses, all was silent but for the tinkling. Treading as softly as I was able, I made my way along it, the taunting sound growing louder. Well, perhaps not louder, but clearer.

It came to an end. So far there had been no sign of a door, so, pressing my hand against the wall, I retraced my steps but a little way when I felt its surface change from rough plaster to smooth; a discrepancy sure to be lost on anyone who had not spent their whole life with the stuff. It was a panel, no doubt about it. I pushed it. It opened. Inside was a thick velvet curtain. I drew it aside. A small, veiled figure turned around, startled, as the greyhounds at her feet flew at me, the bells on their collars drowned out by their yelping.

I stood in wonderment as through the silvery fabric shrouding her face, I caught a glimpse of forehead, of cheek and of neck. Her hair, the shade of an owl's wing, hung in coils below the edge of her veil. I tried to catch hold of my thoughts but they dashed about my head, thumping and walloping into each other, before deserting my brain.

I had died after all; was trapped in some kind of hell where day is night, night day, up down, down up, and veiled women lurk behind walls.

Taking a cautious step towards her, I managed, somehow, to find my voice. 'Please... I am Simone da Benno.' She tilted her head, and with this movement I caught a faint glimpse of her face. 'And, might I ask who you are, my lady?' this was not a time for niceties.

'My name is Irena,' and with those words the world seemed to crash in around me. When you think of monsters, what does your mind conjure up; a gorgon, as Anna had said, or some fearsome creature. But she was neither.

I tried to pull myself together. 'I beg your forgiveness,

I'm not here to harm you. I heard a sound. I only wanted to find out what it was... where it came from.' She did not reply, and so on I stumbled. 'The bells on your dogs' collars... I heard them in the church. I was curious.'

'Such a little sound... and you heard them? I thought I was safe behind the wall. No one could see me and so I supposed they could not hear me. But it seems I was wrong.' Her voice was rich and warm, her words born of a place far away. 'There's a space behind it you see, a hole is pierced through it. And a hidden door with a passage leads here, to my chamber. It's how my steward was able to enter and leave the church with such ease.'

Ivan Kovac was her steward?

'It must once have been used for spying, but now it seems to be forgotten. You might ask what I was doing there. And the answer... watching you.'

I tried to keep a calm expression as she went on, '...as you pained the fresco.' And when still I said nothing, 'The truth is I saw you on the campo, all that time ago now, amongst the other contenders. You were different.'

Tomma had been right then, as ever.

'You intrigued me and so I found myself doing something that never I could have imagined; I told my husband's Chamberlain to add your name to his list. He had sights on another... I had to insist.'

I'd had many a champion in my life but never one as enchanting.

'I thank you, my lady, with all my heart.' And as if it were leading me forward, I moved closer to her, so close that our arms touched. Her perfume of roses stirred me greatly.

Soft lips, hair curling in ringlets or straight as a

waterfall; black, fair or cinnabar. Pale eyes, dark eyes, small noses, straight noses, tiny waists, plump breasts or tiny like buds; such tangible delights till now had, I believed, caused me to be a lover of women. But are not all men thus, craving simply what they can see? Only a blind man would be insensible to such sensations. But I was not blind. I could not see her, knew naught of the form of her breasts, her neck or her eyes, yet...

I had to force myself to listen. 'Before you were brought to his chamber, I hid behind the hangings. And then your apprentice unrolled your drawings... and I was lost. You're touched by the hand of God, Signor Benno. I did not care what sin I might be forced to commit to have you paint our fresco. And when you jumped from the window...'

Gesu Cristo, she'd seen the whole fucking thing.

'I was sure you had killed yourself. Ivan tried to find you, but you were nowhere to be seen. I cannot describe my distress. You were gone and I was left with no more than an image of what might have been. And when I heard they had caught you, had you locked in the dungeon, I ordered your release.'

The mystery was unravelled; I knew it now. 'It was you who saved my life, lady.' I pulled the eye-bead from my tunic. 'And it was you who gave me this?'

'It was meant to protect you against all that is evil. But it failed you. I am sorry.'

I had to explain. 'I didn't... attack ... her.' I meant the Abbess.

'I know,' she said. 'I was there when it happened, behind the wall. I saw her come into the church and hide in the shadows. It was clear she was up to no good. It's why I sent Ivan to help you. But your boy got to you first.'

I stood, as if dumb, as she spoke.

'She's loathsome. They all are. They're not what they pretend to be, but of course you must know that by now. Why set out on a pilgrimage at this time of year? And go the wrong way to Assisi? And why appear at the very time my husband and his father are gone from the city? And then there's the Abbess; her manner, her dress. I could not conceive that even in England holy rules are so carelessly flaunted.'

'Who are they, then, my lady. And why are they here?'

'I wish I could tell you. But whatever the reason, my husband's Chamberlain is involved. He pretends to be a stranger to them, but he's not. What a shock you gave him when he realised you spoke their language, understood what they were saying. It was I who told him to have you to translate their words at the banquet. I hid then too, and listened, and watched.' She gave a little laugh. 'You did not disappoint me. You upset their plans. Which is why they wanted you back in the dungeon.'

'But you would have rescued me, would you not?'

'How would I have known what they had done with you? They'd have been careful, after I helped you the first time. And even then, I only found out you were there when Signor Baldassare told me.'

I need not explain the effect of these words. But she saw it.

'You did not know?'

Language lost to me, I could but shake my head.

'He came to plead for you. He brought your portrait.'

What did she mean?

'Of the Lady Francesca.'

This stunned me as much as a broadsword smashing down on my head... That's what Anna had seen him carrying.

'It's beautiful. She's blessed indeed.'

'I'm confused, my lady.'

'He told me that it had been painted by a man called Simone da Benno, a name that meant much to me. That you had been employed by his master. He wished to show me your skill, but there was no need for I had seen it already. He begged me to let you paint the fresco, but first I'd have to find you. I did not know what he meant. But then he explained. Volsini's men had taken you prisoner, you were locked up somewhere here, in the palace. I knew nothing about this, of course.'

She saw my reaction. I shook myself. 'But why the...' I adapted my words, '...on earth would he want to save me? He wasn't a friend. In fact, I thought him exactly the opposite.'

And what did she say but, 'Then you were mistaken.'

'Perhaps you're as crazy as you seem,' might have been the more honest reply.

'I am sorry, it would take me too long to explain and time is against me.

'I wish you could stay with us, Signor Benno.'

'Benno. Just Benno.'

'But you have to go. Before my husband returns. If it's a choice of believing your story or hers, you are a dead man. And I don't want you to die.'

A blurred glimpse of her face through her veil.

'We must get you away. When the storm passes,

Ivan will get horses and take you to the foot of the hill. I overheard your plans for Naples.'

'I'll come back, my lady, I promise.'

Had she been an ordinary mortal, I would have pulled her to me. But she wasn't, and I couldn't find the courage.

'I shall pray every day till you do.'

And with that, Ivan Kovac appeared at the door and I knew he'd been waiting behind it.

CHAPTER FIFTY-SIX

I said nothing to him, nor did he to me, as he led me back into the chamber. And there he left me alone. The blizzard still battered against the windowpanes, the fire still crackled. I sat slumped before it, mind racing, trying to pull my thoughts back into my head but they whizzed around it with such velocity I could do naught but let them; how to make sense of what had just happened, of the Lady Irena, her shrouded form, her perfume, her arm against mine... her strange and beautiful voice. I could barely turn my mind to thoughts of Baldassare. Yet I had to. He had saved me. But why? Why had he saved me?

Those simple words, 'Then you were mistaken' hit me with force. I was struck by a deep sense of shame. All this time we had been wrong about him. So wrong... I owed him my life, just as I did to the Lady Irena.

And what about Francesca; she had been wrong about him too. Just as she had about Donato. Wild thoughts swarmed my brain. I picked up my cloak. I would slip away without telling Tomma. I had put him through enough already.

The guard didn't stop me at the door, what's more, he pushed open a metal fence-like barrier to let me go back out into the corridor, and it occurred to me that he was there to take stock only of those wishing to enter his lady's chamber, not those who were leaving. In this unknown part of the palace, I made a few wrong turns before I found myself in the passage smelling of beeswax. I strode along it, my face turned downwards. But I needn't have bothered for it was empty, as always. Left at its end and down the narrow steps, the putrid stench of piss stronger with every step. The dungeon door now. I kicked it, with a deal of ferocity I might add. Moments passed then came a sound of jangling. When after long moments it opened, it was not my own shrivelled fly-speck standing before me but a tall creature who had much in common with a scarecrow. He opened his toothless mouth, at least they owned this one feature in common, but before he could enquire as to what I might want, I said in a sullen tone, 'Where's your friend?'

'What friend, signore?' which was a fair question; I couldn't imagine he had any.

'The withered one.'

'Not here tonight.'

'Where is he?'

'Dunno, signore.'

Snowflakes floated down through slats in the grate above his head, but his skull was too thick for him to notice.

'Will I say you was lookin' for 'im?'

I crashed up the steps without providing an answer and pulling my hood over my face, passed the guard on the door, and out I went, into the courtyard. After the warmth of the palace, the blast of freezing wind hit me hard. I wrapped my cloak tight around me and set off for the kitchen. And, just at that moment, the morning Angelus started to toll.

CHAPTER FIFTY-SEVEN

When he left me, I fell into a state of oblivion; I wouldn't call it sleep. And when I felt myself rise into wakefulness, I plunged myself back into that place of bliss where I could feel his arms around me, his mouth upon mine, that part of his body forbidden even to know existed filling me with exquisite tenderness.

And somewhere above, I heard the morning Angelus toll.

CHAPTER FIFTY-EIGHT

The place was empty but for a dozing boy. I slammed the door behind me, causing him to jump from his stool.

It's hard to sound friendly at such an hour, but I did my best. 'I wonder if you can help me?'

He screwed up his eyes and peered at me, blearily. Yes, they were right, he was a madman, wandering around at this godawful hour giving people frights.

Madman was one thing, but at least it seemed he knew nothing about my supposed crime or the fact that I should have been far from the city, not here in the kitchen asking for favours.

'I wonder if you could lend me a knife?' I continued, as if this were the most usual of requests. 'A sharp one.' But perhaps I should do a little by way of explaining... or of lying. 'We need to cut some rope and seem to have lost ours. We're terribly muddled, you know.'

Muddled? Was that the name for it?

Darting from his stool, it being clear he wanted to see the back of me just as soon as he could, he scrabbled about in a box on a table and held two aloft. 'This one, signore? Or that?'

I took them both and, thrusting them into the band of

my breeches, was out of the door and halfway up the steps before he could bid me a joyous farewell.

Down the frozen alley, battling against the driving wind and the agonising pain in my shoulder, thoughts of the Lady Irena filling my mind, the blinding snow whirling around me with such force that on reaching the bend in the lane's turning had I not known the house to be but a few steps ahead, I might have stumbled past it.

A ball of light swelled up through the swirling eddies. Gripped with a desperate horror, I tried to run, but the snow would not let me. I reached the gate. It was open. I didn't give a thought to dogs. Or my plan, if I'd had one. Through the portal. The door and…*Gesu Cristo*…

A great heat filled the hall. I took the knives from the belt of my breeches and made my cautious way towards the fierce glow and crackling and sparking of fire. The door of the dining chamber was open, framing a scene much like Dante's description of hellfire. Flames raged in the chimney so violently I thought the very house might be set alight. And as if not content with the size of the inferno, Baldassare stood stoking it, tossing the contents of one of the drum-like boxes into the blaze.

Unbelieving of what I was seeing before me, I held the knives out at arm's length and took a few steps forward. Sensing a presence behind him, he could have heard naught above the crackling inferno, he turned. With no way of knowing that this was more precaution than precursor to an act of violence on my part, he held up his hand as if to delay me from plunging them into some part of his body. And just as he did, a small figure pushed between us. All those times when I'd thought myself caught in a nightmare… but this was a real one. I laughed. 'Wake Benno... you're dreaming.'

'Sire,' Tomma said, in a steady voice, and I knew I wasn't.

Baldassare stood gaping at me, and in that desperate moment, forgetting what the Lady Irena had told me regarding the fact that he'd saved me, my mind worked too fast. I could but think he'd captured my boy, somehow, taken him hostage... defying my shoulder's disinclination to do my bidding, I lunged forward and held the blade to his neck.

I had only just committed this routine act when there came a 'No, Benno. Stop!' and who did I see before me now, not the Francesca of old, but a thin and drawn-looking waif.

I let go of my grip and as Tomma seized the knives from my hands, she threw her arms around me. 'It's not his fault. None of it is. Oh Benno.'

I held her close and felt, not the glorious plumpness of her belly, but the bones beneath her skin. At least, thank God, she was alive.

'You must help Giacomo, he's been protecting us all this time.' He was Giacomo now? Had I truly lost my mind?

'She's right, sire.' Tomma was peering up at me with very great consternation.

What, *per la sacra amore di Dio?*

'It's like this,' he started, the familiar steadiness of his voice doing much to calm me. 'I came here after midnight, when you were asleep... When Ivan Kovac said we were leaving, I could only think of Francesca. I had one last chance to find her. There's no time to tell you more. Something's happened, the English are coming...'

As if all this were not enough to get my head around,

now he was saying the English were coming.

'They're coming, sire, to raid the house.'

He turned to Baldassare, who stood stock still, face spectral with shock, sticks of kindling still in his hands. Only now did I see it was not the usual type of tinder but fragments of the drum-like boxes piled beside him one on top of the other.

Tomma pointed. 'We have to break them up, burn them before they get here. Quick sire, you have to help us.'

Like a man fallen into a spell-bound trance, I released Francesca from my arms. I had no idea why, but if Tomma said burn them, that's what I'd do. I took one of the boxes and pulled off its lid. But when I saw its contents, my stomach heaved, for there upon a layer of leaves was a wriggling mass of maggots. A sweet smell wafted up from them.

I stood in utter stupefaction, trying to make sense of what I was seeing.

'They're silkworms,' informed Tomma.

And when he got no response, 'Do you not know?'

Still I stood.

'They're worth a fortune. A thousand fortunes. It's how silk is made. From these. All Christendom is after them… It's why they want them, to take them to England… not the actual worms themselves. But, sire, there's no time to explain,' and with that he took the box and emptied the whole lot of them into the fire. They sputtered and spat as the flames lapped up to consume the fat, squirming shapes, the honey smell so strong it all but overwhelmed me.

At that very moment, a ragamuffin ran into the room door, his arms around more boxes. He stopped in his tracks when he saw me. 'Oh Signor Benno,' so thin had Fortunato become, only his voice let me know it was him.

When all the worms and shards of boxes were burned, I drew Francesca to me. She buried her face in my shoulder. Baldassare – or should I now call him Giacomo – turned to Tomma. 'It's time for the books.' He looked so bleak, so desolate, as if his world had come to an end. 'It breaks my heart to let them go. But if the English get their hands on them...'

'I'll bring them,' said Fortunato, who having only just run into the room, ran back out of it again.

Tomma might have known what books had to do with the problem at hand, but not me; I hadn't the vaguest notion what they were talking about.

'The one with the symbols, but there are others too.' And just as before, 'We don't have time, we'll tell you later.'

He turned to Baldassare. 'But I've been thinking. Couldn't we hide them?'

He received a desperate look in return. 'I thought of that too. There's the attic, or one of the stables, but they're not secure and we can't risk taking them with us. If it were only me, but there's Francesca, and to be caught with them, well you know what they'd do to us. There's nothing else for it, we have to get rid of them, then we must get us away, before it's too late. But where can we go? And where can we take Francesca?' He put the questions to Tomma, my counsel clearly being of no value.

'There's always the convent.'

'The convent.' Baldassare's face flooded with joy. 'Yes, the convent.'

'And what about the cave for the books?' added Tomma.

'It's as good a place as any, don't you think, sire?' He turned to me, as if seeking my approval. I was grateful as ever for his salvaging of my dignity, even though it was clear that, unlike his master, he was in charge of proceedings. I could but thank God that at least one of us had a grasp of the situation.

Baldassare gaped at him. 'What cave, signorino?'

'Remember. We went there to find my master.'

Now it was Fortunato's turn. He had reappeared with what I could but think was the last of the boxes, devoid of worms, now filled with books. 'We can take the pony. The guards stole the horses.' This he said to Tomma. 'But we still have him. He's in the stable. I'll go for him now.'

'If only I had my own horse,' said Baldassare. He turned to Francesca and spoke to her gently. 'Get the baby.'

This was the first time I had thought of such things. She took a step towards the door but stumbled. She'd never get all the way up the stairs and back down them again with a baby. Tomma and Baldassare forced her to sit and I went instead.

I found the door to her chamber and turned the handle. A small figure stood in the muted darkness, her shrunken silhouette barely discernible.

'Oh Signore!' cried Dosolina when she saw me. 'Oh Signore.'

I took her in my arms. 'It's all right. You're safe now.'

At which a small whimper came from behind us; she stepped aside and I saw a basket set on the floor, a tiny mite inside it. It stretched its trembling arms and bawled.

'We have to be quick,' I told her. 'We're leaving.'

And on hearing this news, she gave a great wail; a joyful

one to be certain. 'Thank you, signore. Oh thank you!'

Baby in my good arm, my other one, agonising in the extreme, all but carrying Dosolina, we made our cautious way down the stairs. And with her mistress now safely back in her charge, she asked, 'Where are we going, my lady?'

'Benno is taking us to the convent.' It was clear she was trying to control her emotions. 'Sofia's there.' At this an uneasy expression crossed Tomma's face. '...and Sister Agata. All will be well.'

'But I can't,' she stared at us in horror. 'I'll never make it. All that way down the mountain.'

'Please Dosolina.'

'No. No. I can't, my lady. I shall stay here. They won't harm an old woman.'

'Don't worry, madama.' Tomma stepped forward. 'I'll take you somewhere safe. It's not far away.'

What was he talking about? He wasn't going anywhere without me.

By now the baby was shrieking. Tomma took the little creature from me and put it into Francesca's arms.

The shrieking increased.

I knelt in front of her and spoke gently, 'We have to go now. Are you ready?'

'But Benno? You seem in pain.' Baldassare's ordeal had not dulled his judgement. 'It's your shoulder again, I do not doubt it.'

And when I admitted it was, Fortunato was sent back out of the door, and up the stairs to fetch a potion. It came in a bottle the length of my palm. 'One sip at a time. And not too often.'

Had he not been watching, I would have swallowed the

whole sodding lot.

'It'll take a while, but it will work, I assure you.'

Thanking all the gods, and Baldassare too, I took a slug and tucked the bottle into the band of my breeches and did the same with the knives.

Thus it was that a few moments later we passed through the white and silent garden, 'we' being the black and white pony, with whom, since the day of the loading of the boxes onto the cart, we were already acquainted, upon which sat Francesca, ashen-faced; Dosolina shuffling behind it holding tight to its tail; Fortunato, leading it forward; Tomma and Baldassare, for I could not at this late date in the proceedings think of him as Giacomo, with sacks slung over their shoulders filled with the books; the precious one as I was to learn soon wrapped in thick fabric and hidden inside Baldassare's tunic. And I, my shoulder still too painful to undertake such labour, with the tiny wailing bundle tucked inside my jerkin.

We stopped at the gate. Tomma put his arm around Dosolina, gently prising her grip from the pony's tail. My protestations about going nowhere without me had clearly fallen on deaf ears. But where was he taking her?

'The temple, sire. Someone is there who can help her.'

'What someone?'

'The little nun,' he whispered. 'The one you asked me about.'

In normal times I would have replied what, *in nome di Sacro Cristo?* But times were not normal. I took his elbow and led him aside.

'I'm coming with you. We'll be up there and back in no time. Baldassare can hold the fort in the meantime.'

He gave me one of his looks. 'It's not a good idea, sire. You need to get Francesca away. As you say, it won't take long to get up there, and then I'll come back down the hill and find you.'

Strange that in moments like these, requiring of all your concentration, unrelated thoughts burst into your mind. Mention of the temple and, '*Dio*, Tomma. The boys...' I had forgotten about them again.

He glanced up at me. 'Don't worry, sire, they're safe, just as Ivan Kovac said. A servant brought them to the chamber. I told them what had happened. That you were injured but had been treated and were asleep in another room. That you should not be disturbed. That we were going when the blizzard stopped, but that I had to leave them for a while. That there was something I needed to do before we went.'

And for the umpteenth time I could but thank my lucky stars; what would my life have been without him?

'I'll take that then,' I pointed to his sack.

He looked at the bulging shape of the baby inside my jerkin. 'No,' he said, 'it's safer with Fortunato.'

Out of the shelter of the garden, though the storm had calmed to a shrieking wind, it was still so loud we could not hear ourselves speak, which meant I would have to wait till we reached the cave before I could ask Baldassare what in *nome di cazzo* had been going on all this time – worms, symbols, the English, why he had saved me, what the old man was up to... the thugs in the garden, the dogs.

In other words, the whole shitting story.

I hadn't come up with a plan as to how we'd bluster our way through the gate tower, but, as it happened, luck –

or even the Good Lord – was with us. The guards sat before their brazier, upon which they were roasting chestnuts, picking the blackening, crisping kernels from the glowing coals and peeling their skins away. The smell of them all but drove me crazy; to ask if I might have a couple was a thought too far. 'Get through this day, Benno, and you can eat a sackful.'

So intent were they at their task they simply waved us through, and in no more than a moment we were out of the city.

The wind gusted with force, whirling the snow all around us, stinging our faces as downwards we plodded but the baby seemed strangely comforted by its screeching, and soon she settled to sleep. I found myself liking the feeling of her warm plumpness.

The hill path was much altered from that day in September when its misty blueness had set itself upon the drowsy heat of the mountain. I couldn't remember seeing a convent, but even if I had, in such altered landscape I doubt I would have recognised it.

But first the cave.

After what seemed an eternity of slipping and sliding down the treacherous track, Baldassare shouted, 'It's here, I think.' Thank *Gesu* he knew the mountain, for I could see nothing but a vast whiteness stretching about us in every direction. Gripping each other for balance, we came to a stop. He pointed; what must once have been the bog was now a sheet of ice. But at least there was one consolation; it looked a deal easier to cross than the quagmire it had been in its previous condition. How could I have known, that night in the thunderstorm, what was ahead of us, just as I couldn't have known what was ahead of us now.

I swapped Fortunato's sack for the baby; she seemed quite happy in his arms and we left him and the stalwart little pony, Francesca upon it, in the curve of a rock which gave at least a little protection from the driving wind, and with that Baldassare and I set off across the frozen stretch of lake. We reached the wall of rock, it towered above us, and grappled about for a while, pressing our hands against its surface. '*Figlio di stronzo*', the words froze on my lips. I heard Baldassare say something and presumed he was cursing too, but when I turned I saw he was breaking off streamers of frigid ivy. 'It's here,' he smiled at me, 'thank God,' and he pushed through the crack of the entrance. I followed him as he stepped into the blackness, and there it was again, that pungent smell of earth and rotted leaves. He put his sack gently onto the ground; following his lead, I set Fortunato's beside it. He then struck his flint and touched it to one of the tapers he'd had sense to bring with him, then to another which he handed to me. Light flickered around us; a moment and the ivy-covered walls and the dome stretching upwards swelled into view.

Out of the screeching wind, there was no need to shout. 'I'll find a good place to hide them,' he said, 'then we'll press on to the convent. We'll come back when we're finished. I'll tell you everything then.'

And though 'then' was too long a wait, for I wanted to hear it all now, he was right, this was no time for talking.

He picked up the sacks and stepped away from me, his taper gripped between his teeth but, instead of following, off I set in the other direction. At what I perceived to be the place, I pulled back the curtain of ferns and there he was, diving downwards, arms stretched out like wings. And, as before, emotion hit me. I stood in front of him, holding my breath, lost to the world till a voice echoed behind me, 'What's that you've found?'

'Part of a fresco,' I eventually managed. 'An old one.'

'What is this place?' He was the second one to have said this; no need to remind you the first had been Tomma.

Joy and melancholy filled me; I was too stricken to reply. He saw this and with, 'Come Benno... we have to go,' pulled me gently away from the most wondrous of walls that ever I had been blessed to see, or would ever again.

Across the icy bog, we slid our way back to the sheltering curve of the rock. And with the baby tucked back inside my jerkin, the cave and my plunging angel behind us, Fortunato gripping the pony's bridle, off we set down the last stretch of track, the wind wailing around us, preventing even the sparest of conversation, which was just as well for I was left with my contemplations, but I knew Baldassare understood how deeply I had been moved.

We reached the valley which stretched out into whiteness before us. A little way along it, he pointed and we turned on to what once must have been a pathway, but now was a stretch of unblemished snow. We passed beneath an archway, into a graveyard. Until this moment I had thought of Hell as a hot place. But what if it were cold enough to freeze your very soul? Beyond the graveyard we entered a high walled courtyard with painted upon them, though barely discernible through the falling snow, the stations of the cross. The arm of a statue stretched out in benediction from its blanket of white.

The convent rose up before us; a bell hung by the portal.

Baldassare pulled it.

'You speak, Benno,' he said. 'It's better. I have a... reputation here.'

Some time passed. He pulled it again. A grille opened. Eyes peered out.

'Holy Sister,' I tried to keep my voice calm. 'We bring the Lady Favoni to you for your protection. She seeks sanctuary for she is in mortal danger.'

No longer lulled by the screeching wind, the baby started to whimper. By now Fortunato was helping Francesca scramble down from the pony.

She came to my side, tears frozen on her cheeks, and clinging to me, the baby a fat pillow between us, her voice was a whisper, 'Oh Benno. Oh Benno...'

I did not care about niceties of conduct; I pulled her face to mine and kissed her forehead. I would have put my arms around her, held her close, had it not been for the great studded door clanking open.

At this a nun appeared and made the sign of the cross. I took the baby from my jerkin and, kissing her too, placed her in Francesca's arms, and to the music of screeches and wails they disappeared through it and out of our sight.

I stood for a moment to still my emotions. Fortunato stroked the pony's muzzle and turned to Baldassare. 'We should leave him here, signore. It's better. What would we do with him anyway? The Sisters will be grateful to have him.'

And he was right; what would we do with him? He unhooked a small parcel from its saddle – we had no time, or thought, to wonder what it was – tied the pony's reins to the bell and pulled it again. Without waiting to see peering eyes at the grille, off we set, back through the graveyard, past the snow-laden arm jutting skyward, the stations of the cross, along by the graveyard towards what only memory told us had to be the hill path.

CHAPTER FIFTY-NINE

A voice was whispering, 'Sofia.'

And again, 'Sofia.'

I opened my eyes.

A face emerged from the pearly light, but it wasn't Tomma's. Dosolina stood beside me, clumps of snow sliding down from her cloak and plopping onto the floor.

Dear God in Heaven.

She opened her mouth as if to speak, but nothing came from it. I jumped up and threw my arms around her. She was trembling so much I feared she might collapse. I eased her down onto the furs, and as I did I saw the flask where Tomma had left it.

I filled the bowl with his magical liquid and held it to her lips. And though she took but a sip, it began to cast its spell, just as it had for me.

She gazed up at me. 'Sofia,' she whispered again.

I don't think I need describe my shock, my utter confusion. What was she doing here? A very great panic rose up in my heart; something terrible must have happened. But how did she know where to find me?

'They've taken Francesca,' she only just managed the words.

I put my arms around her again; her familiar old plump body felt like a bag full of bones. 'Who took her, Dosolina? Who?'

She opened her mouth but nothing came out of it. I could but pray that Tomma's liquid wouldn't take long to start working.

I peeled off her cloak and wrapped her in one of the furs. 'You're with me now,' I said, very gently. 'You're safe.'

I tried again. 'Do you know who took her? Can you remember?'

And summoning the last of her strength, Signor Benno.'

It was as if I'd been struck by a lightning bolt. 'When?'

'This morning... His boy came.'

My breath stopped in my throat. I dared not raise my hopes for I knew there were three, the sullen one, the one with hair in golden ringlets and...

'Do you know his name?'

'Yes,' she said. 'Tomma.'

I sat for a moment, trying to still my emotions, Happiness is too small a word. I would have to invent another one to describe how I felt at that moment.

CHAPTER SIXTY

We were mustering the willpower to struggle our weary way back up the hill path when Tomma's fuzzy figure emerged through the heightening skirl. And it was here, whilst still on flat land, that I should have pulled him aside, told him about the Lady Irena, that he had been right about the eye-bead, for it was a woman who saved us. But the cold and the need to get on with the task set out before us... it wasn't the right time. I hesitated and the moment was gone.

The wind was behind us, which was a mercy for it helped us struggle upwards. We reached the cliff, crossed the icy stretch of bog, and pushing through the mouth of the cave threw ourselves onto the ground. So cold were we by now, and so exhausted, we could barely find voices to speak. Only Fortunato seemed to have energy enough to move. We watched as he unwrapped his aforementioned parcel and laid its contents before us; a circle of bread and a chunk of cheese. We fell upon the feast, and though the bread was old and the cheese so hard our teeth could have suffered some permanent damage, it might have been manna from Heaven.

My strength at least a little restored and life coming back to my body, now was the time for questions. But first there was something important. I turned to Baldassare. 'Before you say anything, I want to thank you.'

It was clear he had not the slightest idea what I was talking about.

'For what you did.'

Still he stared.

'You came to the palace with the portrait.'

Ah, now he understood. 'I'd have got there sooner if I'd known you were there. Tomma will have told you that we tried to find you, but you were gone. Then I heard of a man who'd been dragged up the hill by the Duke's men, and that's when I went to speak with the Lady Irena.'

Knowing nothing at all of this story, Tomma's seemed far more dumbfounded than I.

But why put himself in danger to save me? And not only me, Tomma too?

'I could not have abandoned you, Benno. You and he were under my master's protection. You'd be forgiven for thinking that he was the one who betrayed you. But he didn't. It was his father.'

All I could manage was, 'Why?'

'It's a long story. I hardly know where to start.'

And where I once would have jumped in at this point to tell him I knew about the dogs, the guards, the old man suddenly able to hear, the dead crow, the witch's sage, something of Tomma had rubbed off on me. And so I said, 'At the beginning.'

'Yes,' he replied, 'that is the best place.'

We drew closer to him.

'It all started when I met Donato. He came to find me in Padua. I was studying medicine there, as he told you, and had become absorbed in accounts of the remedies of other lands; of how they're administered and their effect. Especially those of Cathay. I need not tell you that this is where the merchant Polo made his travels.

'As I read of his adventures, I became absorbed in other subjects to do with that land. I began to search for more information. And that is when I came into the company of a man, a foreigner called Beyefendi Gul. He brought me a bundle of scrolls. He claimed they were medical dissertations, which had come all the way from the city of Yanzou. But they were written in the script of that place; indecipherable lines of symbols... I believe you know what I'm talking about. It was not until after your escape, when I had gained Francesca's trust, that she told me she confided in you about the book she had found. But let's talk of this later; back to Signor Gul. He would sell me the scroll for ten gold florins; a deal of money for a language I couldn't read. But he had a book, a dictionary of sorts, which translated certain groups of the symbols into Latin. By studying it, I could decipher the instructions and make myself a fortune. But I am not interested in fortunes, as you might guess. The art of experiment is what intrigues me. And so I borrowed enough money to buy them both and set myself to learning the language, at least in its written form, and indeed became quite proficient in it.

'That's why Donato came to find me. He wanted to ask for my help. He told me the foreigner, Gul, had made acquaintance with his father. His family were silk merchants. It seemed they were facing a deal of problems caused by Venice, that city being in control of the sale and purchase of the bundles of threads used to weave the fabric, the source of which is the greatest of secrets. It's how they make their great fortune. You must know that all systems there are run by a network of spies and secret police who, by violent methods, keep tight control of all the trade passing in and out of their city. This being the case for the bundles of silk threads required to weave the fabric, the old signore had an irrational fear of falling foul of the establishment and losing his livelihood.

'But what if he could produce his own silk, removing the need to rely on Venice? An undertaking such as that would be impossible unless you found a way to do it. And he believed he had. Beyefendi Gul had convinced his father to buy a book which he claimed set out a new and simpler way of cultivating the threads, or should I say of breeding silkworms, with no need for mulberry leaves and all the usual paraphernalia required for the task.

'Over the years, the old signore had amassed a small collection of books, these being the ones we brought in the sacks... but though they pertain to the general production of the fabric, which is incriminating enough as far as Venice is concerned, this one was different, Gul told him, for it set out the stages as I have said not only of harvesting worms from their eggs, but in a new and faster way, much different from the old, laborious system. Such information is worth a king's ransom, and that's exactly what the old man paid for it. But when he opened it he was enraged for he had been cheated; it contained only pages of what he perceived to be scribbles.

'Now, Donato may be the most soft-hearted and joyous of men but he's clever too. Why bother to fill them with neat rows of symbols if, indeed, that's what they were? He remembered that Signor Gul had mentioned my name. Perhaps if he let me see them, I could solve the puzzle, explain what they meant. And so he set out to find me, with the precious book, of course. In doing so, he was risking everything, for had he been caught with such secret information, well, I do not need to tell you. The moment I saw it I was able to tell him it was written in the language of Cathay. Which made perfect sense, for as you will know, that is where the art of silk-making was developed.'

He was being courteous, of course, for he was aware that when it came to a subject apart from the painting of walls, I knew precisely nothing. And as far as the mysteries of silk were concerned, had not Tomma been obliged to inform me but a short while before that it was woven from the threads of worms.

'But something perplexed me for by now I had learned that books, as such, do not belong to that land, everything there is written on the type of scrolls Gul had sold me. I could only guess that the symbols had been transcribed. And I was right. Written inside the front cover was the name Caterina Villoni. I did a little research. It seems she belonged to a trading family who lived in Yangzou many years ago. And as I began to study it, I realised Signor Gul had been right for they told the secret of how to breed silkworms, but not only that, as Gul had explained in a new and far less complex way. To say I was excited about our discovery would be an understatement of incalculable magnitude, but as I translated the directions set out in the pages, I realised the enormity of the operation. It takes 3,000 worms for every pound of silk; they could never produce enough to set up a viable business. And so I suggested another idea.

What if we experimented with the instructions? Made sure they worked. And if they did, we could take the book, and its translation, to Venice and present it to the Doge, along with our sample of silk. For such a wondrous revelation, we would be richly rewarded. Even I was certain of that.

'I returned to Montevecchio with Donato where, by underhand and, I confess, entirely illegal means, we got our hands on a batch of eggs and started on the experiments set out in the book. The first stage was finding some of the old, traditional boxes used for the breeding stage. They were of a conventional design, which will explain my strange behaviour that night in the corridor. I was afraid you might have known what they were.'

One puzzle solved, now for the next. 'And what about the Latin words inscribed beside the symbols?' asked Tomma.

At this I leaned forward, like a child as a story is about to be told.

'The book was divided into sections, each of which pertained to the separate environments required for this new process. Damp, to start with, then hot to dry them, then cold etcetera. Well, it's impossible to produce such different conditions in one single place and so we were forced to work in various rooms. Of course we had to keep it secret, we had to be careful and be sure to lock the rooms at the end of each day.

'All was going fairly well until two things happened: first the old signore grew impatient. Why was it taking such time to follow some simple instructions? And, second, Francesca gave Donato the happy news that she was pregnant. We would have postponed our experiments in the meantime were it not for his father... and though one should not speak ill of the dead...'

What was he saying... the old man was dead? This shocked me but Tomma seemed unperturbed.

'...I have no qualms about telling the unfortunate truth,' he continued. 'He was avaricious and grasping. He was also a liar. For years he had feigned to be deaf in order to listen to conversations with no one having the slightest suspicion that he was able to hear them.'

But I saw through his pretence from the start and deeply regret that I said nothing of it, even to Donato. I feared that if his father so much as suspected I knew his secret he would find a way to get rid of me, and where would that leave my poor friend?'

I did not interrupt his flow to tell about hearing the old man at the window.

'But anyway, as time passed and we delved deeper into our investigations, he would come to watch as we worked, pressing us on. By now he had rejected the idea of presenting the book to Venice and reverted to the ridiculous notion of producing silk in secret and selling it at enormous profit. We pretended to go along with his plan, simply to keep him quiet. There was little time for Francesca. She became bored and resentful and began to wonder what we were doing. Why were we always shut away working? Why had the doors been locked? One day, in our hurry, we forgot to close the one that led to the study and she thought to find out. That's when she discovered the book. No, not discovered it in the true sense of the word, for it was lying open on the table. Beside it was a bottle of quicksilver. Somehow she managed to spill it. She told you all this?'

'Yes,' said Tomma.

'Of course, as you know, once out of the bottle it's impossible to get back in. Alas, it was the old man who found it. I tried to take the blame; I told him that I had knocked the bottle over but he was too shrewd to believe me. He fell into a rage. The last thing he wanted was for some silly girl to scupper his plans. He ordered Donato to curb his wife's behaviour, to keep her in check; she must stay in the parts of the house prescribed to her or face the consequences. Of course, my poor friend tried to reason with her, unsuccessfully I may add. They argued. The old man heard Francesca shouting that she would go into any room she pleased, that she didn't require his permission.

'This,' he closed his eyes, 'is where things became very much worse. For now, the old man took matters into his own hands. He started to poison… no, let me change that… not poison, simply to drug her in order to muddle her mind, make her unable to think in a clear way.'

Tomma broke in at this point, 'For a while I thought it was the quicksilver. That it must have seeped into her skin. Regarding its power to set people mad.' He had said nothing of this theory to me.

'And I should have thought of that too but I'm ashamed to say that I was too intent on my work with the worms to realise what was happening. I should have guessed when her crow died. The old man tested his potions upon him, upping the dose as he went.'

'Ah,' Tomma nodded. At least he still had grasp of the story.

'Accounting for the fact that a crow is a deal smaller than a human, too little and there would be no consequence, too much and it would die. He must have watched as it took its effect – so many drops still squawking, so many drops drowsy, so many drops dead – until he knew how much to put into the bird's food, then hers, without going as far as to kill her... or not at that point. He was still at the stage of adding the smallest amount when you and Tomma arrived. Things in the house had become so unbearable I had persuaded Donato to go to his olive grove to check his nets, but really to get away from his father, even for a while. And that's when he met you.'

We had simply been part of his plan; we had fitted into it nicely. 'And brought us back with him to keep Francesca out of the way?'

'No Benno, I assure you, Donato doesn't think like that. But his father does. I realise now that you were a godsend as far as the old man was concerned. Having her sit for long stretches of time while her portrait was painted, well that was the very thing he'd been seeking.'

Yes, he was right; I seemed to recall it was the old man who'd asked me to do it.

'Then came the next crisis. That first night when you were dining, a message arrived from a workfellow in Venice. The guild of silk-makers had become suspicious of what we were up to. But how was that possible? Unless they had planted a spy in the house. But anyway, we had to act quickly. Pre-empt them. Our lives depended upon it. If the Great Council of Venice were to discover what we were doing, no amount of explaining would make them believe that our intention had been to present our discovery to the Doge. We would be dead men. You will know of the torture chamber of the three inquisitors?'

I nodded. How could I not?

'And so we concocted a plan. That's why he left in such a rush. He set off with a portion of text copied from the book, but unfortunately, as I've said, we still had no silk. He would request an audience with the Doge, present the precious pages to him as a gift, and explain that he had not wished to do so before he had proof that the instructions did work. At that stage in proceedings having no silk, or indeed even threads, to back up our story, if we were not believed, or if the procedure turned out to be false, we might lose all that we had been working towards, but that was better than losing our lives.

'Of course, we kept all this from the old man. But, as it turned out, this was the perfect chance for him; with Donato gone he was free to increase the doses. By now he had become a man possessed. He didn't care that Francesca was pregnant, that if by some miscalculation he killed her, the baby would be killed too. Of course, as I said, I knew nothing of this at that time.

'I thought to tell you about the book; the real reason for going to Venice in such haste, but I needed time to be sure it was safe to do so. I'm sorry, Benno, but back then I wasn't certain I could trust you. But not only you, everyone I suppose. I took too long however. You escaped that night, and now it was only Francesca, the old man and me. And Dosolina, of course, and the servants.' He looked at Tomma. 'When you appeared the following day, I had to get you away.' Then at me, 'We went to the cave to find you but you weren't there,' then back to Tomma, 'and so I took you to the convent; it was the only place I could think of.

'It wasn't until Francesca fell into a deeper malaise that

I started to notice a strange smell about her. I knew it from somewhere – and then I remembered, it was the same as had been on her crow. I could only think it had something to do with the old man. I searched his chamber and found the herb. Of course, I was familiar with it, what it's used for. And now I knew I had to keep her safe, not only from him but from everyone… everywhere… I couldn't let her out of my sight. Not even to visit the convent where she has a friend, for their apothecary is a skilled woman; it wouldn't take her long to realise she'd been poisoned and if I, the only man of medicine – and potions – in the house, was accused of the crime, all would be finished for us. I had to be by her side at all times. I even slept outside her door.

'It was then I heard that a man had been dragged up the hill by the Duke's men some little time before. It could only have been you. It took me a while to think of a plan, but, in the end, as you know, I went to the Lady Irena.' I put my hand to my neck and touched the eye-bead. I could never repay the debt I owed her, no matter how long I might live.

'I took Francesca's portrait. For safety's sake I hid it in one of the boxes, wrapped in a blanket. I had heard of the competition for a fresco to be painted in the church. I told her that you were the best – indeed the only – one who should do it.'

I grasped his arm and thanked him again.

'She told me she knew who you were, but had no idea they had taken you prisoner. She promised she would release you. And now came the time of real trouble. She sent me a message. She had heard of a plot to raid the house and steal something in it, she didn't know what, but I did of course. I should have asked her to keep this secret between us, to tell no one. But I didn't and she sent her servant to inform the old signore, letters being too dangerous to risk. Which is why he brought the guards and dogs to patrol the garden. And with them there, no one could get in or out. But by now all the servants had run away and there was only Francesca, Dosolina, Fortunato and me. In short, we were imprisoned.

'When Donato sent word from Venice asking me to copy out more of the text and take it to him, and to hurry, I had to think of how to keep Francesca safe while I was gone. Using some of the old man's herbs, I made up a small bottle of the drug and told Dosolina to give him one drop every day. But I hadn't reckoned how deeply she hated him. She emptied the whole lot into his wine. A mouthful was enough. I cannot say how long he's been dead, only the cold has kept him from rotting. He's still on the floor of his chamber with a blanket spread upon him.'

Sacra Madre di Cristo. I turned to Tomma, but, as with the news of the old man's death, this piece of information didn't seem to surprise him. 'I know,' he said, 'we found him there… but the guard dogs had got scent of us. We had to get away. I had to get Sofia back up to the palace. And then I came back to the house.'

Who the hell was Sofia?

'Thank God you did.' Baldassare, misreading my confusion, thought to explain the next part of the story. 'I got back from Venice just as Tomma appeared. I should have been there sooner but as I might have mentioned, I had to take my horse to the blacksmith. It lost a shoe on the hill path, but thank God at least it got me that far. I'll go for him tomorrow... we may need him.

'Anyway, late though it was, I got to the house just as Tomma appeared. A message had come from the Lady Irena. The English were coming to raid the house. Of course, I knew what they were after. The guards had fled with the horses. Then you found us burning the boxes. As they are used for one purpose alone, they were clear evidence of our crime, we had to get rid of them.'

Tomma interrupted. 'We saw you loading some onto a cart. Where were you taking them?'

'They were filled with cocoons. They're made of threads spun by the worms. We had produced them in their boxes in the cellar, but didn't have skill enough to unravel them. Our plans depended upon a successful operation and so I was sending them to Lucca to the one man there who knew how to do it. And then, had circumstances been different regarding time, we would have woven what little amount of silk we could and taken it to Venice.

'But back to the books. Before Tomma came up with the genius idea of hiding them, I had thought to burn them as well. But of course I would have kept Gul's, in case we had to trade it for our lives. That's what the English are after, you see Benno, it, with its instructions. As I have said, Venice rules the world by way of her income from silk, no other place in Christendom knows how to produce it, and before you can even start to do that you need to know how to harvest the worms. If any other land could discover that secret... well, you can imagine.'

Fortunato glanced at me and I could see his reassuring confusion. 'But how did they know about it... about them?'

I supposed this to be a rhetorical question, but, as ever,

Tomma had an answer.

'They must have heard rumours. You were right about the spy. But it wasn't Venice who sent her.'

All three of us gaped at him now.

'It was Volsini. He knew there was something in the house; something of monumental importance and therefore of very great value. He sent her to find out what it was.'

He had lost me.

'Her, sire. That day Francesca almost fainted and I went to find Dosolina. Remember I said that when I left the room a servant woman was listening at the door?'

I searched my brain.

'The next time I saw her she was in the church with the English. She wasn't wearing servants' clothes then, she was in a nun's habit.' And to Baldassare again, 'I don't know how, but she found out about the book, I imagine by standing outside your door and hearing your conversations with Signor Favoni. Just as she did that day with ours. It might have taken a while to realise that the treasure she had been sent to discover was a book that held the secret of silk, and how to produce it in a new way. And so Volsini, determined to steal it, hired some crooks for the job. English ones as you know. Which surely means that his plan was to take it to England, and following its instructions, set up a rival silk trade. What a prize that would be. But after Francesca came across it, you hid it where it could never be easily found, thus they made plans to raid the house.'

Hardly had I caught my breath when, for good measure, he added, 'And I bet you ten gold florins they hadn't come far the day they arrived, that they had been hiding close by.'

I remembered my awed admiration regarding their

ability to speak so clearly, so vigorously, to appear so composed after spending such time in the saddle... added to which, in a snowstorm. Of course such a feat was impossible, but I had fallen for their tale. I could but console myself with the fact that Tomma had too.

'But he doesn't speak English.' I thought to redeem myself, if only in my own mind, this being an uncontroversial fact.

'Di Fassa does. Sofia told me'

Di fucking Fassa. The English weren't the only ones lurking about in disguise. I was an idiot, was I not. The greatest one alive. To be in the company of a shithead masquerading as a painter... and to believe he was one without seeing proof of the fact. Carpini's words came back to haunt me. "...he said there was no doubt that he would win, but I shouldn't worry for he would hire me. He'd draw out the design he wanted, and I would paint it for him."

But he hadn't reckoned on the fact that an impediment to his plan was about to turn up... namely me.

'And something else,' Tomma was saying now. There was more? 'They've got a map of the house. Well, not a map in the true sense, a rough sketch of its layout. The spy woman must have drawn it for them.'

Silence closed in around us. The flaming pitch was spreading over my shoulder again. I took Baldassare's bottle from the band of my breeches and would have swallowed the lot were it not for him taking careful note.

After some moments, Fortunato's voice broke through the quiet. 'We should be getting back up the hill.'

CHAPTER SIXTY-ONE.

'He's right, sire,' said Tomma, 'we have to go. Get back to the boys.'

My boys. A warmth filled my soul. And then we would get ourselves back to Florence. Now that I had my angel... my Virgin, dealing with those fuckheads would be but a piece of cake, and Tomma was right, our Lord de'Medici only need set eyes upon my design. Filled with joyous anticipation, I pushed through the frigid curtain of ivy and stepping back into the gale let myself wallow in the vision rising up in my mind. There was I, as startling as Signor Polo returned from the lands of the Orient, striding through the doors of the Novella, Tomma at my heels. Boys looking up from their grinding bowls, a murmur rising up to the ceiling. 'Who's that?' I could almost hear them whisper.

'Simone da Benno,' would come the reply. 'It's that son of a bitch... Simone da Benno.'

Oh no, that gilded tomb with my name carved upon it wasn't lost to me yet.

Basking in such imaginings, I fell into a kind of daze. I can only thank God for Tomma; he grasped my cloak and pulled me onwards.

I quickened my step. With this shift in my bearing,

Tomma let go of his grip. And now, to the fore of our little group, I led them up through the frigid whiteness, battling against the wind, until through the gusts we could only just make out above us, as if floating in a swirling sea, the blurred shape of the city. After what seemed too long a time, the ramparts emerged from the dim fortress light.

Dusk was setting in by now; the guards on the gate tower had changed. Their compatriots having long since consumed the bag of chestnuts, the shells strewn about their feet told the story, there was nothing to distract them. But that mattered little, for who would have thought us anything other than poor sods struggling our wretched way home.

The three new men looked us up and down. 'Orders,' said the nearest. 'No one gets through.'

Where I would simply have taken them, one after the other, and crashed their heads against the wall, Baldassare held out three coins. They snatched them and waved us on. We waded up through the warren of alleys and as we approached the ghostly shape of the Favoni house, a group of what we took to be soldiers came stumbling towards us through the whipping snow. For a moment we thought they were about to confront us, but they passed without a word. Only a few steps on and we stopped in our tracks as it struck us all at once; whoever they were, they had come from the house. We rushed forward. Perhaps it was folly to imagine that, with no precious treasure there to steal, the place would be more or less as we'd left it. The gate was half open. A glow swelled before us. Pushing forward we saw the door, or what once had been the door for now it was smashed to pieces, and in the hall beyond it a scene illuminated by every candle and lamp to be found, of shattered furniture strewn around. But not all the makers of this mayhem had departed, for now came towards us two men I knew well. The first Mortimer and behind him, the shithead di Fassa.

It's at such times that blind, raging fury descends on my soul; there was no stopping me, even by Tomma. With a great whooping roar, I raced towards them. Mortimer turned to run; di Fassa lunged forward. He caught my neck and thrust me hard against the wall, crashing my head against it. Had he been holding any other part of my body... but he wasn't. His thumb pushed hard on my throat. Stars floated before my eyes. I had misjudged him, he knew how to fight. And he'd have beaten me, had it not been for Tomma who jumped on the *stronzo's* back and clung on to it like a crab, his weight forcing his victim to give up his hold for just long enough to let me kick him in his balls. He stumbled. I kicked again. He fell, and Tomma was above him, holding a knife to his throat.

'No Tomma. No.' I had been a guest in too many gaols not to have learned that killing powerful men is never a wise thing to do. I cared naught for myself, but I did for him.

Holding the fucker's neck, as but a few moments before he had held mine, I thrust his head onto the floor.

'I know what you're doing here, my friend. I will be merciful, however, and let you go. But I warn you, if you should think to return, I'll beat you to pulp and no one will stop me. Don't doubt me,' I added a lie for good measure, 'for I have the ear of Lord Umberto.'

We watched as he sped off into the night, as fast as

his aching balls would allow, and then I turned to Tomma. 'Where *Dio Santo,* did you get that knife?'

'It's not a knife,' replied he, holding towards me the finest dagger I had seen, and I had seen many. 'It's a stiletto. I took it from the waist of his breeches.'

I was laughing when Baldassare stumbled forward to tell us, 'Whoever they were... well, they're running off down the alley.'

Yes, I had let them. But if I had known what I'd find when we got to the palace, I would have cut them into pieces.

CHAPTER SIXTY-TWO

My neck felt as if it had been hung from a gibbet and my head knocked about by a cudgel. Baldassare's medicine was losing its power and the pitch spread over my shoulder had been set afire once again, yet it was with joy that I led my little band onto the campo. This place would soon be behind us. But I shouldn't have been so happy for things were not as we had expected; there was strange movement and bustle, and men at arms coming and going. What's more, a row of sentries stood in a line, barring the gate to the palace.

'No one gets through,' said the one we reached first, but unlike the guard at the watch tower he had the courtesy to add, 'Signore.'

I turned to Tomma, but he didn't need prompting. In a cordially inquisitive voice he asked, 'Why, *Corporale*? Has something happened?'

The sentry said nothing, his gaze fixed at a point floating somewhere above our heads. The crowds milled about us; a very great tension hung in the air. Tomma looked around, and using the same friendly tone asked an old woman if she could tell us. She seemed terrified by his question and shuffled off before he had time to stop her. He ran after her, but she struck out at him with her stick.

Joy was turned now to gut-wrenching panic. We had to get in, get the boys, bid farewell to my lady, tell her about Volsini. And then the evening Angelus tolled, and I knew how we'd do it.

Memory of snowflakes floating down through the grate, piling on a scarecrow's skull.

I signalled to my little band and off we set across the teeming campo. I stopped by the bell tower. 'There's a grate in the pavement somewhere around here.' I was doing my best to damp down my panic. 'It shouldn't be too hard to find it.'

Baldassare and Fortunato looked up at me, puzzled, and though I hadn't mentioned it to him, there was no need for Tomma to ask me why. 'I'm guessing it's the way we'll get in,' he thought to inform them.

Had the place been empty of its crowds, the sentries would not have missed us scraping the snow with our feet. But it was, and they did. Only a few moments passed before Baldassare beckoned us over to his patch where now the dimmest glow of light shone under his feet. We worked together, kicking the snow away, and there were the criss-crossed struts of the grille.

On our knees now we hauled together, but it wouldn't budge.

'We need to smash though it,' Tomma pointed at a snow-covered pyramid beside the bell tower wall. 'We could use one of them.'

Now it was my turn to look puzzled.

'They're cannonballs. Haven't you seen them, sire?'

No, I hadn't, strange though the fact might seem.

But he ignored this.

Fortunato scraped the snow from the pile and there they were, just as Tomma had said. We set to the task of lifting the one on the top, but it was the weight of, well, a cannonball.

Tomma took over. 'Push it off,' he instructed, 'we'll roll it with our feet.'

The campo sloped towards the bell tower, which made our task fairly easy. Gathering momentum, it slid down towards the grate. 'Now,' he said. 'All together.'

With every last vestige of our strength, we heaved it up, then let it drop. It smashed through the wooden struts of the grate and crashed to the floor not too far below.

The dear Lord was surely with us for next came the wavering light of a lantern. A face with which I was well acquainted peered up at us, a petrified look etched upon it. I stretched out in the snow and sticking my head through the shattered lattice, shouted, 'Help us down, you useless dumbarse!'

'You should be more courteous,' said Tomma. 'We might need his help to get back out when we're finished.'

But manners were not to the fore of my mind. He scuttled off. Too much time passed. I stuck my legs through the splintered struts, and despite Tomma's cautions about it not being a good idea, as injury was bound to follow, etcetera, etcetera, was about to jump down when the *cretino* appeared on the scene again, this time with a pole of great length. He thrust it upwards, sticking its top through the grate.

'Slide down it, signore,' he shouted. That a golden coin could ignite such initiative.

'You gave me a fright there, so you did,' exclaimed he when I bumped to the ground, doing his best to sound as if all this was of great amusement.

I would have taken him by his neck and asked if he thought that a fright, what did he think of this...? But Tomma, who by now had reached terra firma, looked at me as if to say, 'What did I tell you up there... don't you ever listen?'

I changed my tack, and chortling along with him at his joke, thrust my hand into my jerkin and pulled out the trusty coin. 'This might help to ease it a little.'

'Ah, signore.' A goat had looked at me once like that.

'Get us into the palace and then...'

He gaped up at us. By now Baldassare and Fortunato had made their way down the pole.

'What are you standing there for?' And this time, instead of putting the coin back where it had come from, I placed it in his open palm, all that was needed to spur him on. As he hurried before us, his lantern bobbing like a boat upon a choppy sea, only Tomma had wit left to ask him, 'What's happened, signore? They wouldn't let us through the gate, that's why we had to come this way.'

'Aint you 'eard?'

I'd have informed him of the fact that if we had, we wouldn't waste our breath asking, but Tomma was born of courteous stock.

'No, signore. We'd be most grateful if you'd tell us.'

'The Lady Irena. They've only gone and broke into her chamber.'

CHAPTER SIXTY-THREE

A voice shouted 'Benno'. Next came a pounding on the door. It crashed open before I could reach it and Anna stood glancing about her.

I started to babble, to tell her why I was... why... we... were here. 'I had to get away from the English. Tomma let me hide here... until he comes back.' Dosolina, lying benumbed beside me, did not wake from her stupor. 'This is my friend's servant. Her name's Dosolina.'

But she wasn't listening. 'I need to find Benno.' She shouted again, 'Where is he?'

I stared at her, open mouthed.

'Don't you know? They said he raped the Abbess. That he was rescued by the Lady Irena. That he's hiding in her chamber; that they've gone there to kill him.'

Tomma's words came back to me. 'She wanted to let the world think he'd... attacked... her.'

'We have to find him,' she shouted. 'We have to go there. We have to save him.'

I did not know who 'they' were, but if they killed Benno it surely followed they'd kill Tomma too.

What would have happened; what would I have done, had not the same rage that helped me save him back in the house, surged up in me now. I thrust my feet into my clogs, pulled my cloak around me and shook Dosolina. Through all Anna's shouting she hadn't stirred. She peered up at me with bleary eyes. 'I have to leave you for a little while. Stay here. You'll be safe. I'll be back soon,' and we were out of the door.

*

The evening Angelus clanged in the darkness as we slid and slipped, as fast as we could, across the snowy courtyard. But when we reached the palace door it was shut tight. We battered upon it. A guard peered through the grille. He cracked it open and that was enough, surprise being a powerful weapon. We crashed into him, toppling him over. And then we were racing through the labyrinth, swarming with panicking throngs. Up the stairway, taking steps two at a time. I would have turned into the familiar corridor towards the Abbess's chamber but Anna pulled me the other way, along passages emptying of the great multitudes, till, at last, she grabbed my arm and pointed. 'It's there. At the end of...'

But she didn't have time to finish, for a group of men appeared from the shadow. We hid in the folds of a curtain and held our breaths as closer and closer they came. We gaped in horror as they passed, dragging something behind them. It was a guard. No, not just a guard, beneath the gore of his lolling head, I saw poor Captain Orlando's face. His throat was cut through to the bone and his body was covered in blood.

I gripped Anna's hand to steady myself and we stood

still as statues until they were gone.

Her face, white as his, she tried to say something, but words wouldn't come.

'Stay here,' I whispered, too loudly.

She clutched my arm. 'No... I'm coming with you.'

'You can't. No one will harm me.' I meant because I was a Holy Sister. 'But they will harm you. Please, Anna, go back to the temple. Stay with Dosolina. I need you to look after her.'

And so, with a very great dread gripping my heart, I stepped out from our hiding place, and turning my gaze downwards as all good and obedient nuns are instructed, forced my feet forward. They slipped on puddles of blood, and I had to be careful to keep my balance, but I reached the chamber. A metal barrier secured its entrance; my heart beat so loudly it would surely be heard by those behind it. I pushed it. It opened. A vast room stretched before me, with tables and chairs toppled onto the ground. Blood spattered the walls and streaked across the floor. All was quiet but for the crackling of the fire in the chimney. In another life I would have turned and run back to the safety of the curtain, but this was my new life, and I only cared about Tomma.

I made my way forward. There was a door at the end of the room. I turned its handle, just inside it lay the bloodied body of a man. His severed head was beside him, and his hands were cut off. I had tended poor innocent lepers in their hours before death, and those with the flux, so emaciated as to seem like living corpses, but nothing could have prepared me for this. I looked down at his head and felt myself gripped with a violent trembling; what if I came across Tomma butchered like him. I prayed that sweet

Santa Chiara would give me strength to go on.

I stretched my arms out like a blind woman and walked a little way into the dark space whispering, 'Tomma, Tomma.' And then I stumbled on something before me and would have fallen had I not grasped out at what I thought must be the wall, but was, instead, a thick velvet curtain. Gently, gently I pulled it a little way open. Light streamed through a window and I saw what had tripped me. A woman's veiled body lay at my feet, a very large sword was beside her... and may the Dear Lord forgive me, for I could only give thanks that it wasn't Tomma.

Some way behind her lay another poor soul, alive or dead I could not know. I forced myself forward, trembling and praying. I looked down through my tears. The Abbess's dead eyes stared back at me. Her face was set in a horrifying grimace and, with her yellow tresses spread out on the floor, her hairless head shone as if polished.

Convulsed with horror, I could not move. A shape loomed above me, but I had not strength to save myself. Hands dragged me roughly into the light... please don't let me die before I've found him.

I looked up; it was the ringlet-haired boy. He placed the point of his knife at my throat. I cannot repeat the foul words he used, but it was clear he thought I was one of the English.

CHAPTER SIXTY-FOUR

Through the corridor we raced, the smell of shit fading behind us, the endless maze of passageways twisting this way and that; a lifetime before we got to Irena's chamber. Blood covered the corridor leading to it and through its now open barrier. Beyond was a scene I can but force myself to remember. We had come from our first place of turmoil, now we entered the next. So far had I ventured into my life, I thought I had seen it all. But not so, for here the blood was not confined to the floor, but splattered all over the walls and the ceiling. And in its midst stood my good lads, clothes shredded, faces cut with deep slashes. Guido had a blade in his hand. Celestino stood beside him, holding tight to one of the English, the point of his dagger held close to her neck. 'No!' Tomma shouted. 'Let her go.'

He did as he was told. The dagger rattled to the ground as Tomma ran towards them and took the little nun in his arms.

CHAPTER SIXTY-FIVE

May God forgive me my exultation when I saw Tomma. Horror reigned around us but he was here; he wasn't dead for if they had killed him my life would be over, and I would have taken the knife from the ringlet-haired boy and killed myself too.

CHAPTER SIXTY-SIX

'What in the name of *Gesu*, boys?' Whatever hell they had been through, we were here now.

'They came. They were looking for you.'

All was still; completely silent.

'Men... With one they called Lord Volsini. They seemed surprised we could fight.'

I could only think what I'd do when I found him; make him wish he had never been born.

The truth is I like fighting and care not if it be with fists or with blades. I am strong and once I get started no one can stop me. But here I saw two brave boys who had stood up to a force far greater than they... my boys, my lads. What pride I had in them.

'The man Ivan Kovac. They wanted to take him. But a woman came. She tried to stop them. And we did too. But there were too many of them.'

A great coldness seized me, I did not need to ask who they meant. 'They killed her too, sire.' All strength drained from my body; I felt I would fall on my knees. 'And...'

But there was no time to listen to what else he might say. 'Go, boys. Now.'

They looked uncertain. 'Back through the passage,

the way you came with him.' And taking Guido's blade, I pushed first him, then Celestino. 'Wait behind the wall in the church, where it comes to an end.'

Tomma signalled them forward. 'Take good care of Sofia. I owe her my life.' It did not seem he wished to let the little nun out of his arms. 'Go with Celestino and Guido.' He kissed her head. 'Stay with them until I come.'

She whispered something so quietly only Tomma could hear what she said. Whatever it was seemed to shock him. I had never seen him look like that.

Thank all the gods they did what I said, Guido all but carrying the little nun in his arms.

I walked across the room, through the open door at its end. Ivan Kovac lay just inside it, his head had been sliced from his body, his sword beside what once had been his hand, but now was a bloodied stump. I took his sword and holding it out before me, stepped into the passageway and by the light from the open door, made my way along it.

Into the Lady Irena's chamber. No need to pull back the curtain, for someone had been there before us. Two bodies lay on the floor.

I knelt by the first and gently lifted the veil from her face. Her expression is still clear in my mind. I see, again, her slightly square face, her eyebrows unshaven, thick and dark against her pale skin, her eyes of palest blue, her nose straight as that of a marble statue, her mouth slightly open, her lips pulled upwards by the scar that stretched from her chin to her forehead. The pool of blood upon which she lay.

All my sorrows came at that moment; the aching sadness, the unbearable torment.

'Come Benno,' said Tomma. This was the first time he'd

called me by my name. I gently closed her eyes and would have stayed with her, mind dumbed, uncaring as to what might happen next, had he not dragged me back through the door.

'I don't suppose you took a moment to look at the other one lying beside her.'

I shook my head.

'It was the Abbess. It's clear that Ivan Kovac killed her, after she killed that lady.'

His words should have had an effect, but they didn't.

'You're not just going to stand there, are you?' Harsh words, but he knew how to rouse me.

'We have to get our hands on Volsini.'

And he was right.

That old raging fury filled me then; and what's more, I knew where to go first.

Back through the chamber, Tomma behind me. Into the passage that led to the church. It took precious minutes to get there, but when we did there was Celestino and Guido standing where I'd told them, both had their arms around the little nun, holding her tightly between them. Her face was white as chalk but flooded with an emotion that went far beyond relief when she saw us, or should I say when she saw Tomma. I put my finger to my lips to signal silence and pushing my Lady's hidden door, Tomma and I crashed into the church.

The Fra sat at his lectern. He looked up at us, terror in his eyes. I grasped him by his fat neck. 'Where is he?' No need to explain who I meant.

He was either struck dumb or cared naught for his life. I took the knives from my breeches and held them to his face. 'I'm counting to ten,' and I started 'One. Two...' His eyes darted one way then the other. 'Three. Four.' Still he was silent, save for loud gulping. At eight, I dragged him from his stool and shook him, much like a fox shakes a rat. 'Nine.'

Gut instinct told Tomma I was going to do it. He put his hand upon my arm, and in a tone less calm than normal, 'Please sire, let me try.'

I dropped the shithead, he crumpled onto the floor. Tomma crouched beside him. He spoke too quietly for me to hear, but when he had finished, and the good Fra had whispered a few garbled words, he said, 'They're heading out to the coast, sire. They can't have got far. If you go now, you'll catch them.'

You may wonder what Tomma had said to extract such information, where I had most miserably failed. And later he told me. I call it to mind, the fable of Aesop; the one of the traveller on the road. The wind and sun striking up a contest, which would remove his cloak first. The wind blew and blew, which only made the traveller hold it even tighter; then came the sun's turn. She shone on him warmly and after a while, well you can imagine what happened.

In other words, 'If you tell us, my master will spare you. And when the Duke returns he will not know that you were part of all this, for we will be gone by that time.'

And had I not thought it often, 'What was a genius lad like him doing as a lowly painter's apprentice?' He never ceased to astound me.

But then, he sought to spoil it all by giving me advice. 'Murdering a priest in his church, it's not a good idea.'

CHAPTER SIXTY-SEVEN

We passed along the graveyard wall. So changed was the scene since the day we had stood upon Corvo's box and watched the Christ figure passing by. The day my life started, though I could not have known it then.

With the horror behind us, we had led Signor Baldassare's horse, retrieved from the blacksmiths forge, down the icy hill path, Dosolina wobbling most precariously upon it, clutching tightly to its mane. Along with my joy at being with Tomma, I was still in a state of shock and confusion. The Abbess had killed the Lady Irena. I prayed that when it came to Judgement Day she would burn in hell, for she had not been a holy woman, but a vicious and fraudulent sinner.

And now we stopped for we were here. Baldassare lifted Dosolina down from his horse. I put my arms around her, and when I could see she was recovered enough I forced myself to smile.

'Are you ready?'

She gave a little half laugh and Fortunato was by her side, guiding her as she slithered forward, Baldassare flattening a passage through the snow as they made their unsteady way forward. More stamping of snow drifted onto the gate. He pulled it open enough to let them through. And even though it was still early morning, the path at the other side had been cleared. I could but think of the little novices sent out with their shovels before morning light.

The horror of her journey down the mountain behind her, only one thing mattered, just as it mattered to me. And now, having less snow to contend with, she picked up her skirts and fairly scurried along, Fortunato grabbing at her with frantic concern. Down by the orchard path and we could see them no longer, the muffled call of the visitants' bell in the distance and silence descended. Snow tumbled from branches above us. I felt my feet freeze, but I did not care for Tomma was with me. He held me close to him, and in the shelter of the horse's steaming body we stood watching and hoping.

Too much time passed before Signor Baldassare whispered, 'I can see something,' he being twice as tall as we were. 'Yes... there are three of them.'

A swell of dread crept up from my belly. 'Please,' I prayed, for if one of them was Canoness Sister Veronica, Tomma and I would have to step quickly into the shadows and let Signor Baldassare say our farewells.

And now we saw them too, coming slowly down the path, Fortunato holding a bundle, Francesca on one side, Sister Agata on the other. I thanked Our Dear Santa Chiara as I ran through the gate towards them, my arms held out wide. Fortunato stood back as we huddled together, and when our tears were frozen on our cheeks, and when Sister Agata said, 'Come, my dears we must not be seen.' And when we had passed through the stamped-out passage in the snow drift and were back on the other side of the gate, Fortunato handed the bundle to me, and this was the first time I held the tiny Sofia Simona. There would be many times in the future, but that was far away from us now. Her sleeping face peeped out at me, her eyelashes so dark against her hood of white rabbit fur.

A tear plopped onto her forehead. I realised it was mine.

'Oh Francesca, I tried to save you.'

'I know. I know. Sister Agata told me. And I am so grateful. I am so sorry.'

I was the one to be sorry, not her. And I felt we might start weeping again.

And all this while Tomma stood back in silence, not wishing to disturb us. But now he stepped forward.

'We have to go away for a little while,' he said very gently.

Her breath seemed to stop in her throat.

'It isn't safe for us here. We have too many enemies in the city.'

She stared at him in horror. Then she stared at me. 'But where are you going?'

'Naples. But we will be back as soon as it's safe. Believe me, I give you my word.'

And when she looked uncertain, he took her hands in his.

'You may not know one simple fact, which is that my master hates his rivals even more than they hate him. He's not going to stay away long enough to let any of them steal his crown. A few months at most, that's all. And your husband will be back very soon, he may even be on his way now. You know he's not to blame for all that's happened. He looked at Signor Baldassare. 'And you know about

362

everything else? Giacomo will have told you.'

She nodded.

And I did too. The last of the mysteries had been solved, for Tomma had explained what the strange symbols were, and the precious knowledge they imparted.

And now Tomma said, 'If the convent permits it, he and Fortunato will stay here with you until Signor Donato arrives.'

Sister Agata turned to Baldassare. 'You will be most welcome, I can assure you.'

'And when he does you have to get away from here. All of you. Go to Florence. Ask for the brothers Pieri, they'll find you a safe place to stay. Wait for us there.'

Sister Agata kissed my cheek. 'Don't worry, my dear, we'll take good care of them until they have to leave.'

Kind and sweet Sister Agata, but there was one last thing. 'I would not ask you, but it's important. No, more than important. Could you take a message to someone? Her name's Anna. She works in the palace kitchen. Thank her for caring for Dosolina, tell her where we're going. That we will be back just as soon as it's safe. I hate to think what will become of her if they find out what she has done. And, so, if you can, please bring her here too. And Francesca, you must take her with you to Florence.'

But she was too overcome to answer and so Baldassare said in her place, 'Be assured Sofia, we will.'

Sister Agata smiled. 'I'll fetch my mantle and staff and go now. This very moment.'

And so it was that Tomma mounted the horse, and when I had placed the tiny Sofia Simona back into Fortunato's arms, he pulled me up behind him.

How hard it was to leave them, Baldassare giving us an encouraging look, Fortunato smiling down at the baby, Francesca's face, white as the snow around us. But, struck with a thought, her expression changed, and steadying herself, she asked, 'And Benno, has he left already?'

Yes, he had gone with the ringlet-haired boy, whose name I now knew was Celestino, and the other one who was called Guido. 'They're somewhere out on the road.' I did not think it wise to add that it was the one that led to Pisa. That they had stolen horses from the Duke's stable and were going to kill the Chamberlain Volsini.

SIMONE DA BENNO 1460–1525

Born in Bergamo, the youngest son of a baker, his early genius was recognised by the Duke Scalieri who, as his first patron, commissioned the paintings in the Castello Lugari.

During an attack on the castle by the house of Urbino, he was captured and imprisoned alongside the English Mercenary Sir Richard Lesley. His ransom being eventually paid, he was invited to Florence to paint a fresco in the Palazzo Medici. During this time, though their styles were very different, he was supported and befriended by Botticelli.

Known as a hothead, frequently involved in feuds with fellow artists, it was one of his quarrels that saved him, forcing him to flee Florence just before Savonarola laid waste to the art in the city. Finding refuge under the patronage of Duke Umberto, it was in the fortified citadel of Montevecchio that he worked on the first of his great masterpieces, 'The Virgin of The Tumbling Angel.' His famous portrait of Francesca Favoni was made here too, which, due to its fragile condition, is kept in a temperature-controlled room in the Uffizi to be viewed by appointment only.

The Montevecchio period onwards is known as his Golden Age and regarded as forerunner of the Baroque. In the following years his work was prolific, the most famous amongst them being his altarpiece, originally intended for the church of Santa Maria Novella.

Embarking upon this second phase of his life, he rescued Sofia Assunta Corrantano from the convent where she was a novice and hired her as an assistant, marking him out as the first painter known to have employed a woman apprentice. Of the many who worked with him, only she was touched with his genius.

Charged with the murder of Ambrogio Volsini, he spent his next few years as a fugitive, working in many cities.

On his death, he left most of his vast fortune to 'that friend of my heart', his one-time apprentice, the eminent banker, Tommasino Trovatello, who, by then, having married Sofia Corrantano, used his master's legacy to build an orphanage for the foundling children of Naples.

Printed in Great Britain
by Amazon

39799640R00214